The Taste of Power

The Taste of Power

LADISLAV MŇAČKO

TRANSLATED FROM THE SLOVAK BY
PAUL STEVENSON

FOREWORD BY MAX HAYWARD

FREDERICK A. PRAEGER, *Publishers*
New York • Washington

F Mnacko

BOOKS THAT MATTER

Published in the United States of America in 1967
by Frederick A. Praeger, Inc., Publishers
111 Fourth Avenue, New York, N.Y. 10003

© 1967 by Verlag Fritz Molden, Wien
English translation © 1967 by Frederick A. Praeger, Inc.,
and George Weidenfeld and Nicolson Limited

Library of Congress Catalog Card Number: 67-20489

Printed in the United States of America

Foreword

Soviet and East European literature is now concerned to the point of obsession with recent history. It is in some ways the literature of an inquest which is likely to go on for many years. For the Russians the experience of 'revolutionary' conditions has been lengthier and more organic than in eastern Europe where there is still a generation which grew up in the culturally 'open' (if in some cases politically harsh and authoritarian) societies of the pre-war years and where it has not, therefore, been so difficult as in Russia to face up to the past. There are striking differences, hence, between the way in which Soviet literature and the literature of the various East European countries once under total Soviet control have come to grips with what may, for convenience sake, be called the 'Stalinist' experience. In Russia the inquest has been gradual, gingerly and bemused. This has not been entirely due to censorship or other external impediments but also to the obvious difficulty of radically revising fifty years of history which have indelibly marked all Russians now living. Thus, for many readers in the West, Soviet literature of the post-Stalin years has seemed tantalizingly diffident and ambiguous in its judgements. This may even be due partly to the classical Russian tradition with its tendency to find redeeming features in the evil and squalid. The Soviet re-appraisal of the past, although it has been going on longer than in any East European country, has been slow and tortuous. The great landmarks have been Ilya Ehrenburg's *Thaw* (1954), Vladimir Dudintsev's *Not by Bread Alone* (1956) and Alexander Solzhenitsyn's *One Day in the Life of Ivan Denisovich* (1962). The latter, with its description of the daily routine in a concentration camp, is so far the most eloquent

5

comment on Stalin's rule, but it is marked, typically, by a certain humility, and the 'meekness' of the hero even led some Soviet critics to compare him with Tolstoy's Karatayev, the *muzhik* in *War and Peace* who has come to symbolize the long-suffering forbearance of the Russian people. One will not find in the Soviet literature of the past decade any clear expression of outright rejection of the past; nor has there been much attempt so far to explore causes or draw conclusions. Some East European writers, by contrast, have not hesitated – once it became politically possible – to settle accounts with their recent history in a decisive and brutally forthright manner. They have done so furthermore in an idiom which seems quite natural to Western ears. Instead of trying to 'assimilate' the past as an essential part – whether one likes it or not – of the nation's historical experience which has to be 'accepted', Polish and Hungarian writers (and now one in Czechoslovakia) have, as it were, spat out the Stalinist experience whole, as something totally alien and repugnant which can never be digested, let alone justified or accepted. The stories of Marek Hlasko (e.g. 'The Cemeteries') and Adam Ważyk's 'Poem for Adults' gave vent in Poland in 1956 to the universal feeling among Poles that they had been the victims of a monstrous experiment to which, however, because of its utter grotesqueness, they had remained spiritually immune. The Hungarians went further in the same year and expressed their revulsion in a revolutionary uprising that had to be suppressed by Soviet tanks.

Czechoslovakia was much slower than her neighbours to respond in literature and art to the new political situation created by the death of Stalin and the Twentieth Congress of the Soviet Communist Party at which Khrushchev, by his admission of past crimes and 'mistakes', loosened the iron bonds which had bound Eastern Europe to Russia. The slowness of the Czechoslovak reaction was due as much to the stubbornness with which the party leaders in Czechoslovakia resisted change (even if it appeared to be licensed by Moscow) as to the unromantic but more than justified caution of the country's intelligentsia. This caution has reaped its reward in cultural

6

terms, if not in political ones. While Poland and Hungary have stagnated, as though exhausted by the heroic outburst of 1956, the Czechs and Slovaks have gradually and unflamboyantly reasserted the autonomy of the creative process. As a result, Prague is currently the most productive (often in a startlingly avant garde way) of the East European capitals. Czechoslovak films which have burst on the world, as Polish ones did about ten years ago, are the most obvious illustration of the scope and intensity of the quiet revolution that has taken place. In literature (except in poetry which does not survive translation) developments have been less spectacular and until the present novel of Ladislav Mňačko there was little prose that could justly lay claim to the attention of readers outside Czechoslovakia.

Extracts from this novel have appeared in the Prague literary periodical *Plamen* (in August and September, 1966) but there seems to be some question at the moment as to whether the whole of the text will be published in the author's own country. It is not surprising that it should have aroused controversy. In its outspokenness Mňačko's novel goes far beyond anything hitherto published in Russia or anywhere else in Eastern Europe.

It is the best portrait so far drawn of *homo stalinensis* and it shirks nothing in its explicit and clinical examination of a peculiarly insidious form of tyranny. Most Soviet and East European works of this kind have focused attention on relatively minor tyrants at the lower levels of the power structure and on their victims, but the central figure in Mňačko's novel is not a mere jack-in-office. As we are casually informed on page 177, he is none other than the 'head of the government'.

The government in question is that of Slovakia (the eastern part of the Czechoslovak Republic, which though very close ethnically and linguistically to Bohemia, has a different political history), and the city in which the action takes place is clearly Bratislava. Many readers will thus be familiar with the physical setting of the story from the film *The Shop on Main Street* to which, in historical terms, it is indeed a kind of sequel. The time span of fifteen years occasionally specified in the story refers to the post-war period from 1945 to about 1960, i.e.

from Slovakia's liberation from the puppet-régime set up by the Germans to a time in which the post-Stalin relaxation had really begun to make itself felt. The intervening years saw the seizure of power by the Communists in 1948 and the savage purges of the late forties and early fifties which were more devastating in Czechoslovakia than anywhere else. The indiscriminate persecutions which followed the Slansky trial in Prague in 1949 swept away many of the leading figures in Czech and Slovak public life. The best known Slovak to be involved was the country's Foreign Minister, Vladimir Clementis who was executed as an alleged accomplice of Slansky. One of Slovakia's most outstanding writers, Laco Novomesky, disappeared into prison for many years and, after his release in 1963, he has played a crucial part in the recent cultural ferment. As Mňačko shows us, large numbers of humble bystanders were also caught up, quite uncomprehending, in the witches' Sabbath. Although the outlines of the story are now familiar, Mňačko is the first writer to tell it through the eyes not of a victim or a pawn, but of a prime mover. True, the anonymous 'statesman' is dead (the novel's framework is a description of his funeral), but his career unfolds in retrospect in the mind's eye of his friend, a photographer, who has witnessed every step of his progress from war-time partisan to arbiter of his country's fate. This 'candid camera' technique is ideally suited to the author's purpose of ruthlessly exposing the discrepancy between the statesman's public image and his private life. Mňačko's subject and the conclusion at which he arrives (it is baldly stated at the end of the novel in so many words : 'Power corrupts') would be banal if it were not for the surprising but convincingly demonstrated proposition that power maintained by terror has a bitter taste all of its own. What is remarkable in this story is not the gradual corruption of an idealist by the fruits of office (this is universal) but the sickening fear which gradually makes the 'statesman' into a craven figure almost devoid of tragic quality. In totalitarian conditions power not only corrupts, it also enslaves and unmans those who exercise it.

It is usual in discussing works of this kind to emphasize that though they are mainly of documentary interest, they also have some literary worth. Mňačko's novel can be wholeheartedly recommended on both counts. It is a superbly concentrated narrative, which as a study in human frailty achieves the essential universality that distinguishes literature from mere reportage. It will be read as an outstanding work of Czechoslovak prose long after the conditions it relates to have receded into history. It is, however, of immense value – in this respect it has an almost text-book quality – for anyone interested in the mechanisms of totalitarian politics. It incidentally strips away the glamour, or even grandeur with which in their heyday the Stalinist régimes of Eastern Europe impressed admirers and enemies alike. Behind the awesome façade it was all much more shabby and sordid. What is astonishing in retrospect was that these post-war governments in Eastern Europe managed to project such an aura of ascetic idealism. Mňačko utterly destroys the lingering myth. One consolation to be derived from the horrors of the Stalin period is that they have provoked a literary and artistic response from such writers as Solzhenitsyn in Russia and Mňačko in Czechoslovakia which is curiously ennobling. In this respect the literary scene in Eastern Europe now appears less bleak than in the West where writers are not easily able to find common ground with their readers. The reasons for the brighter prospects in the East were well described by Vera Blackwell in a recent issue of *Survey* (April 1966):

'The treatment of ethical and existential questions awakens a lively response from a very wide public precisely because the experiences which led to their being asked in the first place were widely shared. During the fifties both the writers and their future public were exposed to many corrupting influences; they were also forced by the circumstances to flex their moral muscles almost daily. Some cracked under the strain, some were strengthened. As Nietzsche says, what does not kill me gives me strength. Very real decisions between good and evil had constantly to be made; and often they

9

involved the ultimate choice between life and death. In other words, the experiences were not only shared but were also pretty drastic. Which means that the writer, the dramatist, and the poet do not have to whip themselves into a sense of life by heroin or by sexual perversions, nor is it necessary for them to shock the public in order to attract attention. What is in demand is not titillation of the senses, but an honest presentation of facts as they were during the fifties and as they are now, a sincere search for truth.'

In conclusion, it should be stressed that Mňačko is not a lone and embittered opponent of the present system in Czechoslovakia. He is a 'liberal' Communist who is generally considered to be an apologist for the régime. He is a member of Earl Russell's 'Committee for the Investigation of US Crimes in Vietnam' and, according to a report in the Czech newspapers in January 1967, he recently returned to Prague from North Vietnam where he reported the war in dispatches widely published in the Soviet and East European press.

His new novel may well bring him into conflict with the conservative wing of the Czechoslovak Communist Party but it is an encouraging sign that at least part of *The Taste of Power* has already been published in Czech.

Max Hayward   *St Antony's College, Oxford*

March 1967

One

On the black-draped catafalque the dead man lay in state, his feet towards the great hall's entrance.

A sheet of glass covered the lacquered black coffin, so that the crowds who would come to say farewell to the departed might once more gaze upon his face and form.

It seemed to Frank that he had seen the coffin somewhere before. For a moment he wondered whether it was not the same one that had been used on the last occasion of this kind: it was very like it. But that was absurd of course – the coffin must have been made to measure for this occasion.

In any case, he thought, the coffin is ridiculous. The basic purpose of coffins is to protect the remains of a human being from the earth. They should be solid and firm to match the nobility, wealth and importance of the dead man and to resist mould, corruption and chemical change. Frank had seen coffins made of pewter, lead, silver, marble and granite – some simple, others, for the more noble departed, adorned with precious stones or surmounted by a marble effigy, so that when they contained only a heap of crumbling bones, they might proclaim the greatness and immortal glory of rulers, kings, magnates, geniuses and tyrants – or commemorate the vanity of rich men who, even after their death, wish to show the world what they were able to afford.

But this coffin served none of these functions. The dead man was to be cremated in two days' time. Nothing would be left of him but a handful of dust, the contents of a small urn. So why the expensive lacquered coffin, so brightly polished that it showed the marks of the fingers and palms of the men who had placed it on the catafalque? Oh well, thought Frank, the dead man must lie in something, after all. In something, and on something.

The body was dressed in a black suit, a snow-white shirt with a dark red tie, and patent leather shoes with pointed toes. Once, a long time ago, the dead man had made a point of always wearing an open-necked shirt and had laughed at Frank for his white shirts and carefully knotted ties. Frank, he said, was a bourgeois – he himself despised ties. He even wore his open-necked shirt to the wedding at which Frank had been his best man, though by then this had begun to count as a grave breach of social decorum. Frank could still remember the disgusted frown which the registry office official had worn throughout the ceremony.

Frank himself had long ago given up wearing ties on all occasions: ties irked him, and when he had no choice but to wear one he felt ill at ease and constricted. It was a professional requirement, in a profession which he had long detested, and putting one on brought home to him the full pointlessness of his existence. His favourite dress was now a coarse coloured shirt and a shabby suède jacket.

But in the meantime the dead man had gradually acquired a reputation as the best-dressed man in the country. He must have spent a long time in front of the mirror every morning adjusting the tie which had become the symbol of his success, an accessory of his charm – and for Frank, who knew him so well, a proof of his increasing hollowness.

Times change, thought Frank with a sigh – and not only because of the dark red tie that had been chosen for the dead man out of the infinite variety of his wardrobe.

No, it was not only the tie – nor was it only the memorial torches which had just been lit at the dead man's head. They were not real torches but powerful electric lights, set in shallow bronze bowls and shining up at the ceiling. Memorial torches, contemporary style.

At the dead man's feet was a glass case containing his orders and decorations. They were numerous, for he had been fond of them, craved them and created opportunities of getting more and more. Indeed, one wondered how much of his whole career he had devoted to securing this or that gewgaw which was not yet in his collection. Regardless of the occasion he used to appear with three rows of coloured ribbons decorating his chest. Frank gazed with interest at the metallic display of crosses and grand crosses, stars, plaques, medals. Almost all the national decorations were there, as well as a good many foreign ones. Frank looked for one star in particular, one that had caught his eye when he had last seen the collection in the dead man's villa. Yes, there it was. If anyone even noticed it now, he could hardly be as surprised as Frank had been on that occasion. It was a foreign order that every recipient in the country had, at a particular time, returned as a gesture of political disapproval. So the press had reported, but now it appeared that the dead man had kept his. Why? Did he not realize the risk he was running? A word in the right quarter from any of his enemies would have meant the end of his career, and possibly much worse besides. He surely could not have been so naïve as not to realize how dangerous it was to remain in possession of this trinket. Everyone knew he had received it. It had been pinned to his breast in a solemn public ceremony, amply recorded in documents and photographs. When Frank saw it at the villa it had made a strange impression on him. Perhaps the dead man was so fond of medals that he could not bring himself to part with this one, despite the risk. But perhaps there was something else – a last spark of dignity and resistance, even of protest.

Frank's eye kept returning to the star. A great, rich object blazing with ruby light, it seemed somehow unsuitable for the dead man – indeed it had long been so, perhaps even from the very moment it was conferred upon him.

At any rate he had come to no harm through it, even though Galovitch knew he had not given it back. Perhaps that was an explanation. He had kept it, and no harm had come to him.

Even so, it was strange that he had kept it. Perhaps after all it did suit him a little. And, try as he might, Frank could not help feeling a certain pleasure in the star for the dead man's sake. Perhaps everyone, even Frank himself, had been a little mistaken in him. Perhaps he was not, after all, exactly what Frank had thought him to be ...

'Don't stand around here.' A brusque voice interrupted his thoughts. He stepped out of the way of two men who laid a large, heavy wreath at the dead man's feet. An expensive one, made of fir branches intertwined with hundreds of red carnations. Where on earth had they managed to get so many? Most of them must have been flown into town, probably by night. The men leant the wreath against the glass case and spread out the two ribbons on the ground to either side, one red, the other in the national colours.

All around, the finishing touches were being put to the scene. Upon the black velvet curtain that concealed the far end of the hall and the passages leading to the rear of the building, they were hanging a portrait of the dead man, a huge enlargement of his photograph, together with his initials and dates of birth and death, the inevitable gilt laurel branch and an inscription commemorating his life and deeds. In the left-hand corner of the hall they had erected a small laurel bower made up of hothouse plants standing in large wooden tubs, also swathed in black. The mourning throng were unlikely to realize that such a bower, which is *de rigueur* on such occasions, does not serve a purely decorative purpose. Frank, however, knew that all kinds of things might take place within its shelter during the two days' lying in state. Women who had fainted, overcome by the sight of the coffin, would be carried to it, and from within it attentive eyes would watch the procession of the dead man's fellow-citizens, scanning every face and ready to intervene at the first unscheduled incident.

Frank was well aware that almost everything on this occasion must be planned and allowed for : it could not be otherwise. But at the moment preparations were still in full swing : knocking of hammers, rustle of paper, heavy steps thudding on the concrete floor and from time to time an irreverent oath. When people eventually filed through the hall, it would not occur to them that men had been working all night to get things ready.

The dead man lay unperturbed by the bustle around him. His face, smooth and placid, had an air of solemn dignity. His complexion was fresh and he looked as though he were sound asleep. One could imagine him at any moment opening his eyes, lifting the glass cover and looking out in amazement at what was happening around him.

But this was an illusion, a feat of the make-up artist. Frank had been in such halls of death before: he knew what measures surrounded this last phase of bodily existence. Perhaps the dead man's last moments had been far from the placidness his composed features might suggest. Perhaps death had come as an enemy, to be fought tooth and nail; perhaps the hands, now quietly folded in his lap, had been stretched out in desperate, convulsive gestures, so that his fingers had to be broken before they would lie straight; perhaps he had tried to scream at the last moment and the death agony had bared his teeth in an unnatural grimace, so that the attendants had had to loosen his lower jaw – this and much more they might have had to do in order that he should lie serenely as he now did upon the catafalque. But by tomorrow the thick covering of rouge and powder would begin to melt in the heat generated by thousands of mourners and by the arc lights, his nose would grow thin and sharp, his eyes would sink into his head and his complexion grow yellow. It would not matter much then: the first day of a lying-in-state is the important one. It is then that guards of honour and people of consequence pay their respects to the dead. And in two days' time, at the final ceremony, the coffin would already be covered by its lacquered lid.

Up above, in a concealed gallery, the musicians were beginning to tune their instruments. From time to time there came the trill of a clarinet, the rumbling of a double-bass or the roll of a kettle-drum. But these sounds did not make the same impression as in a concert hall. There, the tuning of instruments is a kind of solemn introduction, a promise of pleasure to come and a normal part of the proceedings. It's a long time since I went to a concert, Frank reflected, his thoughts wandering: I haven't even played a record for ages. He had a large collection, by world-famous artists. Why had he got tired of them? Perhaps because not even the best equipment can begin to reproduce the atmosphere of a concert-hall with its preliminary noises and coughing, the tuning of instruments, the applause and the shining, grateful eyes of the audience. Stereophonic sound and high fidelity were all very well, but records could never replace the glamour of a live concert, the inimitable tension, expectation and devotion of hundreds of listeners.

Here, on the other hand, the keening of unseen strings from above had a disturbing, unnatural and unpleasant effect. It seemed to Frank that this music was meant for the dead man, that these violins and cellos were mocking and calling him names. Once the heavy bronze doors were opened, a different music would be heard, but that was somehow not for him. In any case, he could no longer hear the musicians. What were they to him?

Frank could not see the musicians and they could not see what was going on below. They would remain unseen throughout the lying-in-state. They were, after all, only an accessory, a sentimental adjunct in the creation of a mourning atmosphere, ludicrous but harmless.

And what am I? he asked himself. Am I not just another accessory in the creation of a spectacle of national mourning? I may not be so invisible as they – every now and then I shall have to leave my corner behind the open bronze doors – but even when they can all see me they won't take any notice, nobody ever does, I am just part of the scene. Thousands of people must have seen me again and again, but if you asked any of them what I looked like they wouldn't have the faintest idea. I'm a man without a face, or rather my face is this thing which hangs on a strap in front of me, the lens of the big Hasselblad camera – that is myself . . .

Frank smiled at his own thoughts. The public anonymity in which he lived and worked had long ceased to bother him,

16

if indeed it ever had. He had had plenty of opportunity to realize that a man's privacy is one of his most precious possessions, enabling him at least occasionally to stop playing a part and to be himself. He himself had no thirst for fame or popularity – he had grown out of that. His dislike of work and his morbid moods and attitudes had other causes. He was a producer on a large scale of public faces – retouching, supplying, popularizing – a part of the machinery that created public legends of the greatness of little people, the importance of the insignificant and the beauty of the ugly. Once, at the beginning, he had looked for something else. Not now . . .

Here, then, was where he would stand. Not, of course, through the entire ceremony. Frank was no beginner, he knew almost to a minute when his presence was and was not required. The funeral staff, whose office was just behind the curtain, had shown him the programme for the whole three days. It was an exact programme and would, to the best of everyone's power, be followed exactly. It would be disastrous – and somebody would be in trouble – if anything unexpected should happen, but in Frank's long experience nothing ever had. Whatever else goes wrong, a state funeral must go smoothly.

'Nothing must go wrong at a state funeral,' Frank had said to the security policeman at the back entrance who had been reluctant to admit him at first. Frank had argued that he needed to study the layout – he had displayed all his documents, including the special card authorizing him to be present at all ceremonies, he had brandished the paper signed by the head of the secret police; in reply the man merely shook his head, he had precise instructions that no one was to enter until the lying-in-state began, and nobody was allowed to use the rear entrance except people with special red invitation cards. All the same, he did realize that a state funeral must go smoothly, and in the end allowed Frank to enter.

A confused noise came from the corridor behind the black curtain. Into the hall, to which the workmen were putting the

17

finishing touches, marched a group of men dressed in their best clothes: all solemn, all in black but for a few senior officers in uniform. They were led by the dead mean's private secretary.

'Will you please stand in a semicircle, comrades,' he commanded them, 'and we will practise taking up positions round the bier. May we have the first guard of honour, please?'

The first group of six, who had been members of the dead man's private office and his close collaborators, moved away from the rest. The private secretary motioned them back behind the curtain.

'From the very beginning, please – now the march into the hall, just as if it was the real thing . . .'

The six men went behind the curtain and returned two abreast. In this fashion they marched to the head of the catafalque and there divided to take up their positions – three to the left and three to the right. The private secretary dashed about, directing, correcting, explaining, praising – that's right, comrades, the march on was exactly right, that's the way to do it, will the others please take notice, now the next guard please, we'll practise the relief: the six at the catafalque stay where they are until each man has a relief standing opposite him, then the first six go off, they form up in twos in front of the catafalque, the second six take a single step forward into their places; now once again, please . . .

The secretary was in his element – if one of you comrades should feel an itch or a tickling in the nose, anything like that, please ignore it, it wouldn't look dignified, you should be like granite, comrades, absolute granite, and please, before coming on do check one another's appearance, whether your ties are straight and so on, this is a solemn occasion, comrades, it must go off properly . . . you've all been in the army, I don't have to tell you which is your right and which is your left, the sign for the relief to come on is the little red light above the entrance, when it shines for the third time you step forward . . . let's try it just once more, comrades, right from the beginning . . .

The secretary surpassed himself, jumping about like a chimpanzee. He had quite forgotten the dead man: this was his own day, his great day as commander of the guard of honour, which had suddenly brought him power over politicians, generals and artists. There he was directing and commanding them while they stood before him like so many children, hanging on his every order. Today, for a few minutes, he was their lord and master, entitled to admonish and criticize, more, to determine their positions – for in a guard of honour it matters a great deal who stands where, and it was he, he alone, who decided upon their grouping and the order of their appearance.

Frank too felt as if the main person present was not the dead man, but his private secretary. This was in fact the only service that the secretary would perform for his master, since he had joined the dead man's staff only shortly before he fell ill. Frank had never seen him before, he did not know where he came from or whether his wife was blonde or brunette. This would be his one and only service, the first and the last, since the new minister would probably bring his own private secretary with him – but what if he did not, what if he should take a fancy to the present one? Hence all this energy and zeal: the private secretary was responsible for the guard of honour, and that must be a success. Everyone must see what a success it was!

Frank smiled to himself. What a tasteless comedy! Here were the men of power and dignity, going through their paces. Admittedly good organization is needed on such occasions, but this was too much. After all, the dead man was present, under the glass coffin-lid. But he was secondary, none of them paid attention to him; he was there for the audience's benefit and these people were actors for the others to gaze at and whisper 'That's so and so' and 'That over there's so and so.' This was why they were rehearsing and practising so hard: they were about to give a public performance, and this was something that they all liked doing.

Frank could remember another comedy of the same sort,

the annual 'dress rehearsal' at the presidential palace, when every year two hundred people practised the ceremony at which they came forward to receive state decorations. Or those curious elections to the town council, where chosen individuals rose to propose the election of chosen candidates and all present raised their hands to signify assent, knowing that the real elections would take place two hours later. No one protested, no one rose and left the hall – on the contrary, they regarded this idiotic charade as a test of discipline and obedience, indeed an honour. Did any of them, he wondered, come to realize later that things might be done differently?

Anyway, he went on photographing the rehearsal until he had used up a whole spool. These people were all used to the glare of flashlights and it did not enter their heads that anybody might be making fun of them. No one noticed him except the private secretary, who shot him a grateful smile, begging with his eyes: That's the picture I want, you must do me an enlargement, it'll be a knock-out – me giving orders to six generals!

In earlier days, when Frank took unsuitable pictures in this way from obviously unsuitable angles, he had always felt slightly nervous. What if someone should notice that there was something fishy about the photographs? But in time he realized that there was nothing to worry about. He got used to the fact that nobody saw or noticed him. He belonged to the scene and was part of it – nobody on these solemn occasions noticed the photographer any more than they noticed the shutter of his camera. So for a long time he had been taking illicit, compromising, unedifying pictures with insolent self-confidence. The only reason the secretary had noticed him was that he was a new man, still unused to the game.

Two

In one of the numerous offices at the back of the building there was installed for the period of the lying-in-state an official whose existence and function were unknown to millions of his fellow citizens. Frank sought in vain an appropriate designation or title for this important personage. Chief of Staff (Funerals)? Grand Master of Ceremonies? Chief of Protocol in Charge of Funeral Rites? Government Interment Officer? State Mourner in Chief? He racked his brains, but could not think of anything more suitable. In any case, this man was in full and absolute charge of all the arrangements. The funeral commission which had been appointed took its orders from him. He determined the order of appearance of the successive guards of honour and the delegations from factories, offices and institutions and how large these delegations should be; he laid down when and for how long the deceased's widow should be present in the ceremonial hall, and the arrangement – according to priority – of the wreaths beneath the catafalque; he prescribed the length of speeches and the order of speakers; he approved the programme of funeral music, and the entire arrangement of the great hall.

Frank did not know his name. Nor could he imagine what this man did, or where and how he operated, during the intervals between state funerals. It was surely impossible that this highly secret person, this specialist, had no other job of any kind. But certainly he must know the funeral business inside out: a layman can scarcely imagine the intricate organization and elaborate staff work that is required for a state funeral to go off properly. The crowd of mourners must file past the coffin smoothly, without awkward gaps. The lying-in-state was to last two days; it would never do for all those who were to file past to turn up at the same time. The official, who had plenty of experience in such matters, estimated the total crowd at two hundred thousand. The question of who came when was not one to be left to chance. While the dead man's relatives were present, the line should consist of people from his home town. This sort of thing had to be planned, checked and organized. It would be embarrassing, for instance, if a delegation of artists' unions should appear at a time when Galovitch formed part of the guard of honour. Galovitch hated artists: he would scent provocation at once. What had to be arranged was for his arrival to coincide with that of a delegation from the biggest factory in town. Hundreds of such details were the official's province. He had to think of everything.

And indeed he did. From the experience of previous funerals he knew that the presence of too many photographers takes away from the dignity of the ceremony and disturbs its mourning atmosphere. Press photographers are a terrible nuisance. They get under statesmen's feet, run about when everyone is standing at attention for the national anthem, scramble for the best places, lie on the ground, shin up trees, crawl around on the grandstand like apes, blind people with their incessant flash bulbs, get on everybody's nerves and intrude where they have no business to be. So the secret official had given orders that there was to be only one film camera, one television camera and a single photographer from the official agency. Frank, who had experience of such ceremonies, was the photographer chosen. He was not called the 'banquet reporter' for nothing.

Here, then, he would stand for the next two days, quiet and unnoticed, half hidden by the massive bronze door and emerging from time to time to take photographs; above all, Galovitch must not be left out. Galovitch standing at attention, Galovitch delivering the funeral oration, Galovitch condoling with the bereaved widow – all this must and would get into the newspapers. Frank sometimes felt that the chief purpose of funerals, official festivities, receptions and other state occasions was to get Galovitch into the newspapers yet again. And then, of course, a picture of the scouts laying a wreath and of some old woman at the catafalque, wiping away her tears with a white handkerchief. Frank was an old hand, he knew how many pictures the newspapers would print and what subjects they must not omit. He would have to take about two hundred, though, in case the editors accused him of shirking. Two hundred negatives was about the norm for a funeral. Of course, he wouldn't keep at it the whole time. What would there be to do all day long? He knew the whole timetable of the ceremony, when he should be there and when not.

Frank had long ceased to have any illusions about himself and his work. Of course, whenever he turned up with his camera people would smile encouragingly and slap him on the back, but in fact they regarded him as a nuisance, a necessary evil. Necessary of course, since nowadays you couldn't imagine a career, or a reputation, or a promotion without photographs. In all Frank's experience as a reporter he had never met anyone who refused to be photographed. Occasionally someone would make a fuss and brush him aside, saying give it a rest, don't be absurd, but they didn't really mean it. People couldn't wait to get into the newspapers – the moment they caught sight of the pointing lens they would crowd to be in the picture, and as near the front as possible.

Frank was the official reporter, known and trusted, always to be seen amongst the great, in drawing-rooms, on reviewing stands, at high-level meetings to which only a select few are admitted : he was one of the few to whom all doors were open, a familiar figure, recognized and admitted with no identification – except for the Hasselblad camera, the Open Sesame.

A political meeting, a festival concert, a statesman's visit to a factory or cooperative – Frank photographed them all, as he had been doing for over twenty years now : microphones by the thousand, and speakers' rostrums. The rostrums were all alike and the microphones did not differ much, but the faces and figures behind them changed incessantly. A celebrity without a microphone ceases to be important and becomes a common, expressionless face: but that doesn't matter, in the press it's only behind the microphone that a public man is really a public man. It's only then that people realize that his calling is to announce and declare things to his fellow-men, and that he actually has something to announce and declare to them.

Frank's private archives included fifteen May Day parades – pictures of the function as a whole, and detailed views of individuals. Recently, when he had compared the earliest photograph with the previous year's, he had been unable to find a single face common to both. What had happened to the great, the memorable faces of fifteen years ago? Where was the strong man who had lifted a child on to the tribune from its father's arms? Or the other, whose picture, acknowledging the nation's cheers, had occupied half a page of newsprint? Did anyone even remember his name? It would have been the worse for Frank if he had failed to take this man's picture at that time, or had over-exposed the film. In those days it was unthinkable that the newspapers should appear without his photograph . . .

These people despised, abused or laughed at Frank, but they needed him, and when they met him they spoke honeyed words of gratitude and pretended a cordial interest in his affairs. But it had happened more than once that when he was out of uniform, that is to say without his camera, these same people had failed to notice him. This was not deliberate – they were literally unaware of his existence. Without his camera he was nobody: it alone gave him some semblance of importance. When they greeted him they were really greeting the lens – for its sake they were ready to adopt poses of ludicrous dignity, to smile when they felt like crying, to look solemn when they felt like laughing, to feign interest when they were bored to death. They wanted to be immortalized, and only a photograph could do that. They wanted the present moment preserved for eternity, with thousands hanging on their words, and only newspapers could make life eternal.

Newspapers are kept in archives and bound, one annual volume after another, they outlast man's temporal life and they record only the doings of exceptional people. One day it might be cinema personalities, another day female bosoms – the newspapers are the social authentication of a man's importance, the true selectors: among thousands of scientists they know only a few, among thousands of officials they know only the most eminent. Here too there are major distinctions: it is one thing to see oneself in a group photograph and another to appear on the front page of a newspaper in a speaker's pose at the microphone. Then there is oneself alone in close-up, perhaps even an official portrait . . .

A man whose name and face have never appeared in the press is anonymous, he is the man of whom the photographed orators so often speak: the man in the street, the ordinary citizen, the working masses, the crowd, the mob, the hoi polloi – in short, the common people. It had always infuriated Frank to hear these words from the lips of speakers, whoever they might be. Who are you, he thought, to presume so? What is so exceptional about you compared with the little, simple, ordinary people? Is it because you fought in the rising, or the revolution? Frank knew hundreds who had fought and fought well, and when the fight was over they had taken their flasks of unsweetened coffee and gone to work an early shift in the mines. Some of them used to know you in those days, he thought, they know who and what you are, and what do you suppose they think when they hear you call them plain, ordinary, average people? Just a rhetorical phrase? Maybe, but it springs from some kind of psychosis, it has deep roots somewhere in you, in your sense of being something greater, one of the elect, a privileged being . . .

Frank knew where these exceptional beings came from and could guess accurately how far they would go and how they would end. He more than anyone else had immortalized their appearances on a large scale. In this way he had helped to create a thousand giants, who still enjoyed immortality in his own rich archives. He could even remember the names of some of them. Otherwise, they had fallen into total oblivion. Giants? Occasionally he met one or other of them on the street. They were those to whom others now referred as little, plain, average, undistinguished people.

Experience had taught Frank scepticism. When on some public occasion he heard the words 'We ordinary people...' he thought to himself: Aha, so you want to get on, do you? He had known people who used to talk in this way: then, later on, they made a tiny alteration and it would be 'The ordinary people....' Once the dead man here had roared from the tribune 'We ordinary, simple people ...'; later, the talk was all of 'our plain, simple countrymen'.

A rhetorical turn of phrase? But the man lying here in state was proof that it was more than that.

Frank had once been a passionate photographer. Mountains, rivers, romantic sunrises. In those days photography was still a luxury; he had belonged to a set of young people, among whom only he possessed a camera. Naturally they kept begging him to take pictures and he did: groups, individuals, excursions, sporting events, demonstrations. Curiously enough even then he photographed hundreds of people but hardly ever appeared in the pictures himself, except when somebody said 'Come on, Frank, you stand with the others and I'll take the picture, then we'll have you in as well.' Frank had never been especially keen on this. He took more pleasure in the picture of a deer, or a fisherman sitting on a willow branch, than in a photograph of himself. But he liked taking others if it gave them pleasure.

Afterwards, this casual occupation became his daily bread. As a 'banquet reporter' he moved about from one show or function to another, photographing incessantly. He was not alone, there were others doing the same job, and it sometimes happened that he snapped one of them rubbing shoulders with the great, or that one of his colleagues did the same to him. If the picture was for some reason important, the reporter would be eliminated by the retoucher's art. Stenographers, chauffeurs and photographers are out of place in such pictures: they fall under the heading of the 'broad masses'.

He gazed at the photograph that hung before the black velvet curtain. It was an enormous reproduction: at least ten years old and not a perfect likeness, as the statesman's angular features had filled out somewhat since then. But the great man himself had liked this portrait and had never wanted another.

Portrait photographs were not Frank's speciality, but for the sake of old times or of some caprice the dead man had insisted on having a portrait done by him. Perhaps it was meant as a mark of favour, or to repair a blunder?

Frank had taken hundreds of trial photographs. None of them met with the statesman's approval: in one he looked too soft, in another too hard, in one the height of the brow was wrong and in another the expression of the eyes was too weak. In yet another, he looked 'too much like a civilian'. Frank, tirelessly snapping the shutter, found this amusing. He had hit on a pose which he knew was right and would please the great man, but he kept on taking more pictures, obliging his subject to take up unnatural attitudes, to make faces – now smile please, we want you to look pleasant, but not so much as to blur the firmness and determination of your features, just the suspicion of a smile . . . no, don't frown, you're starting to get wrinkles . . . now gaze into the distance, to symbolize the way ahead of us . . . a firm, decided, forward look . . .

Frank knew what efforts people were capable of, just for a single portrait. He had once persuaded a crazy actress that the maximum of concentration is expressed in the face of a person sitting on the toilet. After developing the picture, he had begun to think that there really was something in it.

For two solid months he kept on visiting the statesman at his residence. When he got tired of it, he pulled out of his portfolio the first photograph of the series. The statesman beamed.

'You see, it was worth the trouble after all!'

The portrait was a good one, fulfilling all expectations and answering to the statesman's conception of himself. Dignified but kind, young but wise, firm but magnanimous. In short, a personality.

Frank received by post an unexpectedly large fee, which he sent back. This caused a row with his wife, who of course could not understand his action. All that money!

In former times, Frank had done his job with interest and enthusiasm. He had imagined himself as the chronicler of the revolution, its ardour and its victories: he caught its young features and its rapid pulse, he wanted to be on the spot and he was there. He was there when the nation rose against the Germans: his pictures were among the few records of those days in all their beauty and ugliness. Later, he was present when the reactionary politicians were driven out of their offices, when he did for the press a successful series entitled 'Now he has to go about town on foot'. He was convinced that such men would never again sit in positions of importance, that a clean sweep had been made. His imagination was lively and his work was full of ingenuity and wit. He was present wherever anything of interest was going on. He enjoyed the busy, varied life of those days, full of drama and vicissitudes, and he wished to catch it in all its uniqueness.

Then, all of a sudden, things changed. One could no longer publish any pictures one liked, no matter of whom or what they were. Each had to be approved by a special commission, which mercilessly excluded all evidence of human frailty. If an official had bad teeth, he mustn't be shown smiling. The commission was careful to ensure that a particular individual was sufficiently in the foreground compared with his humbler colleagues, and that his appearance matched his importance.

Frank continued to be present. He was present when the monasteries and convents were closed. From that expedition he brought back a full set of pictures, recording scenes to which only a chosen few had been admitted. The series was much admired, but was never published. Frank could not understand why. The whole country knew that the monasteries had been occupied by the workers' militia – why should the story not be published? He was told that the pictures might be exploited by foreign reactionary propaganda. Why, thought

Frank to himself, what have we done that we should be ashamed of before a lot of foreigners?

But there was also another side to being present. Frank saw the élite, those worthy of being photographed, in intimacy and at close quarters. Hysterical actresses, conceited prize-winners, political bigwigs, regional and village bosses – there is scarcely any profession in which it is possible to see so much of the other, unofficial, unguarded side of human affairs. And he could not remember a single case of a person who did not wish to appear in some way other than he really was. Taller if he was short, handsomer if he was ugly, younger if he was getting on in years. Accordingly, a major retouching department grew up within the laboratories of the state press office. Wrinkles? Away with them! A person rumoured to be out of favour? Rub him out! Contemptuous sneers were transformed by the retouching artists into cheery smiles.

Frank saw the underside of life because he was only a big lens : no one needed to act a part before him unless the camera was actually pointing at them. It was strange how people who in those days had to watch every word talked freely on all subjects in front of chauffeurs and photographers. Frank was an eye-witness to their petty quarrels, their ludicrous fighting for spoils and perquisites, their angry outbursts, intrigue and slander, their greed, the vices which they carefully concealed from the world – in short, their other selves. He was allowed everywhere, because he was the creator of personalities that would resist the assault of time.

All those journeys, a hundred, two hundred, three hundred miles, in a large, comfortable car next to some notability on the way to a public celebration: how much he was able to hear and see on such occasions! But watch out if the picture of this unimportant function did not appear on the front page of the newspapers! For whenever that happened it was, of course, the photographer's fault.

Frank was still gazing at the dead man's portrait. How many times had he reproduced that face on celluloid? A thousand? Two thousand? He couldn't remember. From the negatives stored in his archives he could have composed a fantastic documentary on this man's life, his greatnesss and littleness. A high-spirited lad of sixteen riding on a cow. At seventeen, a young revolutionary, about to hit a gendarme on the head with the rifle which he has just snatched out of his grasp. Then handcuffed and being taken off to jail. Then addressing an excited crowd which is rhythmically shouting the slogan 'Work and bread!' Then kissing Margaret on the river-bank. Emptying a bottle of gin at one swallow. Jumping into a deep river from a high bridge. Climbing up a steep rock. Gazing thoughtfully into the flames of a camp fire. Wearing two belts of machine-gun ammunition and leading his men into the attack. During the retreat, exhausted, dragging himself painfully over the frozen snow. Grasping a tommy-gun and cursing as he blazes away at the Germans. Frank had caught him at a thousand unguarded moments, just as he really was, when he had nothing to pretend and no one to pretend to.

But Frank's archives, carefully hidden from the world, recorded other moments in the life of this historic personage: for example, being slapped by a female orderly whom he was pestering, or squatting in the forest to relieve himself while his bodyguard stood on either side of him, looking away it is true, but still on duty. Or again, sitting at a concert during the interval, all alone among the empty seats, snoring, with his head sunk on his chest. Frank had recorded all his faces, not only the one he was now looking at. And even the ones which the camera had not caught would never slip from his memory.

Frank disliked his job and would, but for one reason, have thrown it up long ago. If he went on patiently snapping one microphone after another it was because of a peculiar and perhaps somewhat perverted ambition, which at times grew to positively manic strength. This was to record the other, the averted face of the world in which he lived and moved. An expensive pastime of which nobody knew, not even his wife. Or, if she did, she never asked Frank what he did during those long hours in the dark-room. A dark-room is a mysterious sanctum in which outsiders have no business. Frank gave her to understand that he was developing or enlarging pictures, and sometimes he actually did. But most of the time he spent over his collection of photographic curiosities, for which he had devised a special hiding-place.

It excited him to feel that he was playing with life and death in this way. If he should be discovered, he would be done for. There were thousands of unique pictures which he had taken during his career. A parade of folly, a riot of vanity, a debauch of cowardice. A stark naked general dancing the *csárdás*, to the loud applause of female guests, among the cakes on a banquet-table. A collective orgy by a group of rural district bosses. A well-known actor splashing about in a pond, naked except for the ribbon of a state prizewinner. Picnics, parties, flirtations, quarrels. A party of deputies gormandizing in the restaurant-car of a special train which was taking them to view the devastation of the war-torn country, while half-naked children stared at them from the platforms. The wife of a prominent politician making love with her chauffeur on the steps of her summer villa.

Political love-affairs. A minister smiling broadly at a colleague about whom he has just said in a ceremonial speech that he is the best son ever born to mortal woman. The same minister denouncing the same colleague as a despicable abortion and emissary of hell. Yes, others had smiled on one another in this way – Galovitch on the dead man, for instance. One day they had cordially shaken hands, and the next day one was branding the other as a common criminal and traitor.

Frank's wife would sometimes reproach him : 'Why don't you photograph castles, ancient buildings, folk-dancing, the Tatra mountains? Why don't you do a book about animals or flowers or butterflies? Or nudes? They pay well these days. Other people do all right for themselves, and we never have any money.'

Frank knew this. They never did have any money. Sometimes, when he was in a good mood, he would say : Just you wait, I'll buy you a yacht and we'll sail round the world. He knew that his collection of 'curios' was unique. But he also knew that nobody would ever see it. He did not know what a luxury yacht cost, but he liked to know that he could have one if he chose, even though he never would choose. He had ceased to care about becoming famous. Not at any price. He had photographed too many celebrities to wish to be one of them.

Three

The first guard of honour, composed of members of the dead man's personal staff, had taken up their places around the catafalque. This time it was the real thing. In a moment the bronze doors would open to admit the endless queue of citizens who were to file past during the next two days. The dead man's former servants looked solemn. Until now, the confusion of the day had left them little time to think of him. Now they would have ten minutes in which to do so, standing at attention around his coffin. Ten minutes can be a long time – infinitely long . . .

Frank knew them all. He certainly knew more about each one of them than they knew about one another. None of them had really liked the dead man, although he had chosen them to serve him out of a host of other candidates. Why indeed should they have liked him? After all, it was he who used to proclaim that there is no such thing as friendship in politics, that friendship is a dangerous thing for a statesman.

Anyway, now they had ten minutes in which to think about him and lament his death, or mentally reproach him for it. It certainly complicated their lives vastly. Whatever they might have thought of him, at least he had represented security. Relative security, no doubt, but even that is better than none. They had got used to him, knew his weaknesses, and how to make up to him, knew his daily routine and had adapted their own to it: everything had its own rhythm, its own regular cycle, order and stability. Now suddenly it was all being thrown out of gear. Another would take his place. Who will it be? Me? The man in front of me? The man behind me?

The man in front can't stand me and I'd be out on my neck. As for the man behind me, I can't stand him and he knows it. He's a nitwit, I couldn't bear to work for him . . . But supposing they bring in someone from outside? Some other bigwig? Could Galovitch bear to let someone else get the job? He's had his eye on it for long enough. Well, if he gets it, that'll be the end of me. This much was clear to each one of them – Galovitch would be the end of him.

But of course it might not be Galovitch, it might be someone else they had never dreamt of as a possibility. Would that be the end of them too? Yes, it would. One after another, they would be pushed out to make room for the new man's friends. Each of the mourners could remember well enough how the dead man had summoned them from the country, years ago, when he himself had been raised to power.

No, it's the end all right. Whoever it is except me, it's the end. An outsider – the end. Galovitch – the end, the absolute end . . .

Frank knew them. He knew the look in their eyes which betrayed their thoughts. He could tell what they were thinking now and what they would be thinking about during the next few minutes. Frank did not see their future quite as pessimistically as they did. The end? Well, up to a point, but not altogether. They wouldn't drive around in such a big car, but still not a small one. They would work in a less important office, but still quite an important one, and they'd even be able to choose which office they would like to work in. Not which they were qualified for, but which they would like. They would move into smaller villas, but villas they would still have. No doubt they would cease to draw expenses for rent and fuel, and they might have to do without a servant.

What would they do in their new jobs? Gradually, unobtrusively they would get rid of the staff they found there and bring their own men in – people they knew and could rely on. They would appear less often in the press, and not on the front page. But they would still be mentioned, the country would not wholly forget them.

If I were standing among them now, thought Frank, would my eyes have the same insecure and frightened expression? He didn't know. How can a man imagine the expression of his own eyes? At any rate, he was glad that he wasn't among them. What would have been the point?

Among them? ... They all had the pasty complexions of officials. Lack of exercise showed in their protruding bellies. Driving to and from the office, to meetings, receptions and celebrations, to inspect rural activities; an armchair at work, a comfortable sofa at home. A hunting trip once or twice a year, a month at the seaside on a private beach, a sixteen-hour working day: sixteen hours or more of sterile consultations, self-contradictory resolutions, committee meetings which take note that the targets fixed by previous committees have not been met and which fix targets which will not be met either. They have no time for anything, they are harried and they harry themselves even more, snowed under with thousands of illusory problems which prevent them concerning themselves with real ones.

All of them were fat, as if cast in a single mould. To give them their due, Frank could remember them as tough revolutionaries, in the days when the revolution itself was tough. Since then, the revolution had softened around the edges and so had they.

Like the dead man here. He too had once been a tough character with sharp edges. But in the last photograph Frank had taken of him he had a vague, washed-out expression, commonplace eyes and flabby cheeks, in fact he had run to seed. Frank knew this was not the usual way of things – generally men attained their final and definitive appearance at about the dead man's age, while in younger photographs they looked like milksops – as their character took shape, so did their appearance. But the dead man had had much more the air of a personality in his youth than in his later years: his sharp profile had started to lose itself in unhealthy fat, he had lost individuality: his pictures could no longer be published without retouching, otherwise he would have had a white oval blob instead of a face and he would have exploded once more in fury at those scoundrels of press photographers.

Frank and the dead man had been friends from early school-days. From then until recently they had been constantly together, in good and bad times. They had even survived the hardest test in the life of two men – that of being in love with the same woman. Without the other, Frank had felt that he was not a whole man.

What did the dead man mean to him today? A photographic subject, nothing more. For many years Frank had attached himself to him with dogged endurance. He had wanted to seize him, to hold him in his entirety. Later, he had avoided seeing him at close quarters, but then began again to seek him out determinedly, following his every step and decision, his concerns and his setbacks. He was curious to know what could happen to a man such as the dead man had once been, what could become of him.

The estrangement between them was not a sudden or dramatic event, but quiet and imperceptible. If Frank had been asked what he had against him, he would have been puzzled to reply. It was not even that their paths wholly diverged. They continued to meet, sought each other out and enjoyed being together. Frank could still not explain exactly what had changed. It was simply that they used to like and understand each other and no longer did so. These things happen.

Towards the end, the dead man had actually begun to be afraid of Frank. Perhaps he felt that Frank knew too much about him, and remembered what had happened to those about whom he himself knew too much. But by that time he was afraid of everything – even of shadows. Shadows there were in plenty, and each day increased their number.

Frank approached the catafalque and took a long look at the face of his former friend. He was surprised to find that he felt nothing whatsoever. Neither grief nor any other emotion. In general, the sight of death inspires feelings of tenderness, contemplation and respect for the departed. Frank felt nothing. A man who meant nothing whatever to him or to the rest of mankind had passed away. Of course, as long as he lay there people would feign everything that is customary during such shows, while the crowd filed past the catafalque in its tens of thousands. Organized bereavement, organized mourning, organized sorrow . . .

The invisible orchestra in the gallery struck up the first bars of the funeral march. The six men who formed the guard of honour stood even more rigidly to attention. At the same moment, two men tugged open the heavy bronze doors. The clock in the nearby tower began to strike eight o'clock. Frank photographed the first members of the public as they filed in, and then stepped for a moment outside the building. There they stood in their hundreds, frozen and waiting, stamping about in an icy wind. The long line of citizens dressed in black, who had come to pay their last respects to the dead, began to stir, to move forward. Delegations from trade unions, co-operatives, societies, political and social institutions of all kinds advanced to lay wreaths beside the catafalque. An attendant showed them discreetly where the wreaths should go, in accordance with the importance of each organization.

The members of the crowd were doubtless hardly aware as they moved past that there were some people who did not leave the hall: the attendants, and those whose business it was to watch. These men saw everything, and each had his special task. Were there enough people waiting to enter the building? There should be at least an hour's worth at any given time. The man responsible for this was experienced in calculating crowds and knew how many persons could pass the catafalque in an hour. If the queue outside became too short he would report to the funeral commission's office, where another official would reach for his telephone and ring up a factory or a school. The flow of people must be kept even: it would be awkward if there were gaps or if there were suddenly no one in front of the catafalque. In fact, it was all too well organized: the mourning procession did not have the air of a genuine display of grief and sense of loss. But perhaps nobody really wanted this: what mattered was numbers, overwhelming numbers, two hundred thousand citizens saying farewell to the dead statesman in the space of two days. After all, each of them who passed by knew well enough that his death was no great loss, he had long since been consigned to oblivion, for several months now he had been as if nonexistent – only his sudden illness had saved him from public disgrace and ignominious expulsion from office.

Yes, the illness which had no doubt been preying on him for a long time had saved him and others a great deal of unpleasantness. It was, as everyone knew, mortal and incurable. There is no point in making a public scandal over a dying man. At one time, indeed, the authorities would have made no bones about doing so, but nowadays a natural death was considered a better form of exit than a political showdown which meant washing loads of dirty linen, bringing too many things to light, precautions, organization. It was better like this. The dead statesman was no longer in anyone's way and no longer had the power to harm.

The laying of wreaths was a decided relief in the slow, monotonous rhythm of the procession. There were many of them: Frank could guess fairly accurately how many there would be. Apart from the two which were deposited before the doors were opened, they were all alike, consisting of brushwood and artificial red chrysanthemums. Natural flowers were scarce and expensive at this time of year. Frank was surprised to see, here and there in the crowd, someone holding a bunch of cyclamen or even of red carnations. He was especially intrigued by a girl – she could not have been more than eighteen – who laid upon the catafalque three branches of white lilac. Could she be a relative? Hardly, or she would not have come alone. A bouquet of that sort might cost anything up to a hundred crowns – a lot of money for a girl of eighteen, several pairs of stockings' worth at least. She couldn't have any close connection with the dead man: she belonged to a generation that might just have heard of his name and position, or known that from time to time he delivered one of those turgid and boring speeches in the main square. But perhaps he had helped her in some way? Perhaps he had removed difficulties in the way of her entering the university, or had her father released from jail at her request? She was an attractive girl, and pretty women always got more out of him, although still not much. Or perhaps she was just naïve and slightly eccentric, sentimental about funerals?

Death in any form is a serious matter. People themselves become grave when they are confronted by it. Frank knew how people's faces darken when they suddenly encounter the funeral of an unknown person, how their expression clouds over as they reflect, if only for a moment, on the transitoriness of life. The people here were walking on tiptoe, even though their steps would have been noiseless on the soft red carpet.

A group of primary schoolchildren, awe-stricken and blue with cold, were just approaching the catafalque. They gazed around them, puzzled and a little frightened. They could not grasp much of what was going on – apart from one or two who might have lost some near relative, they could as yet know nothing of death. Frank looked angrily at the teacher who had brought them. Why, in heaven's name? These six-year-olds must have had a long stand outside in the cold. What was the point of it? The children skipped out again into the icy weather. For a little while they would still be bewildered, overawed and quiet, and then they would start chattering and forget about the queer place where some old man lay on a high bed draped in black.

The procession continued to move forward. Whatever the people in the crowd might have thought of the dead man while he was still alive, here they felt the presence of death and were cowed by its majesty. But were these thoughts directed towards the dead man, or rather towards death as such? Were they moved or frightened by his end? Had any of them known him, had they cause to be grateful to his memory, did they now feel a sense of irreparable loss? Frank scanned the faces of the individuals who had just filed past the coffin. Did they show any trace of human sympathy or grief? Those who could not remember his name or who blamed him for things that had not been his fault – did their faces now show joy, malice or relief?

Frank had attended several state funerals in the past, and at some of them people had had tears in their eyes. Today, all eyes were dry. The dead man, extolled by the press and radio as great and unreplaceable, was alone, with none to bear him company.

Of course, the ceremony was impressive. For some reason Frank could not understand, people like funerals. The organization of this one was perfect: penetrating, uplifting, mournful music was wafted down to the ears of the crowd and reverberated from the cut-glass of the great chandelier, the electric memorial torches burned, one guard of honour succeeded another, the scene was full of reds and greens, film cameras were at work and the ceremony was being televised 'live' – whichever way the citizen turned he was assailed by the organized atmosphere of mourning. Yet it all somehow lacked significance, in spite of the flags at half-mast, the black-rimmed portraits in shop windows, the broadcasting of funeral music, the special television programme, and the thousands of mourners. During his life many had cursed and despised the dead man, many had spread unsavoury tales about him, whether true or false, but now it was not worth while to do even that any more – he was dead, he was no longer there. The great man had become too insignificant to excite anyone's sympathy, to be worth even a sneer or a malicious gleam in the eye. Was it really so? Could he really be so unimportant as that? Did his death fail to move even those whom he had injured? What about those?

No, even they were unconcerned. Nothing was here but death: a serious matter, but beyond it nothing at all. Nothing and nobody.

Frank was just photographing the group of six boy scouts who had relieved the six generals, when something happened. A subdued gasp was heard in the hall, people stood still for a moment and glanced with curiosity at the entrance doors.

Frank distinctly heard the involuntary 'Ah!' which escaped several lips. He did not need to turn round. He knew what was happening at the entrance, it could be felt in the atmosphere and read in innumerable pairs of eyes. So that was she! They had all heard much about her, most of it unfavourable. So that was what she looked like! Even through the veil that covered her face, you could tell she was a handsome woman. They said the two of them hadn't got on well together, in fact that they had fought like cat and dog. She used to play around, they said, and he used to beat her whenever the fancy took him.

The nearby clock struck eleven. So the widow had come. The people in front of her stood to one side. She had come with the dead man's father and sister, and she was escorted by her brother, the ambassador. The drama of her appearance must have been felt even up in the gallery. Two musicians moved their heads, and the strains of the dirge wavered for a moment.

She's still pretty, the tigress, thought Frank, and many must have been thinking the same. Everyone, especially the women, stared at her with bold curiosity. Her legs – oh! Her sable coat – ah! Her hat – my goodness!

Frank too had a long look at her. Her legs were long, slender and beautifully formed. The coat was from Moscow and the hat from Vienna. The sheer stockings, bag and gloves were from Vienna too. Clearly, she had been warned in plenty of time that there was no hope left.

Frank caught himself divining the contours of her figure under the fur coat. She could have come in a sack and still made the same vivid impression. The mourning garb enhanced her charms. A few curls of sunny blonde hair peeped out from under her hat.

Frank turned his eyes away from her.

The diplomat led his sister gently towards the catafalque. The crowd remained stock-still, and Frank felt a shiver of curiosity. What would she do? How would she react to this encounter? She behaved with dignity. She stood for a moment looking down at the dead man; her face, pallid for lack of sleep, was visible through the transparent veil on which every gaze was fixed, but her lips did not tremble, she remained composed, no tears showed in her eyes. Not a movement, not a gesture, not a sign of emotion. Cold, austere, dignified she was, but unmoved by sorrow. Behind her, the dead man's sister broke into a long-drawn, whining sob of grief. The widow stepped back, took her by the arm and led her to the other side of the catafalque, where three chairs had been placed in readiness. The widow took her place on the middle chair, with the dead man's father on her right and his sister on her left; the ambassador stood behind her. Frank felt his admiration grow for the official who had organized all this behind the scenes. Perfect stage management – even down to the business of the three chairs. Or perhaps this had been prearranged between him and the others?

At a funeral of this sort a chair is the widow's privilege, it belongs to the occasion, and accordingly there she sat. Frank was pleased, very pleased by her performance: she was not acting a part or pretending feelings that she didn't have. She was the late statesman's widow, a role which entails certain obligations: she was prepared to comply with them, and that was all. Protocol required that she should remain there for a quarter of an hour and so she would, but no one need hope that she would fall in a faint or break out in hysterical weeping, that it would be their happy chance to witness a sensational tragedy or a sensational comedy. For this, Frank respected her.

She would not have an easy life from now on. She would be attacked from all sides, her every step would be watched, the scandal-mongering would not abate but would even be intensified for a time. Her villa would be taken away, many things would become more complicated, she would have to restrict herself in many ways; however big her pension was, it would be no substitute for the privileges she had enjoyed. But was she really so badly off? She would still be a beautiful woman – the Western sports-car was hers, and once the turmoil of interests around her had died down she would be able to live avidly, as she had always wanted to, and free from the restrictions which her position had hitherto imposed on her. She herself might well feel that this was her day of liberation, that she would have an easier time in future.

It was whispered that she was the mistress of a certain famous actor, who came to her villa secretly by the back door. This, as Frank knew, was the purest gossip. The villa was watched day and night by the secret police, and she wasn't such a fool as all that. However, he had sometimes seen her car, a conspicuous one, parked in a certain side-street. The actor in question did not live there, but Frank knew who did. It was part of his job to know where prominent people lived ...

There must have been something telepathic in Frank's gaze, for she suddenly turned her head and their eyes met. Frank did not look away, nor did she. Frank narrowed his eyes a little as a sign of greeting or sympathy. He did not expect her to answer, she didn't like him, but she too dropped her eyelids, so slightly that only he would notice. He aimed the big lens at her, and she started as if to say Don't, what are you doing that for? He shrugged his shoulders imperceptibly: I can't help it, I'm not here for fun and neither are you, I know how you feel, but there'd be trouble if I turned up at the office without a picture of you, there has to be one, it's only right and proper. And what harm does it do you anyway?

The clock chimed the first quarter. The widow rose, followed by her companions, and her brother escorted her to the exit, where two attendants needlessly cleared a path for her. All those who stood by knew who she was, and would have made way unasked.

Watching her receding figure, Frank suddenly started violently. Good God! Where was Martin? Why had he not come with his stepmother? He was the dead man's son, his own flesh and blood – even if his father had thrown him out of the house after that unpleasant business during his student days in Moscow. Was it possible that an estrangement of this kind could be prolonged, in medieval fashion, beyond the grave? Martin was his only son and Frank knew he had loved the boy – perhaps he had not cast him off of his own free will, perhaps it had cost him pain to do it. Why hadn't he come? Was it he who didn't want to, or had the widow prevented him? The stepson and stepmother hated each other, they had done so from the very first moment, with the sort of hate that never dies out and stops at nothing.

Once upon a time Martin had ridden on Frank's knee and had been allowed to knock him out at boxing, provided he first ate up all his spinach. That was when the dead man was still living with Margaret, his first wife. Frank had enjoyed being with them, the dead man had not yet discovered himself to be a great statesman, he still thought more of others than himself. Later on, Margaret was no longer presentable enough for him: she hadn't kept pace with his development, and she was getting fat. The divorce had very nearly wrecked his career, but what good had the career been to him anyway? But for it, he might not be lying here today . . .

Margaret was always placid, always cheerful and indulgent towards his moods. He was constantly having affairs and she knew it – as she once said to Frank, he's a stallion and there's nothing to be done about it. Frank had foreseen the crack-up in their relations rather sooner than the dead man himself. When the final breach came he was living in the capital, but he heard all about it from there. The news of the divorce did not surprise him. The blonde bitch – as he used, in those days, to call the widow who had just left the hall – knew what she wanted and had got the dead man exactly where she wanted him. Frank was only surprised that he had had the political courage to risk breaking his neck in this way. At that time such things were still judged severely, and Galovitch was there to notice whenever he made a wrong move.

Frank by then had ceased to feel any special tie with his boyhood friend: in his own mind, he had broken with him some months earlier. But he was sorry for Margaret. He often thought of her and kept telling himself that he would find out where she lived and look her up whenever he should pass that way. She was a splendid woman: her idiot of a husband didn't know what he was throwing away. She had managed to create an oasis of peace and certainty at the centre of his stormy life. No other woman could have done this for him, and certainly not the blonde. Frank had expected that the divorce and remarriage would do him a lot of harm, but on the contrary, he had continued to rise until he became the chief man of the province. Nevertheless, whenever Frank saw him he could not resist the impression that the decay and dissolution of his personality dated from that one fateful step. Even his vital spirits were not adequate to the blonde's passions and her bohemian way of life. Frank had long been convinced that it was she who kept urging him to climb higher and at the same time dragegd him ever further into the depths.

Where had she come from, and how had she got into his office? Frank had suspected from the first that she was planted there by Galovitch. He sometimes laughed at this idea, but there might after all be something in it. Galovitch was capable of anything. Was she too? That he didn't know.

Anyhow, wherever she came from, one fine day she was there. Frank remembered it well . . .

The strong man of the region – the firm, outstretched arm of the revolutionary government. When they sent him to these parts they had said: We have chosen you because we believe in your qualities. It's a bad area, too big for its boots, all kinds of skulduggery, nothing works properly. Purchases, deliveries, production, communications – everything's in a mess; the Catholics are getting out of hand, the farmers won't join the cooperatives; go out there and knock it into shape, be watchful and firm and ruthless if you have to be. Off you go, we're behind you, we'll help you and we'll expect results.

So he went. He was persevering, firm, ruthless when he had to be, tireless and incorruptible. Day and night he was on the job, travelling about the country and turning up unexpectedly at trouble spots or where a shake-up was needed. He agitated, argued, begged, threatened, shouted, clapped men in jail without caring too much if it was legal – he had full powers, courage to take decisions and strength to act. He was a local Hercules with the superhuman task of cleansing thousands of Augean stables, and he did so in the full knowledge that the task might be the death of him. He would wake Frank up in the middle of the night: 'Come on, we have to be in the frontier zone in the morning, I don't like travelling alone at night'; or he would burst in on the night shifts in factories and sit with the workers, finding out where the shoe pinched them, giving orders and rectifying mistakes to the best of his power. The means at his disposal were limited, but in those stirring revolutionary days he was, with all his short-comings, the right man in the right place, full of indestructible energy and dash and – despite his occasional excessive severity – understanding and broad-minded. Later on he had far greater means and more powerful instruments at his command, but by then he was no longer the same man.

Frank and he had been close friends for many years, they liked being together, and although it was not in accordance with regulations he kept Frank informed of all his problems and discussed impending operations with him: Frank became his confidant, his unofficial adviser, his conscience. Frank used to warn him not to let politics go to his head, but he only laughed and retorted that he had no time left for a political career, any-way he would burn to a cinder before they recognized his services. In this he was wrong, success did come to him, and in the end he did not burn out but slowly rotted. Meanwhile they enjoyed each other's company and went on many long night trips together. These furnished Frank with plenty of interesting material – the country was on the move, he was moving with it and thanks to his powerful friend he was able to see many places to which others had no access.

The great man trusted Frank and confided in him about everything. He sometimes complained of the people around him, how few of them could be relied on – each one was out for what he could get, the revolution for them was a matter of mouths and bellies, not brains and hearts.

'If ever you catch me about to do something stupid or

dishonest, kick me hard in the shins,' he once said to Frank as they were returning from the funeral of a comrade, a former partisan, who had taken bribes and shot himself for fear of retribution. But when Frank did so later on he took it amiss, and this was probably the beginning of their estrangement.

The great man's office, where Frank visited him almost every day, was run by an extremely efficient personal secretary. Although it was the custom in those days to call everyone Comrade, she for some reason was always known as Mrs Hornak. Whenever Frank arrived she greeted him with a friendly smile and set about making coffee. Frank was very fond of her and was also glad that in this respect too, his friend had not succumbed to what was becoming the prevailing fashion. Mrs Hornak was middle-aged and unglamorous: her speciality was brains, not legs.

One day Frank arrived to find the outer office empty. He scented something strange and alien about the atmosphere. A red sign glowed over the inner door – Do Not Enter. Frank took a chair. Mrs Hornak would be out any minute. He did not feel like going further, though he could not have explained why.

Suddenly the inner door opened and a tall, radiant young woman came out. The kind of whom one cannot doubt for an instant that the gold of her hair is real. She had a shorthand-pad in her hand and looked in some bewilderment at Frank, who had installed himself comfortably at the coffee-table.

'What can I do for you?' she asked uncertainly.

It was Frank's turn to be disconcerted. He stood up, unable to tear his eyes from the apparition.

'Nothing, thanks,' he smiled. 'I came to see the boss.'

'The boss? Oh, I see,' she said, recovering composure. 'I'm sorry, but the Chairman is engaged. He can't see anyone.'

'He'll see me,' Frank replied, with a certainty which again seemed to perplex the young lady. 'You're new here, aren't you?' he added superfluously. Then, ignoring her protesting gesture, he stepped to the door and threw it open. He found his friend staring dreamily out of the window into the distance.

When he saw Frank looking at him from the doorway he started perceptibly. Then he walked rapidly across the room, took him by the arm and led him into the outer office.

'Let me introduce my new secretary,' he said, but with constraint in his tone.

'My friend here can come and go as he likes,' he added. 'And now, would you please make us some good strong coffee?'

The words sounded affected and self-conscious. The situation was clear as day. Frank felt like whistling with surprise. So that was how things were! Well, after all, it had to come some day, goodness knows it was inevitable, the normal and natural thing. It was the previous situation that had needed explaining, not this.

However, while they were alone he could not help asking 'What about Mrs Hornak?'

His friend turned round in his chair and said:

'I had to have her transferred.'

'Where to?'

'The archives department.'

Frank asked no more questions: everything was clear. Anyway, what was the harm? The blonde looked as if she had something to offer and knew how to offer it.

The conversation refused to flow smoothly. Frank's arrival at the critical moment had caught his friend unawares. He felt a little cross that the other had told him nothing when they had last met two days before; after all, these things didn't happen at a moment's notice. But this very fact confirmed Frank's certainty that he knew what was afoot. However, he also knew that such things seldom work out happily and without complications when the relationship is that of boss and secretary. If matters had got so far his friend ought at least, for form's sake, to have put her in another department or, better still, not have her in the office at all. You couldn't hide things in an office.

The other's thoughts were probably running on similar lines, for he suddenly said:

'She's very efficient. In spite of her looks.'

'You know the sort of jokes people make about such things,' remarked Frank.

'The personnel department took her on – I didn't choose her. I had to get rid of Mrs Hornak because of an indiscretion of hers – a small one, but it mightn't have been so small next time.'

Frank was amused by his defensive tone. You needn't lie, old chap, he thought to himself, you won't pull the wool over my eyes, and why should you try? I understand you and it's no business of mine, anyway she's jolly attractive and you might have done much worse. But you always were a lucky devil.

'She's a stunner all right,' he said aloud. 'But listen, don't go off the deep end all at once, keep a little back to be on the safe side.'

'What on earth do you mean, go off the deep end?' said the other with a smile; but it was not a friendly smile.

Just don't be too confident, Frank thought. This is an odd business, it's beginning differently from the ones I've known before. It's the first time you've hidden something from me and the first time you've tried to throw dust in my eyes. Why shouldn't you have her if you want to? I could go for her, that's certain. What if people do tell jokes about it, what if it's the commonest thing in the world – I reckon you deserve the woman, you have a sort of right to her after all you've been through. But take care, that's all – and don't forget Galovitch!

The blonde brought in the coffee. As she went out again, they both gazed at her legs admiringly. Then they looked at each other and burst out laughing.

'She's got what it takes, eh?' said her boss, slapping Frank on the back. This made them both feel better: the tension which had been growing disappeared. Frank said:

'You ought to keep her out of the way somewhere.'

'What kind of a bourgeois do you think I am? Nobody does that sort of thing nowadays.'

'Do you think we manage any better? Don't we do exactly the same?'

'What rubbish you talk. Surely you've known me long enough!'

And so they dropped the subject. Frank's objections were rubbish and that was that. But it couldn't make any difference to their friendship – they had weathered other storms together.

None the less, as he left, Frank took a final glance at the blonde Venus and met the challenge in her eyes, and he had a presentiment that everything was going to change between them. She knew what she wanted and was going for it tooth and nail. It was an old story: the woman who wants a man does her best to cut him off from his friends in the shortest possible time. Until she has managed that, she cannot feel sure of him.

She was a tigress. She attracted Frank, but from the very first moment they disliked each other. He began to visit the office more rarely. The coffee wasn't the same any more ... and he felt that he was no longer so welcome as formerly.

He also ceased to visit his friend in his villa overlooking the city square. He felt embarrassed in Margaret's presence. He had no desire to play the part of a stooge in the game of make-believe that was developing. Margaret was not just anybody, he had been best man at their wedding, not that that would have meant so very much, but there were older and stronger ties besides.

Frank did not have to see everything in order to know what was going on. His friend's new condition absorbed and engulfed him more and more. He became less energetic, less of a martinet: he went on tours more and more often, and people began to ask one another what sort of official trips these were. Frank begrudged him none of this: he was happy, what more could he wish? He might be laying up trouble for himself, he might singe his wings or come a cropper, but what then? Happiness is not measured by time or any other scale. You either have it or you don't, and when you do, it may be marred or destroyed but it cannot be made as if it had never been.

But one man's happiness is always paid for by someone else. And Frank could not ignore the fact that in this case the other person was Margaret. Besides, there was something else that worried him. What if the whole thing were a snare spread by Galovitch, and his friend had fallen into the trap?

As it turned out, this was not so. The divorce and re-marriage were much talked about, generally unfavourably, and this might have been Galovitch's opportunity, but he did not seize it. He did not thunder against the declining standards of leading comrades who had sacrificed their revolutionary vigilance for the sake of comfort and unworthy lusts. He did not lament that those who should be giving an example to the nation were themselves sinking into a moral slough. Perhaps Frank had mistaken the position after all. Perhaps the girl really had been put there by the personnel department. As it happened, she was not only a perfect blonde, but also a first-class shorthand-typist and excellent at dealing with people. Perhaps there had been nothing whatever between them when he first saw her, and all that had come afterwards. Be that as it may, it certainly had to come sooner or later. Frank had seen plenty of these office love affairs. What happens? The boss, laden with responsibility and overwhelmed with work, organizes directs, intervenes, sits up late into the night dictating reports, speeches, proclamations, has no time for rest or his family or anything else, slogs away for sixteen hours a day and more, wears himself out struggling till he grows pale and withered with the strain of insoluble problems. Then one night, dizzy for lack of sleep, he will cease dictating for a moment to wipe his brow and say 'Where was I? . . . I've lost the thread . . . I feel as empty as a drum . . . Comrade, we must stop for five minutes, I must have some coffee, good and strong, you know how to make it . . .'

Nowadays the great man kept a bottle of brandy in his desk. This was something new – it used to be vodka. New, but not especially disquieting.

Perhaps it had happened like this –

Some time previously, in the middle of a midnight dictating session, he too had paused and put a hand to his brow. This was not play-acting, he was genuinely tired. The coffee was good and strong, but the perfect secretary confessed that she did not like vodka. Later on, there were other such evenings and other such dictations, after which he would drive her home. The poor girl lived a long way off and it was well past midnight. When they parted, he took her hand. Perhaps he would have liked to draw her to him, but was it done? Was it the proper thing? Had not his friend said something about the kind of jokes that were going round?

As for the secretary, she was a treasure. Glorious hair, beautiful eyes, classic legs, yes, but she could also type at eighty words a minute. Willing, well-trained, good-humoured, she knew her way about the maze of files, could find anything the moment it was needed and knew telephone numbers by heart. She also admired her chief. He was tireless, strong, clever and gentlemanly. He had far too much on his shoulders, poor man, but he was tough and was equal to the burden. Towards her he behaved correctly and properly: she knew she attracted him, but he never gave the slightest sign of this. People made such silly jokes – of course they weren't only jokes, this wasn't her first job as a secretary, but he was different. She could have wished at times that he wasn't so completely different; and indeed she knew he wasn't, from the unguarded looks he sometimes gave her.

At any rate, he was considerate, and he didn't have a sofa in his office. (Her last boss had had one, but it didn't get him anywhere.) And he drove her home whenever he kept her working late. Would he accept if she asked him in for a cup of coffee? He might – of course he would. Should she try? Maybe – but she preferred to wait a little . . .

Strange ideas I'm getting today, thought Frank with amusement, as he recalled this ancient history. I expect it was really all quite different.

But was it really? Or was it very much as he imagined?

Of course it might not have begun on the sofa which two

strong men one day carried into the statesman's office, nor with a late-night invitation to coffee. It might have been on an official trip to the Tatra Mountains – a genuine one, people did make such trips, even at week-ends. There her boss and his colleagues would have sat till late in the evening over one of those pointless discussions on the development of tourist resorts—discussions that she knew, even if nobody else did, would never be translated into reality. She would be taking the minutes, and some time after midnight someone would say that there was no reason to go on sitting there without a drop to drink. The mountains. Wine. The moon . . .

She would have been fast asleep when a gentle knock came at her door.

'Who is it?' There was no need to ask, but it sounds better.

'It's me.'

'But I'm in bed.'

'I forgot something. It's important.'

'Couldn't it wait till the morning?'

'I might forget it again.'

She hesitated for a moment. It is proper to hesitate for a moment.

'Wait a second, I'll put on a dressing-gown.'

Then she opened the door. As she stood there he seized her in his arms and crushed her to him, then lifted her and carried her to the bed. She kicked and struggled a little, but not more than was fitting.

He fumbled clumsily with the button of her dressing-gown, tugged at it and finally tore it away with a piece of the material. Was this the right time to say I'll buy you a new one? In the end, he didn't say it till later.

It all happened so suddenly that she could not refuse him. The first words she uttered after the moment when he seized her were: You're mine, you're mine, you're mine . . .

What an idiot I am, thought Frank once more. This kind of thing might have happened many a time, but not between those two – they were , not made for that sort of waiting. Frank could still remember how the widow had looked that day, many years ago, when he left her presence for the first time, and also on the day when he had been transferred to headquarters and had come, as in duty bound, to take his leave.

'You see, you little worm,' her eyes had said to him, 'you wanted to stand in my way, didn't you? A fine figure you used to cut, and look where it's got you. Stand in my way! and all I had to do was to waggle my little finger if you made a nuisance of yourself, you puppy!'

I wonder if she loves him at all, he had wondered. Not anxiously, purely from curiosity.

It was a strained leave-taking. Frank was vexed with himself afterwards for having gone. They sat over their glasses of brandy and had nothing to say to each other. His former friend was lamenting that he never had enough time for anything, that life was getting too complicated. This self-pity was new, it wasn't like him.

'I'll miss you,' the great man went on. 'And don't forget to look us up if you're ever round this way.'

Frank well knew that he would not be missed and that he would not look them up. 'Of course I will,' he said. They both knew that he would not come.

In the street he met Margaret. This was a relief, it would spare him one last, painful visit.

'You've been avoiding us,' she said sadly.

He wanted to fob her off with a phrase about having too much work, but the words would not come.

'Yes, I have.' With these words they had said all that there was to say.

'This is a ghastly time,' she went on. He nodded. Indeed it was. As they stood there, Galovitch flashed by in a new eight-cylinder car with the registration number 001. So he had won that battle and got his way at last: the bitter tussle, followed by the public with malicious glee, as to who should have the lowest registration number in the province. Frank, watching the car swerve round the corner, heard Margaret's voice behind him:

'Where does she come from, anyway, the peroxide blonde?'

So he wasn't the only one who couldn't get the girl out of his head!

'She's not peroxide. You'll have to face it, she's not ...'

He could not escape being invited to dinner with the family. He did his best, but Margaret insisted and he could not refuse. 'It's not for my sake, but Martin's. You must see him.'

To all appearances, it was just like old times. Margaret cooked an excellent meal, the boy put Frank down for the count with an expert left hook, but the old intimacy which had linked the three adults for years was gone for ever. The air was full of unmentioned problems which occupied their thoughts more than the words they spoke. Margaret put a bold face on it, she gave no sign of worry or discomposure, she did not even sigh.

Frank said to himself: I'll stay for another half hour and then say I have to pack. I don't suppose they'll press me to stay.

Soon afterwards, Margaret and the boy left the room. Frank got up to go, but his host led him out on to the big terrace overlooking the main square. Here they had stood for many an hour, leaning over the parapet and enjoying the spectacle of bustling life below. Once again they looked down upon the chattering strollers in the dimly-lit square.

'I'm sorry about this evening,' said his host. Frank made a gesture of indifference. What was the use of talking?

'We're getting divorced,' the other went on in a firm, matter-of-fact tone.

'Well, it's your own affair.'

'Of course. But I'm worried about Margaret.'

'You needn't be. She can look after herself.'

'I know. But there's also Martin.'

Frank said nothing. Of course there was Martin, but what was he supposed to do about it?

'I won't give him up,' said the other with fierce determination.

Frank felt like saying something to the effect that it was not yet time to talk about giving or not giving up, that this would be for the courts to decide and that in such cases they usually assigned custody of any children to the innocent party. Then he realized that he was being foolish. The courts? Who were the courts? Martin's father would be judge in his own cause, he would tell the courts what to decide.

'It's no use,' he said finally. 'I can't advise you and I can't help you.'

'Yes, but all the same, I think it's better if you hear it all from me at first hand.'

Again Frank did not answer. There had already been one occasion in their lives when it would have been better for him to have heard something from his friend at first hand. The same thought probably passed through both their minds. It would all have been much easier if they hadn't been in a similar situation once before.

Frank looked down at the square, where hundreds of young people were taking their evening walk. He remembered another occasion when they had been standing by this very parapet on a fine Sunday afternoon, watching the townsfolk take the air for the first time after the long seclusion of winter. They had been talking about the Junoesque proportions of a local beauty and whether she would fulfil the promise of her figure. Suddenly Frank jumped on to the parapet, commanded his friend to adopt a dramatic pose and photographed him in such a way that the entire square and its population were seen as a background. The subject of the photograph grasped its theme at once and clearly did not find it distasteful. Frank still had it in his files – the lord of the city and of the country round about, dominating the festive crowds in their Sunday best.

All at once, his friend had said, as though in a trance:

'You know, what if something should happen? Suppose someone got loose with a machine-gun? I tell you, this place isn't a home, it's a fortress.'

Of course, thought Frank, machine-guns. His generation can never stop thinking about them – our side's and the enemy's. Those were great times all right, cruel but somehow beautiful, the fronts were clearly drawn, our guns here and the Germans' over there . . . He liked the way his friend had said it. An old, crazy romantic – but this was precisely the most likeable thing about him . . .

And then suddenly he shuddered at the relativity of human ideas. Machine-guns, machine-guns – against whom, for Heaven's sake? Against the festive crowd down in the square? What in God's name could 'happen' from that quarter? Surely the revolution had made a clean sweep of all that kind of thing and, as everyone believed, for good. What on earth did the representative of the victorious people, who had raised him to power as one of themselves, mean by talking about machine-guns? Did he not believe in the people's victory? Was he afraid? And if so, of what and of whom?

Frank still shuddered when he thought of that conversation years before. And one memory brought back another. This time, his friend was already Secretary-General and the first man in the province. They were driving away from some official function. By this time they were already practically strangers, but linked by too many past events to be able to pretend that they had nothing to say to each other. They were sitting in the back, and the great man's personal bodyguard was next to the driver. Another big car full of security police brought up the rear. Suddenly the bodyguard's head drooped onto his chest: he had fallen asleep. The statesman noticed this, shook him furiously and barked:

'Comrade! Do your duty!'

The bodyguard started awake and reddened with shame. A trivial incident: Frank found it unpleasant, but he soon forgot it. Now suddenly he remembered it again. For goodness' sake, what was the duty of a bodyguard in a car whizzing along at sixty miles an hour? What the hell could happen? An attempt on the great man's life? Was he really afraid of that? And if anything so fantastic should happen, what on earth could the bodyguard do about it in a car travelling at that speed? No: it was panic – sheer panic.

Frank could remember another such case of panic. A strange incident, comic or tragic as you cared to look at it. One of his fellow-reporters, who specialized in theatrical first nights and cultural events generally, had once asked him to take his place at the first night of a new play. Frank wondered why the other had chosen him, as they were not exactly friends. The answer had been: 'Well, it's partly your affair, some of the bigwigs will be there.' Whereupon Frank had declined. But the head of his department had in the end assigned him to the job in very much the same terms. Actually, one particular 'bigwig' had turned up, and it was obvious why. For some time now people had been talking about his friend and a certain young actress who was appearing in the new piece. There could be no other reason for his friend going to the theatre: ordinarily he never went except on official occasions, and then he was bored to death. The theatre manager knew, of course, that someone important was coming, and the whole place was in a high state of tension. It was a golden opportunity to raise the question of the theatre's need for renovation. A small snack had been prepared for the distinguished guest in the private lounge, where a word could conveniently be dropped in conversation about the necessary half million or so crowns.

During the interval Frank met his former friend in the foyer. The other, in an expansive mood, laid an arm about his shoulder and led him off mysteriously towards the lounge. The party consisted, beside themselves, of the manager, the director and the actress, whose part was finished for the evening. A table was spread, with two bottles of wine and some sandwiches – the simplest kind of between-acts snack.

So they sat down. The manager began to talk about his problems, while the director opened the first bottle and began filling their glasses. Just as they were about to drink a toast, a door leading to the stage opened and a woman in a black suit appeared. Frank had seen her before and knew who she was. She for her part had clearly not expected to find a party in progress. She stopped short in evident embarrassment, then walked rapidly through the lounge and disappeared into the foyer by the other door.

The statesman gave a start, dropped his glass on to the table and demanded in a sharp, nervous tone:

'Who was that?'

The terrified manager began to explain haltingly that it was a co-director, a certain Madame Pavlin. It was quite clear to everyone that something unforeseen and inopportune had happened.

'You mean Madame Marton, don't you?' said the great man.

The manager tried to gloss it over. Yes, of course, Marton was her married name, the other was her stage name, but as soon as her husband came out of prison she was going to get a divorce, otherwise they wouldn't have dreamt of taking her on . . .

'Oh, she's on your staff, is she?'

The manager collapsed, but the director stepped into the breach. She's jolly good at her job, and after all she's worked her passage, she spent two years in some godforsaken country hole, they gave her the best possible references, and anyway she can't have had anything to do with her husband's anti-state activities, otherwise she'd not have been released and certainly never allowed to come back to the theatre.

The statesman was still staring at the glasses on the table in front of him.

'Is she in tonight's performance? Has she anything to do with it?'

The manager began babbling that a first night is a special occasion for the entire theatre, not only those who are in it or who have helped to put on the performance, the theatre is one big happy family. By this time he had forgotten about the renovation and his few hundred thousands: he was sweating, scared out of his wits, he could see that he was in disgrace.

But which of the two was the more frightened? Suddenly, to Frank's amazement, the statesman reached for his untouched glass, thrust it into the hand of the bodyguard who stood behind him, and commanded:

'Wash it!'

Frank turned aside sharply. Was it possible? Was such a thing really possible?

Frank watched the slow-moving train of black-clad citizens as they passed before the catafalque. His head throbbed with memories: machine-guns, wash it, do your duty – and suddenly he wondered how the dead man had come to know this woman. Where could he have met her? Was it just that she had gone to him to plead for her husband, the engineer condemned for high treason? Or was there something else? He mentally recalled the scene. She had come in, stopped in astonishment and perhaps fear at what she saw, and then stepped nervously across the room and out again . . .

No, it didn't seem as though there was anything else. One mustn't always look for hidden motives in everything, and if one did – well, Frank had his own ideas.

The dead man had been scared – terrified. Well, after all, he himself had helped to create a psychosis of hysteria and universal suspicion. If you assert something long enough, you end by believing it . . .

And yet Frank had known him at a time when he was not afraid, when he used to proclaim, loud and clear, that his life was the revolution and the revolution was his life. In those days it had sounded sincere and not pretentious, and in many a tight corner Frank had had occasion to realize that it was indeed so. What then had happened to him, and when? When had he come to attach a different value to his life than the revolutionary one?

Was it the blonde? Frank had known about his friend's other affairs, they had discussed them together in ribald detail. But when he saw this charmer for the first time he had realized that it was something new and different, and the sequel had amply confirmed this.

During their first nights together she might have said: 'Listen, darling, you mustn't try so hard – do save yourself a little bit for me.'

And perhaps he had said to her during one of those nights:
'The revolution's important, but you are everything.'

Anyway, had they been in love with each other? With the
love which consumes, elevates, pardons and justifies everything? Had they? Or at any rate, had it been so on his side?
Frank had no idea.

Well, if it was love – what good had it all done him?
done him?

Frank puzzled in vain. He would never know when and
how the dead man had begun to alter his maxim to: I am the
revolution and the revolution is myself.

Was it the blonde's doing? Perhaps. But not hers alone.

Four

From his position behind the door Frank had a good view of the entire hall. The black of the catafalque was gradually disappearing under the accumulation of wreaths and flowers. The guard of honour continued to be relieved every ten minutes. The unseen music played on – Chopin's funeral march, the *Eroica*, Tchaikovsky's andante cantabile, the second movement of Dvorak's cello concerto, parts of Smetana's tone poem *Tabor* and of Brahms's fourth symphony. The mourners paused for a moment, gazed at the dead man's face, moved on to sign the album provided for condolences and then returned to the world of life, the cold and their daily cares.

Frank never tired of observing the changes in people's faces and thoughts on such occasions. Even before leaving the hall people were comparing notes with their friends or relations and commenting in subdued voices on the statesman's life and death : some of them actually now said for the first time what they had thought about him all his life. Fragments of sentences, judgements, condemnations drifted to Frank's ear. He looks just as if he were alive. He was only fifty-two. Mourning becomes her. She'll find someone to take care of her all right. This'll take her down a peg. Never know what to believe, do you? They say he was a bit of a lad too – used to choose his secretaries by the colour of their hair. Oh, he wasn't such a bad bloke. Did a lot of dirty work, though. Well, *de mortuis* . . .

A crazy idea shot through Frank's mind – what if this whole place is bugged? If it wasn't it ought to be. Not so that people could be brought to book for a silly or incautious remark, but as a lesson – not to the dead man, who was past profiting from it, but to whoever took his place. His successor should be listening to what people had to say now, if only so that they might say different things if ever he were the central figure at a state funeral.

Some of the scraps of talk sounded pointless or even absurd, but all in all they gave a fairly accurate, none too flattering impression of the dead man's life and works. Suddenly Frank heard:

'He was a coward in the rising, and no mistake.'

Frank turned sharply to see who had spoken. Clearly some self-important know-all with a taste for besmirching reputations. Frank knew how the dead man had behaved during the rising: he had been constantly at his side. His friend had commanded one of the finest partisan detachments. He had been courageous, calm and level-headed, able to cope with the worst emergency. What had happened later with Judith was a different story. During the rising itself Judith was all right and so was he, and so were the things that had taken place between them.

As a commander he was decisive and imperious. He was vain, and an exhibitionist in action, but he did not engage in it foolhardily and did not treat his men as cannon-fodder. At the same time, he was ruthless and perhaps needlessly cruel – although Frank to this day could not say whether his cruelty was in fact needless or not. He had been shocked when his friend had shot out of hand a soldier, a mere boy, who had fallen asleep on guard duty. But soon afterwards, through the fault of another sentry, the Germans had caught the detachment by surprise on the hillside and were shooting them down like rabbits. Frank knew what it was to fall asleep on guard – it had happened to him once. Perhaps it had also happened to the sentry on that fatal night. Frank never learnt what became of him. Perhaps the Germans found him asleep and cut his throat, or perhaps they crept past without even noticing him and he was awakened by the rattle of gunfire.

Frank remembered what it was like to stand on guard and fight the rising wave of fatigue, to feel your eyelids grow heavy as lead and the pupils begin to roll upwards – your consciousness is suspended for a moment, the fraction of a second only, or could it be longer? and it's no use biting your finger to ward off sleep, or rubbing your eyes with spittle. The others are sleeping all around you and you have to keep standing in one place – you can't walk about, because the enemy might hear you, and the noise of your steps might prevent your hearing them. And you mustn't sit down, because then it would be that much harder to keep from falling asleep.

Everyone must have fallen asleep on guard some time or other, if only for a brief moment, and some at least for a moment long enough to seal the fate of many of their comrades. Everyone had given way to sleep but the commander had left them all in no doubt that whoever did so was risking his own life.

Would he have shot me too? Frank used to wonder. Would he have shot me if he had found me asleep, or would he just have given me a shove and said Wake up, you bloody fool?

He couldn't tell which was right. For some time after the boy's death Frank had told himself, to excuse him, that the Germans never came up the mountains by night anyway. But once they had, on the very night when the sentry failed in his duty, and that glorious, almost legendary partisan group had been decimated. All those fine men killed on account of a single guard! But the commander had never said to Frank: There, you see. Remember all that hysterical fuss you made? Well, was I right or wasn't I?

In fact, they never talked about the matter afterwards, although as a rule they reminisced about everything. Frank could never imagine how his friend could live with the memory that he had shot out of hand a seventeen-year-old boy who had fallen asleep on guard. But after all it was his friend who had to live with it, not he.

Anyway, that night the detachment was cut to pieces. The legend that the Germans were afraid of the mountains was a reflection of the partisans' own fears. The enemy had attacked at night, caught them sleeping and burnt the rough Alpine huts over their heads – it wasn't a battle but a slaughter. Five of them had survived, and there was nothing for it but to take to their heels. Five, including one woman and one wounded man who had to be carried on a stretcher improvised from a coat and two branches. Stumbling, falling, floundering in the snow, they managed at last to drag him to the summit. The wounded man kept groaning, lamenting, protesting that it was no use trying to help him, that he would rather have a bullet through his head at once than endure the frightful pain. But the commander had decided that he must be brought to safety. God knew what sort of safety he meant: the Germans were certain to round them up, they were for it as soon as the night came to an end. Still, they went on carrying him. The three of them took it in turns, since Judith was a woman and tired and exhausted into the bargain.

But they came through. In the course of the night they somehow broke through the circle of death, making their way along the crest of the range. For some reason they had persuaded themselves that if once they left the crest they were sure to be killed. For a partisan the mountains are safety, the mountains are himself, and the higher they are the safer they are – there was no particular logic in this, but there wasn't much in partisan warfare anyway. So they kept doggedly to the ridge which represented their only hope of escape. They were desperately tired – nothing exhausts a human being so much as defeat – and Frank kept saying to himself: Another step and I'll fall down, another step and I'll fall down; but he took many steps, perhaps not more than he'd ever taken in his life at a single time, but heavier – each one was the heaviest he had ever taken.

The commander was in front, the two other men carrying their wounded comrade and Judith bringing up the rear, when their chief suddenly hissed: 'Lie down!' Frank stopped, thinking it was an order to rest, when the commander repeated in a louder tone: 'Down, you fools, it's the Germans!' Frank felt as if he had received an electric shock: all fatigue was gone and replaced by panic fear – this was the end, the absolute and inevitable end.

So they lay there. Frank stared into the darkness, his eyes wide open. For a moment he felt a wild, ridiculous hope: perhaps they hadn't seen them! But of course they had: through the darkness could be heard smothered commands, a rustling noise, the sound of metal scraping against metal.

'Don't shoot,' whispered the commander. 'Don't shoot unless they do.'

Why? thought Frank. What difference could it make, when the Germans were already lying a few feet away from them in the darkness? But of course it did make some difference. Even though they were done for, there was some point in not shooting first at dead of night, when whoever did so would fire into the blackness at an unseen enemy and, in so doing, would present a clear target himself. I wonder if they're thinking the same and waiting for us to start, thought Frank. An uncanny and terrifying silence ensued. The Germans did not shoot. Frank could not see what they were doing, but clearly they too were lying on the ground and waiting. Apparently they were, after all, a little afraid of the mountains and of the night.

Frank's head felt as if it would split; his head was beating wildly, the tension was unendurable, the seconds dragged out longer than minutes, the minutes were longer than hours and the hours were longer than eternity.

'What the hell are you waiting for?' said the wounded man in a hoarse whisper. 'They want us on toast, and that's where they've got us.'

'Shut up!' hissed the commander. 'It's a question of nerve, that's all.'

Frank smiled grimly. Nerve? Who had any nerve left? The Germans had, they could afford to.

But in the end it was the Germans' nerve which gave way first. Perhaps only a couple of seconds sooner than theirs. Frank heard what sounded like a muttered order to retreat, then a noise of movement in the darkness, more scraping of metal against metal, a muffled oath, the crackle of dry branches underfoot, a dislodged rock tumbling down the mountain-side.

Then everything was still again. A solemn, awe-inspiring silence. In the middle of it, Frank seemed to hear Judith moaning and gasping. He put it down to nerves, but the wounded man's ears were better.

'My God, they're fucking,' he murmured.

This seemed to Frank so fantastic that he burst out laughing. He got out his torch and flashed it into the darkness. There he saw Judith's white thighs uplifted and immediately heard a smothered voice saying: Put out that light, damn you!

'They're fucking, aren't they?' repeated the wounded man unnecessarily.

'Yes, they are.'

'God damn and blast it!' said the other with feeling. Even though at death's door, he would clearly have liked to be in the commander's shoes. And why not? Suddenly Frank felt the same thing, violently. After all, a man isn't a block of wood. A few minutes ago the Germans were here, and this lascivious devil just goes and tumbles her where she stands. Good God alive! What would he do to one of us if he found him rolling a girl in the snow ten feet away from the Germans? I wonder if he's put a tunic underneath her at least?

When they came down from the mountain-top at dawn, the wounded man had a high fever and was delirious. They made their way cautiously into a village which they knew, found the house of the mayor appointed by the Germans, crossed the yard and knocked at the door.

'Who is it?' said a man's voice timidly.

'Open up!'

'Who's there?'

'Never mind, open and you'll see.'

'I won't. You've no business here.'

'All right, if you want the house burnt down over your head.'

The mayor opened up. He was trembling in every limb.

'You know me, you treacherous bastard,' said the commander. The other's teeth were chattering. 'You know me and know who I am. We've got a wounded man here, he's got fever. You're going to look after him. If anything happens to him, there's not a bolt-hole in the world where you'll be safe from me.'

He shoved the man aside and motioned to the others to bring the wounded man into the hut, where the mayor's wife was wringing her hands.

'The Germans – they'll hang me,' said her husband, trembling like an aspen.

'The Germans'll be here a few more weeks. We'll be here always. Take your choice.'

The mayor opened his mouth to complain further, and the commander struck him across it so that it bled. His wife was more sensible. Without a word she prepared the bed, which was still warm from her own plump body. They laid the wounded man on it just as he was, without taking his boots off.

'You'll get a doctor, understand? The Germans mustn't get this chap, and he's not to die either.'

The mayor nodded obediently, while his wife looked at him with reproach. Now you see the trouble we're in. What did you want to take this job on for, you ninny?

The wounded man's friends touched his cheek in sign of farewell and departed. They felt consoled by the thought that they had done all they could for him and that there might be some hope. In any case they couldn't have carried him with them across country without help.

They spent the whole day resting in the forest. At one moment Judith leant over to Frank and said :

'About last night – I'm sorry.'

Frank laughed good-humouredly.

'Dear Judith, it was splendid. You've nothing to be ashamed of.'

'You know what he's like.'

When night fell they moved on. They had heard of a band of

partisans in the vicinity called the Ivan group. Frank knew little about them – they had been operating on the other side of the mountains. That evening they fell in with them by chance as they were crossing a main road. Even in the dark it was clear that they were something out of the ordinary, well-armed and well-clad. There were about thirty of them. Their commander, a Russian, listened briefly to the new arrivals' story and permitted them to join the group. They trooped along the high road, for all the world as if they were going to a fair. They even had two cows with them, harnessed to a cart.

Before long they branched off on to a side road leading towards the mountains. After about an hour's march they came to a farmstead and entered one of the buildings : it was empty, but there was a fire lit and it was warm.

'All right,' said the Russian, 'take your things off and make yourselves comfortable.'

Frank was about to stow his weapons in a corner, but his friend stopped him.

'Wait a bit.' He turned to the Russian commander. 'What's going on here?'

The Russian was eyeing them curiously, almost with amusement.

'So you say you've come from the Klak mountain?'

'We don't say so, we have.'

'Our information is different. Nobody got away alive from the fight on the Klak mountain last night.

'Yes, they did. We did.'

'Well, you'll have to prove it.'

The Russian whom they called Ivan went on to maintain that the Germans had combed the mountain on the previous night and that not even a mouse could have slipped through their patrols. Anybody could come along and say he was a survivor. Even a spy.

Frank's friend refused to be drawn.

'We're dog-tired and hungry. We want to eat and sleep, nothing else. We can talk about all the rest in the morning.'

Frank was afraid that the suspicious Russian would lose his

temper, but, surprisingly, he agreed. Meat and brandy were fetched. Hell's bells, they do themselves well here, it's like peace-time.

The Russian offered them cigarettes, a whole packet each. Frank noticed that his eyes rested for some time on Judith.

'Have you had enough to eat?'

Frank nodded; his friend said nothing.

'There's some hay upstairs. You can sleep as long as you like. And tomorrow we'll talk.'

They went up the steps into the loft. Frank threw himself down on to the hay and went to sleep at once. He must have slept for a very long time. Suddenly he awoke in a cold sweat. He had been dreaming that the Germans had surrounded them, that he had reached for the tommy-gun beside him and had found it was not there. Then he awoke, full of relief that it was only a dream. He reached for his gun. It had disappeared.

Frank sprang to his feet and awoke the others.

'They've taken our guns.'

Things looked bad. They went downstairs. There was nobody in the house, only a young fellow standing in front of the door with a rifle in his hand.

'Where are our weapons?' said Frank furiously. The youth shrugged his shoulders.

'Commander's orders.'

'Where is your commander?'

'You can't leave the house. They've gone out on an operation.'

The nerve of this kid – if you slapped his face, his head would fly off.

'Calm down,' said Frank's friend. 'It'll sort itself out.'

Frank wasn't at all sure that it would. He didn't like the situation and he didn't like the Russian either.

In the evening the group returned from their operation. They all had brand-new boots and clothing and brightly-polished weapons. The cart, drawn by a horse this time, was laden with sacks of sugar. So that was the kind of group they were.

The Russian came into the house, accompanied by several armed members of the band carrying cartons of cigarettes. They had plundered a grocer's, a tobacconist's and, only yesterday, the stables of some village. If the Germans had succeeded in wiping them out, it would have been a relief to the entire countryside. Unfortunately the Germans did not devote much attention to bands of this sort.

'The robbers,' whispered Judith.

'Why have you disarmed us and why are you keeping us under guard?' demanded Frank's friend.

'That's enough,' said the Russian sharply. 'I'll ask the questions. You can have your arms back, but first we must find out who you are. We have to be careful, this whole area's full of spies and traitors.'

'And do you propose to find out about us?'

'We have our methods.'

Frank's friend rose to his feet and carefully unpicked part of the lining of his coat. He drew out a crumpled piece of paper and handed it to the Russian, who read it attentively: it was evidently written in his own language. After he had read the few words it contained several times over, his manner became more subdued.

'*Kharasho,*' he said at last. 'Give them back their guns.' Two men did so.

'Do you want to stay with us?' asked the Russian uncertainly.

Frank wanted to say no, and it was clear that Judith too would have liked to refuse. The Russian's words had not sounded like an invitation, and it was plain that he would have been glad to see the last of them. But, surprisingly, Frank's friend said that they would stay. For a moment the burly Russian's eyes flashed with unconcealed anger, but he could do nothing about it. Frank looked round at the others. For some reason, some of them looked pleased at his chief's decision.

'*Kharasho,*' he repeated sulkily. 'If you want to, stay. But I enforce iron discipline.'

'Discipline can never be strict enough,' said Frank's friend with a smile.

So they stayed, and got to know what sort of a group it was. One night they would occupy a brandy distillery and hold revels there, next time it would be cigarettes, and then the Russian would get tired of beef and want a change of diet. Meanwhile the newcomers were still treated with suspicion. They were allowed their arms, but felt themselves permanently under surveillance. Frank tried several times in vain to strike up a conversation with one or another member of the group, but it was clear that the Russian had forbidden this. Frank felt like an outcast among his own countrymen.

Spring came earlier than usual that year. The Red Army was not far off, fighting desperate battles for possession of the mountain passes. And here were partisans whose operations were directed against tobacconists and distilleries, who robbed farmers of their livestock and spread terror throughout the countryside. Frank discovered that the mountain farmers and the partisans had no contact with one another. The peasantry were afraid of them. Wherever they held their drinking bouts, the inmates of the house would huddle in a corner, with fear and suffering in their eyes.

Judith once said to him 'Don't leave me alone. That Ivan looks at me so strangely.'

Frank had already noticed this. He replied that there was nothing to be afraid of, but it didn't sound very convincing. He was conscious of the unenviable position of himself and his friends amongst the silent, forbidding members of the larger group. They were in their power and under constant observation, their every word was listened to and they could not even talk freely to one another. Perhaps they could slip away from them unobserved. Frank suggested this to his chief, who only replied 'Take it easy.' But Frank felt that something must and would happen soon.

And so it did. It was a fine Sunday in early spring : the front was quite close, Soviet fighters swarmed over their heads. The group were marching along a path beside a young forest, when the Russian ordered a short rest and posted sentries. It was, Frank knew, an aimless foray, like so many others they had made. The Russian ordered them to polish their weapons. The men vigorously set about cleaning their rifles and tommy-guns, with which they had probably never fired a shot in anger. Three dozen well-armed men – by partisan standards, quite a respectable force . . .

Suddenly the Russian hissed out an order. Frank did not catch what it was, but the men instantly took cover. Frank looked around, but could see nothing suspicious. A solitary farmer, wearing his black Sunday suit and hat and a white shirt, was walking deliberately along the field which bordered the wood. An ordinary, idyllic Sunday scene: the farmer was probably out in the fields for the first time after the long winter, to see how the crops were doing. His manner was carefree; a lark twittered somewhere over his head.

Ivan beckoned two of his men and, quietly but emphatically, gave them an order. A few moments later, they withdrew unobtrusively. After a while, Frank saw them approach the farmer from behind. After a short conversation one of them motioned with his rifle and the man followed them into the forest. He was elderly and his eyes darted apprehensively to and fro. Frank could not hear Ivan's questions or his replies. After a while the burly Russian drew a black notebook out of his pocket, leafed through it for some time and put it away again, having evidently found what he was looking for. In a loud voice, so that everyone could hear, he ordered the two men to take the prisoner aside and guard him well. The farmer looked round in terror for help or an explanation, but encountered only silence.

Ivan came up to Frank. There was something ominous in his expression.

'All right,' he said, 'now we'll see what you're good for. This man is a blackguard. His name is Machala, he's a fascist and a German spy. You – he pointed to Frank – are to shoot him. That's an order.'

The Russian drew a huge revolver out of his pocket and held

it out to Frank, who involuntarily withdrew his hand. The thing was ridiculous. The man couldn't possibly be a German spy. It would be murder.

'He's no spy!' exclaimed Frank indignantly. This was evidently what the Russian had been waiting for.

'So you refuse to carry out my order?'

'That sort of order, yes!' shouted Frank. 'I'm not a murderer.'

The Russian's eyes darkened.

'So now we know where we stand, my fine friends! You don't mind sharing our meat and vodka, but you won't shoot a German spy, is that it? Because you're hand in glove with them – you're all traitors like him. I knew it from the start!'

At that moment he received a fearful blow which toppled him to the ground like a felled tree. Frank's chief had struck him across the nape of the neck with the side of his hand. As the Russian lay gurgling and gasping the other planted one foot on his throat and kicked the revolver out of his hand.

'You swine!' he roared. 'If you move an inch I'll stamp on you like a snake!'

All this had happened before anyone had time to do anything. It was a fantastic and dangerous moment: rifles were levelled from all sides at Frank and his companions, it only needed one man to press the trigger. But Frank's chief remained master of the situation.

'I am a special agent of the partisan staff,' he said in a clear, firm voice. 'From now on I am in command. Anyone who doesn't like it has got five minutes to get away. All of you who stay will obey my orders unconditionally.'

A single shot rang out. Frank's friend drew his revolver and fired twice at the man whose rifle-barrel was still smoking. He collapsed in a pool of blood, hit through the neck.

'Any more?' the chief demanded. No one moved. The men stood there, frightened and cowed. The Russian stayed where he was on the ground, rolling his eyes like a dog in panic fear.

'Stand up, you swine,' said Frank's friend, kicking him again. The Russian got slowly to his feet.

'Let's see that notebook,' ordered the other. The Russian pulled the shabby black book out of his pocket. The chief glanced at it, spat contemptuously and tossed it to Frank, who leafed through the pages. They contained nothing but musical notes.

'What are you, a composer?' said Frank.

'I play the piano,' answered the Russian quietly. He was by now completely reconciled to his fate.

'Shall we disarm him?' asked Frank.

'No. You can keep your arms,' he said to the Russian, 'and it'll depend on you from now on what we do with you when your people get here. Either you'll fight with us, you bastard, or you'll be handed over to the NKVD as a thief and murderer. And that goes for all of you – do you understand?'

The men bowed their heads. They understood, and some of them at least were clearly pleased at this turn of events.

'All right – get ready to move,' the chief ordered. Then, turning to Frank, he added for all to hear: 'You can look after Ivan. If he does anything in the least suspicious, put a bullet through him. I'm making you personally responsible.'

So the chief once again had a detachment under his orders – and not of the worst quality, either.

After they had been marching for a good while, one of Ivan's men moved closer to Frank and whispered mysteriously: 'He had a jolly fine pair of boots.'

'What do you mean?' said Frank, puzzled.

'The farmer. That Machala chap. A jolly fine pair . . .'

Frank spat in disgust. They ought to have shot the Russian while they were about it. He resolved to do so at the very next suitable opportunity.

Remembering all this, Frank felt very much like spitting once again, but the hall with its funeral trappings was hardly the place. Not even when some miserable know-all had just passed by and whispered to his equally miserable companion:

'He was a coward in the rising, and no mistake.'

75

Five

The procession of mourners had settled into its steady, pre-ordained rhythm. No wavering of the line, no gaps, no bunching, and above all no unforeseen incidents. Frank reckoned that thirty persons were passing the catafalque every minute. By the end of two days the number would have reached over thirty thousand, and thousands more would assemble on the square outside to witness the final ceremony. For Frank, the mourners' faces had merged into a blur, he no longer distinguished their features or peculiarities: they were all alike, all serious, all devoid of sympathy. His interest had become so blunted that he did not immediately notice that something unusual was taking place: a scuffling noise and a knot of people by the main door.

'Clear out!' – the incongruous command finally attracted his attention. Looking towards the entrance, he saw that the doorkeepers were trying to hold back a young man who was struggling to get into the hall. Frank knew who it was – he recognized his voice.

The newcomer wore a shabby, padded coat and heavy boots encrusted with tar. His hands were black and chapped, and he himself was dirty and unkempt. Thrusting aside the two attendants he rushed in, gazed wildly about him and went up to the catafalque, where he remained standing. The witnesses of this curious scene looked on with confused and puzzled expressions. Who was this young hooligan, and where did he think he was? What business had he to mar the solemnity of the ceremony? Even though none of the crowd had any personal ties with the dead man or any great respect for him, they were outraged by the intruder's behaviour, as though it had in some way affronted their own dignity. Each was clearly putting it down to the depravity of modern youth.

The secret organizer of ceremonies himself appeared from the passage at the rear end of the hall. He stood in a corner, looking perplexed and indignant. The attendants whispered in his ear: he shook his head – no, that would be still worse, let him alone, he'll go away in a minute and then things can return to normal. We can't risk having a disturbance, let alone a fight!

Almost every eye was bent angrily on the impious young man, till it appeared that they were witnessing a far from commonplace tragedy.

The grimy youth with the tousled hair, with tar on his boots, hands and face, stood alone beside the dead man, nervously twisting in his fingers his cap with its broken peak. All at once his shoulders began to heave with sobbing, he laid his head on the glass coffin-lid and moved his lips inaudibly. Then he pulled himself together and ran out as though the devil were at his heels.

While the young man was standing beside the catafalque Frank had emerged from his corner and focused the camera on him – then slowly lowered it.

You sentimental idiot, he rebuked himself. What a shot that would have been!

The picture certainly would have been a precious addition to his secret collection; but he could not bring himself to take it.

Instead he ran out in pursuit of the young man, down the frosty street. When he caught up, he laid a hand on his shoulder from behind.

'Martin!'

The boy still had tears in his eyes.

'Oh, Uncle Frank!'

After a moment he burst out: 'My father ... why is everyone so beastly about him? When he was alive and could do everything they were all afraid, and they're taking it out on him now that he's dead.'

'That's absurd, Martin.'

'They're glad. They're all glad he's dead. That bitch wife of his is glad too.'

Frank wanted to reprove him, but what was the use? No one would ever get it out of Martin's head that the blonde was to blame for his father's downfall and for his death as well. So he merely said:

'You should have come with her, you know. In your best suit...'

'I? With her? With that bitch? She'll be in bed with that fancy man of hers before evening.'

'Oh, stop it, Martin!'

'She's a tramp, and you know it as well as I do.'

Frank knew it was useless to contradict him. In any case, what if it was true, and she really was going to spend the night with her 'fancy man'? Who could blame her? Was she supposed to sit at home amongst wailing women, pretending a sorrow she did not feel? Of course, it was a startling enough thought – the defunct statesman in his coffin and his widow in her lover's bed. Frank remembered how she had looked today. Black suited her to perfection. And it might be a novel and exciting sensation to take all the black things off one by one – the sable coat, the hat, the gloves ... the dress, the sheer stockings, the slip with its black lace, the black brassière ...

'You might at least have changed your clothes.'

'I couldn't. I didn't mean to go at all. I don't know what made me. I had to – I just dashed away from work for a minute. We're putting down asphalt on the main street. It's a rush job for the procession tomorrow.'

They walked along for a while in silence, each buried in his own thoughts. Martin was thinking about the 'tramp' who had ruined his father's life, and Frank about the new surface on the main street – to be laid in three days, in the dead of winter. How long could it be expected to last? A month? Two?

'You must come and see me some time, Martin. You know where I live. And if you should need anything...'

'Thanks, uncle, the pay's quite good.'

'That isn't what I meant. Listen, it's cold, come and have a cup of coffee.'

'I can't, I've got to get back to the job. But you come and see us, mother'll be pleased.'

'Is she with you?'

'She lives at my place. I'm married, you know, and we're expecting a baby. The flat's not much, it's on the other side of the river. But do come, uncle.'

Frank took down the address, as though he really meant to come, and said 'All right, I will some day.'

The young workman hurried off. He had grown into a handsome lad. Frank remembered their mock boxing matches. Looking at Martin's sturdy figure, he thought that he would not like to connect with his left hook nowadays.

Once, about six years before, Martin had seen Frank driving past him in the street and had waved at him. When Frank stopped, he said: 'Give me a lift, uncle.' Then after about a hundred yards he asked Frank to stop again and let him out.

'Where do you want to go, then?'

'Nowhere. I just wanted to see what it feels like driving in such a tiny car.'

What had the tough roadmender in common with the cheeky lad of six years ago? Nothing, but he had found himself. And this was more than his father had ever done . . .

Six

Frank did not feel like going back into the hall. It was cold in there, and there was no point in hanging around all day. He had photographed the widow, the dead man's personal staff, the generals and the scouts' guard of honour. The old woman with her simple tribute could wait till tomorrow, when his editors would expect more pictures anyway. Galovitch he had got already and would have to take again when he made his big speech in two days' time, so what was there to wait for now? The flags on their staffs rattled in the icy wind, the street-lamps were lit – every one of them, thought Frank – the procession route was being re-surfaced, the burnt-out neon light tubes were being replaced. From every shop-window the dead man's portrait looked out on to the dismal street: sometimes framed in black, sometimes with his initials below, sometimes accompanied by a slogan: our great son has left us, his grateful fellow-countrymen will not forget, the working class salutes him . . .

The grateful fellow-countrymen were at this moment scurrying glumly up and down the street. They had neither the time nor the inclination to think of the dead man. Perhaps, like Frank, they were noticing the lights and thinking Well, its about time, or else wondering why there was suddenly such a surplus of electricity. To and fro they scuttled, wrapped up to the eyebrows, ill-humoured, their eyes watering in the bitter wind. The dead man stared from every shop-window at the passers-by, and at the grimy town with its streets full of potholes, including the main street which was being hastily repaired. No one had thought of cleansing the gutters of their congealed heaps of ordure, which, together with the mottled façades of the houses, intensified the gloom of the drab winter's day. In the open spaces, parks and squares where there was no traffic, the untrodden snow was blackened by the fine rain of ashes which poured incessantly down from the dozens of factory chimneys and which got into the streets, into flats and into one's lungs. Today, at least, the wind had blown away the stink of hydrogen sulphide which hung perpetually over the town, the product of a large chemical works nearby. Just outside the town there was a sign welcoming motorists, but the smell had usually welcomed them long before.

Across the frozen roadway the wind drove scraps of paper which had fallen from a passing van. Passengers hung in bunches on the screeching trams. Pedestrians waded through a greyish morass composed of snow, ashes, salt and grime. The forecast that morning had promised a thaw. If it came, things would be even worse: the loose, frozen mess on the pavements would turn into black, oily mud.

There was a long queue in front of a fruit-stall. Some lemons had arrived. Frank thought: We've got so used to it that we stand in queues like sheep, people nowadays can hardly imagine life without them.

At other times of year the streets didn't look so bad. The dead man had chosen a bad time for his departure. He himself, of course, had never seen the town in such a state. He lived up on the hill in his big villa, where every morning the housekeeper swept away the snow from the pavement and the steps, and a big well-heated car stood waiting to take him to the baroque palace which served as a residency. When had he last got his shoes wet or slipped on the icy pavement? For years past the only walking he had done was on the hunting trips which had become an escape, a passion, a compensation and a joy. If he ever looked at the town it was through the windows of his villa or of the luxury car, or, once or twice a year, from the festively decorated saluting base on the main square.

Frank had not envied the great man his life. What was there to envy? Of course he had a comfortable villa, but he worked at higher pressure than others and had a more urgent need of rest: he was in effect always on duty, and if anything happened he could be woken up at any hour of the night. Frank could switch off his telephone and nobody would care, but the statesman had some telephones on his desk that could never be switched off.

He needed a fast, comfortable car because he travelled a great deal and often at short notice, when an emergency arose in some remote part of the country. He needed a gardener too, he needed good clothes, in fact everything that serves to maintain a high position – all this he could, would and must have, and only a few ignorant people would begrudge it him.

His work was not such as to excite envy either. Day by day he had to cope with dozens of more or less important problems, many of which he did not understand but for all of which he was responsible. It began with the morning mail. The creation of a chemical combine, a flat for an actress, an application from a writer for the allocation of a motor car. He had reserved to himself the right to make special allocations of cars, and as a result a lot of paltry requests appeared on his desk which could have been dealt with by a junior clerk. Naturally the public applied to him with all their troubles; a well-organized office could have coped with most of them, but he insisted on deciding everything himself. Consequently, instead of governing the whole region he found himself dealing with vehicle allocations and housing privileges, and taking the final decision on whether a student with a doubtful political record should be allowed to go to the university, or whether a certain embezzler should be let off the remainder of his sentence. Instead of reckoning in billions he frittered away his time with thousands. Thus in the end he became a sort of panjandrum, an omnicompetent official, submerged in detail instead of determining broad lines of progress. He decided the rights and wrongs of everything, made pronouncements on artistic questions he knew nothing about, presided over discussions on agriculture one day and hydraulics the next. At one time he became indignant over the inefficiency of the railways and took over their supervision personally, but failed to achieve any improvement.

Naturally, each of his failures was somebody else's fault. As time went on, the whole nation became in his eyes a headless, faceless mass, to be taken by the hand, led, protected and punished, but on no account trusted: doing everything to spite him, envious of him and scheming to deprive him of power. In his later years he had ceased to trust anyone. They had all betrayed, deserted, deceived and disappointed him: no one was to be relied upon any longer.

On one occasion he flew into a rage on receiving the report that a cement factory which he had solemnly opened a few years before had been based on a deposit of limestone so inadequate that, given the factory's capacity, it would be exhausted in two or three years. He went in person to the spot, had the planners put in jail, and sacked several heads of departments; the building engineers, who had nothing to do with the decision, got stiff sentences for sabotage.

Had he really forgotten? Or had he not paid attention at the beginning? Had he forgotten that it was he himself who took the absolute and final decision as regards the site of the factory? Or that when he went to lay the foundation stone, a deputation of local officials and experts had pointed out to him that the factory would be up-wind and would cover their town, one of the prettiest in the country, with a film of white dust? They had brought an alternative plan which they themselves had worked out in the light of local conditions, and which would have placed the factory on the other side of the valley, directly under a limestone mountain. Under their plan, millions would be saved and their town would remain a jewel of the countryside.

Could he really have quite forgotten his reply to their urgent pleas and recommendations? He probably had. But Frank, who was present when he snubbed the deputation, could remember him saying: 'I'm not going to have the country's industrialization messed up because of a lot of small-town prejudice.' Having said which, he turned his back on them. The townsmen shrugged their shoulders and went away – indignant, injured, frightened. And so today the limestone was brought to the cement works by means of a cable railway two or three miles long, from a quarry which had just been opened at the foot of the very mountain where the local experts had wanted the factory to be sited. The town, sure enough, was permanently covered by a dirty white layer of heavy cement dust. If, after being there for an hour, you passed a hand across your face, the sharp dust would scratch it so that the blood came.

Today, as he lay there upon the bier, a delegation had come from that town to pay its last respects, and among its members were two of the men on whom he had once turned his back . . .

As the years passed he must have come to realize that some of his strokes of the pen had brought disaster instead of benefit. But it was always the fault of others. They were trying to cut the ground from under his feet, to discredit him and frustrate his efforts; they even brought him false documents to sign . . .

It finally got to the point where he was afraid to decide anything. This made him only the more determined to secure his personal position, to usurp ever-increasing powers and to concentrate all authority in his own hands. Not in order to rule – that ambition he had renounced – but in order to maintain and fortify his position, to feel more secure. Nevertheless he was still afraid – desperately afraid of one man who was outside his range, whose position was equally secure if not more so. He was afraid of Galovitch. He guessed, quite rightly, that Galovitch was after his neck.

Frank had long foreseen that it would come to this. By then he and the great man were no longer friends, but he still wondered whether he should not seek him out and warn him of his own forebodings. But it was an idle thought and it came too late. Later still, he ceased to care one way or another. Only once in recent years had he again had occasion to feel sorry for his former friend . . .

Seven

The banquet had been a disaster. The great man had got drunk, lost his temper and offended a foreign diplomat. Tact and moderation were not his strong suit even when sober. The diplomat had turned on his heel and walked out. Frank wondered how matters would end: according to the rules, his friend would have to send a written apology. It would have pleased Frank to see him in the role of a penitent. From his earliest childhood he had never been known to admit that he was in the wrong, or to own up to anything. However much his teachers and parents thrashed him he would neither cry nor utter a word: he would not give in or take back anything he had said, even when he knew perfectly well that he was to blame.

The incident with the consul put an end to the banquet. Frank, who had taken all the pictures he needed, was lingering near the kitchen amongst the attendants, waiters and drivers. You could always get an extra drink behind the screens there, long after the guests' glasses were empty.

Suddenly the statesman himself appeared in the servants' quarters. He was cross and tired and demanded a glass of brandy.

'You've had a busy day, comrades, you've helped to make the reception a success, let's drink your health ...'

Then he noticed Frank in the corner with a brandy-glass in his hand. Frank had the impression that he was glad to see him.

'Hallo, you old rascal!' he exclaimed with a grin, 'You know where you're well off, don't you?' Then, feeling perhaps that he had been over-familiar, he went on in a stiffer tone:

'You bloody reporters give us a lot of trouble.'

Frank assumed an innocent air. He didn't know what the great man was driving at, but he disliked his tone. Statesmen had a way of dividing people into categories: We and You. Frank had his own opinion about who gave trouble to whom. Anyhow, it was no way to talk to an old friend. Still, there was no point in getting into an argument about it.

The great man swallowed his brandy at a gulp, as they had done in their youth when they vied to see who could hold more, and instantly called for another. He wanted to drink, to get drunk and to blot out the memory of the inauspicious evening.

He noticed Frank looking at him quizzically. Perhaps he realized why, for he put an arm round his shoulder and said:

'I don't mean you, of course.'

'Why?' said Frank, now in open mockery. 'Don't you count me as a reporter?'

'That's different. I mean those scribblers in there.'

By this time it had dawned on him that he was cutting an undignified figure in front of the chauffeurs and waiters; or perhaps a distant memory took shape in his befuddled brain. Suddenly he grabbed Frank's arm and said:

'Come along. You've never been at my place. You don't know where I live.'

Frank understood the reason for this sudden intimacy. The other desperately wanted to go on drinking, and he needed a companion. Nowadays he had no one to drink with, and he was not yet so far gone as to drink alone. Besides, Frank reminded him of the days long ago when they had shared a bottle of vodka and had good times together. But those days were past. Frank too felt like drinking, and unlike the other he could choose where and with whom. He tried to get out of it: it was late, perhaps some other time, they must both get some sleep, there was work to think of . . .

'You and your blasted work!' exclaimed the statesman angrily. The words burst out involuntarily, but they clearly expressed what he thought of his former comrade. You miserable little twirp of a reporter . . .

'I didn't mean my work,' said Frank with a sneer. 'Naturally, that doesn't count. I meant your work as a statesman.'

A waiter behind him sniggered audibly. It wasn't every day that you heard one of these photographer chaps make fun of the bosses.

The great man almost exploded, but with a visible effort kept his temper. He shot a thunderous glance at the audacious waiter, who scuttled away as fast as he could. It would be a long time before he was allowed to serve at another official banquet!

Then, with outward calm, he repeated his invitation to Frank. 'Come on, old friend, I've got better brandy than this at home, we can sit and talk as we used to in the old days. I need it.'

Yes, indeed, he did need it. He had learnt all too quickly to give orders and make everybody jump to his slightest whim. But did he really believe that he and Frank could sit and talk together as they had in the old days?

Frank started to refuse even more firmly. But just then the blonde appeared in the passage. Ignoring the waiters and attendants, she said to her husband:

'I was pretty sure I'd find you here.' Then, seeing Frank, she managed an 'Oh!' of surprise. Frank bowed ceremoniously.

'It's a long time since we've seen each other,' she remarked.

Frank could not resist answering: 'I saw you a quarter of an hour ago.'

'Yes, of course, I know. That isn't what I meant.'

'He's been avoiding us,' put in the great man.

'Yes, he has. We're not good enough for him.'

'Oh, shut up!' barked her husband suddenly. Frank felt embarrassed. Surely they weren't going to start quarrelling here?

'I've been asked to have a drink at your house,' he said. The blonde smiled ironically. Her look said: 'So even you're good enough for him nowadays.' But for some reason the thought seemed to give her pleasure.

'Well, then, let's go,' she said. 'I wouldn't mind a drink either.'

They went out. The banquet hall was deserted. Half-full dishes, brimming ashtrays and empty glasses were scattered about on the tables.

They sat in the back of the car, with the usual bodyguard beside the chauffeur. Frank felt the blonde's nearness, her scent and her provocative charm. The years had done nothing to impair it, rather the contrary. But had she got what she wanted? Had she not imagined something quite different? Frank knew they lived a cat-and-dog life: such things can't be hidden, and anyhow that single 'Shut up!' was more eloquent than a cartload of rumours.

No one said anything in the car. All three of them felt a sense of constraint, the foreboding of a wasted evening. Frank was as fond of drinking as the next man, but not anywhere and with anybody: to sit over the best brandy in the world and have nothing to say to one another is a torment. Frank felt awkward – he had disliked the blonde from the first moment he saw her; she was beautiful all right, but, my girl – so he addressed her in his thoughts – I've seen plenty of beauties like you, just as ambitious in their day, just as fond of life and glitter – one of them is bent and withered and cleans the stairway in some flea-pit hotel, but at least she's lived and had her fling and got something out of it all. If you have to say goodbye to something, you can say goodbye to it. But what sort of a past will you have to look back to? – you who are first lady in the land, which, let's face it, is a good deal different from being a lady.

Supposing you come down to washing stairs – and you may – will you be able to stop on the landing with a warm feeling inside you and think of the young partisan who used to turn your head? Or will your best memory be that god-awful banquet this evening? I watched you the whole time – sitting at the head of the table with boredom all over your face, looking disgusted at the other bosses' fat frumps of wives, opening your eyes in horror as they stuffed sweets into themselves in a way you don't dare to any more. I saw you turn your face away when some old battleaxe in armour-plated brocade, the height of local elegance of course, bent down to talk to you and you caught the whiff of her sweat. Is it such a great thing to be first lady among those old trouts? At least they're at home with one another, they don't have to put on an act, they can sit down to a great big round table loaded with cream cakes and tear your reputation into little shreds. They're the people who belong in baroque drawing-rooms nowadays, they feel at home there and it's no good your despising them – they despise you much more and they're right to, because you are the intruder, not they.

Was it really the chandeliers and the bright lights that you wanted? You live amongst them now all right, every week there's some anniversary, some reception, some festivity. And you have to smile at men you don't give a damn for and who are bores into the bargain, and shake hands with equally boring women and chatter about dress-makers and the weather, and look sour when you meet men you do care for – because every smile of yours is an act of protocol, it may be an absurd system but it has to be obeyed. You have to go to a gala night at the opera when your favourite actor's in a new romantic comedy. You can never go where you'd like to or eat while you like or love whom you like, because someone is watching every step. Is that the sort of life you wanted, in the days when you thought you could choose?

People tell tales about all the lovers who come to see you at the villa, not just in ones and twos, the more the merrier, you're supposed to be insatiable. But that villa is guarded by two secret policemen, and the housekeeper and gardener and charwoman are on the same payroll. So who would be such an idiot as to come by night to the villa of the first man in the country, by that famous back entrance which may or may not exist, to make love to the first woman in the country? And how would you dare to let anybody in at that hour of night? Not on your husband's account, of course, but from fear of Galovitch, because you're well aware that the people shadowing you are not just security guards but morality guards too. Anyone who goes to see you up there has to identify himself and someone writes down the time he arrives and the time he leaves. Oh, I dare say you might get a kick out of making love under state control in that fashion, but the men in your circle are a cowardly lot, my dear – it might cost them their career and a good deal more besides, and, forgive me for saying so, however attractive you may be, I for one wouldn't care to sit there cuddling you with someone outside looking at his watch to see how long I was staying. And I doubt if you would like it either.

Perhaps somewhere tucked away in your memory is the thought of a forest glade on a Sunday afternoon, with a shy, inexperienced young man touching you and arousing feelings that frighten you but which you can't resist. What can you do about that today? Nothing. Life is no longer a question of what you can do, but what you may or must or should do . . .

I wander about a lot in the evenings, the town is a sort of kingdom at that hour, and sometimes I see your car parked in a side-street – not always the same one. I suppose those are the times you hear what women need to hear – how lovely, how beautiful you are – but no one will ever say these things to you in the morning, because you can't stay that long, you have to go the minute the concert programme comes to an end. Your season ticket is for Thursdays, every Thursday evening from half past seven to half past ten, and at exactly ten forty-five the secret policeman up at the villa will make a note in his diary . . .

And what about your husband? Of course, he was never particular, in that sense you're wasted on him. But he has even less freedom than you. He can't let on that he's going to a concert – he hasn't the courage or the imagination. So he changes his secretary. You were the first in the series. Every so often the buzzer will sound in his outer office, the girl will go in with her notebook in her hand, the Do Not Disturb sign will be switched on, and just to make sure he'll lock the door as well. Maybe that's enough for him. But, my dear good girl, it isn't a life for a normal man. He knows that visible and invisible eyes follow him wherever he goes. Four guards, no less, follow him everywhere, and even when he goes to the lavatory one of them stands in front of the door. And each time he undresses a new girl on the eighteenth-century sofa, don't you think he worries himself to death wondering, as I once did, where she's from and whether it wasn't Galovitch who sent her there? Or maybe the latest is an agent of a foreign power, or even a modern Charlotte Corday?

What sort of a life is that? – unnatural, sterile, cut off from one's fellow-beings, the prisoner of one's own power.

Once upon a time he divorced for your sake. It might have cost him his career, but he wasn't important enough in those days, he got away with it, and now you're stuck with each other. No chance of a divorce or separation now – statesmen don't do that. Of course, he might divorce you and stop being a statesman, but he isn't brave enough. Anyway what could he do afterwards, how would he manage? And why would he do it in the first place? For another woman? You were the other woman once – you know how it turned out, and so does he.

Years ago, the King of England abdicated on account of a woman, at least that was supposed to be the reason. But your husband can't give up his position, if he did his enemies would be at his throat at once. The only way he can get out is by being kicked out, or having a heart attack . . .

All these years later, Frank could still vividly remember that drive to the statesman's home : he could have repeated word for word the thoughts which had then passed through his head.

At last they stopped in front of the large villa, where Frank had not set foot before. As they arrived, lights instantly went on in the garden, over the front door and on the stairs. A man in civilian clothes, standing by the gate, raised his hat as they passed : nobody acknowledged the salute.

Frank had never been in the villa, but he knew its history.

It had been built during the war by a rich man with friends in high quarters, on an excellent site with a superb view of the town and river. Its internal appointments soon became a by-word. After the war, it was transformed into a nursery. Frank could not imagine what had possessed his friend to take it over as his home, to the indignation of the whole neighbourhood. Of course, someone else might have had the idea first and his friend might have been presented with a *fait accompli*. Never-theless, even if the nursery had already been turned back into a luxury villa, he should have refused to live in it. There were plenty of handsome villas overlooking the town and it would have been an easy matter to find state reasons for dislodging any of their occupants – it need not have been children who suffered.

As they entered the spacious hall, Frank looked about him. One wall was entirely covered by bookshelves reaching to the ceiling. He looked around for a ladder, but saw none. In one corner was a large round table, a leather sofa with a small bar next to it and three comfortable leather chairs. In the opposite corner was an ornamental fireplace. A soft carpet covered the floor from wall to wall. One end of the room consisted of a single broad window. The wall near the entrance was hung with pictures, and in an alcove was a portrait of the blonde. Frank looked at it curiously. He could tell by the style who had painted it. It was an excellent likeness, and knowing the painter he could roughly guess how many sittings she must have given him.

He sank into one of the big chairs, while the blonde placed a bottle of brandy and some glasses on the table. Then she sat down, eyeing him closely. This caught the great man's attention.

'I thought you were tired,' he said tactlessly. Her eyes narrowed with contempt for a moment.

'I feel better now,' she said. 'I'd like a drink too.'

The great man wanted to get rid of her, and restrained him-self with difficulty from saying so straight out. However, he too sat down, and they touched glasses. The blonde drank with enjoyment, which appealed to Frank. His friend tossed down the brandy at a gulp, and she immediately poured him a double.

The atmosphere was constrained, nobody felt like talking. They were probably already sorry they'd invited him. Many unspoken memories hung in the air between them. Well, if he wants to sit together like old times, here we are ...

The silence was getting on Frank's nerves. He stood up, glass in hand, walked over to the books and began to look at their titles. The blonde, from her seat by the table, said: 'Those are my husband's books – I keep mine elsewhere.' Frank understood what she meant. The books were dead ones, stowed away in no sort of order, exactly as they had arrived from the publishers. If she had a collection of her own, no doubt she picked out the ones she wanted first, and the rest ended up here. It wasn't a library, but a repository of books that no one would ever take off the shelves. One can always tell whether books are living or lifeless. One day all these would find their way to some second-hand dealer and even he wouldn't want most of them.

But what shocked Frank most of all were the pictures illustrating the great man's life. There he stood on a speaker's platform, holding in his arms a child in national costume; amongst a crack team of woodcutters; drinking a toast to celebrate the gathering in of the harvest. As a commander of partisans, scanning the horizon with eagle eye, operating a machine-gun or giving the signal to attack. Or again as a leader of working youth, surrounded by his comrades. Every single one of these pictures were copied from one of Frank's photographs. They had even used the same faces, except that the woman in the partisan scenes did not look like Judith. When Frank came back to the table, his host avoided his glance and nervously clutched his double brandy. The blonde looked on amusedly. This eloquent, wordless conversation went on throughout the time they sat there. The host was not so fuddled as not to perceive that the silence had an edge to it. He burst out:

'Anyway, he's a damned good painter. A realist, not one of

these people who paint your ear where your knee ought to be.'

Why did he fly off the handle in this fashion? Frank realized that the picture must often have been discussed before. He could not resist pouring a little oil on the flames.

'What, you call that realistic? He's foreshortened your hand in one picture, and in another he's given you a squint.'

The blonde's grey eyes narrowed, this time expressing delighted agreement. Frank was startled. Were things really so bad between them that it amused her when her husband was held up to ridicule? But the other was aware of nothing: he merely frowned sulkily. The hand too short? He'd never noticed it. A squint? Well, artists were a pack of good-for-nothings, everyone knew that . . .

Frank knew the man who had painted the series, and could imagine how it had come about. He would have turned up one fine day and announced with due modesty that he was looking for material on the history of the rising and the revolutionary movement, in order to do a set of commemorative paintings. Preferably photographs, which could be a source of deep inspiration to the painter who knew how to use them. Then, several months later, he would have brought the lot along, not asking for any fee of course, just the price of the frames. And so he would get the Artist's Order of Merit, and be able to boast in the club that he hadn't got it, like some of his colleagues, just for being fifty or sixty years old . . .

The portrait of the blonde, which hung opposite Frank, continued to attract and tantalize him. She herself was sitting beneath it. In some curious way the picture caused him, for the first time, to feel respect for her. Whatever else she might be, she was a personality, it was she who counted here and not her husband. The painter had succeeded in expressing more than one would have surmised from a casual glance at her face. He must have worked hard at it . . .

'Set me back twenty thousand, the swindler,' said the great man, interrupting Frank's thoughts.

'Well, of course, the more famous the artist, the more he can get away with,' laughed Frank. But this too failed to irritate the great man, who was past noticing that he was being made game of.

The blonde suddenly rose and said: 'Excuse me, I'll go and change.' As soon as they were alone, Frank's host swallowed his brandy and poured out another stiff one.

'She makes a fuss if I overdo it,' he explained needlessly. Having seen his rate of consumption, Frank was not surprised. He knew how this sort of bout usually ended: he had seen it once with Judith. The great man either drank himself insensible or went berserk.

Frank took another look at the portrait. This woman must once have thought that she had got what she wanted, but she had not and neither had her husband, who didn't know what he had got in her anyway. Nor did he know how to treat her. He had been glad to make her his own in the days when everything about her was new, dazzling, uncertain, and when she attracted him more and more. Then, once she had become his property, he neglected her, not realizing that a woman like that cannot be neglected with impunity. Some women are quite happy to be an ornament, a brilliant accessory, a badge of success. Not this one. She had wanted the whole of him, to be shared with nothing and nobody. His career? Fame, wealth, position? No doubt, but above all she wanted to possess him completely, and that was impossible. That was where she had gone wrong. She probably begrudged it when he came home tired out from a long journey, while she sat waiting. She expected him to be always smiling, caressing, spoiling her, a lover for twenty-four hours of the day ...

When she came back into the room, she was wearing a plain black dress and had taken off her jewellery. The effect was well calculated: the whole place seemed filled with her enticing presence. Even her husband was aware of it and gazed at her with greedy admiration, which she ignored. Her indifference exasperated him. All right, if that's how you want it ... He gulped down yet another brandy, and poured out a fresh one.

She laid a hand on his, saying: 'Don't drink any more. You know what the doctor said.'

The crafty bitch knew what she was up to all right, she wanted to make him drunk. Of course, after the remark about the doctor he would drink even more. Trying to frighten him with the doctor in front of an old friend who had known him in the days when he was indestructible, when he could drink a bottle of gin and go off to a dance none the worse for it. He'd show them! He got up unsteadily and opened another bottle. The blonde shrugged her shoulders: she washed her hands of it, she had done her best, there was nothing more she could do. So that was the kind of protest she made when he 'overdid it' . . .

Frank had once seen a man drink two bottles of raw spirit in the course of a single night. One might still do that and live to tell the tale, but no one could drink at the rate this man was doing and get away with it. He did not in fact last another hour. His jaw stiffened, he began to babble, his eyes grew bloodshot, he fell into a semi-stupor. He tried to grab the glass, but missed it.

Frank felt that he too had had enough to drink. He started to rise, but she waved him back into his chair.

'Let's have another. I feel like it. You pour.'

'Just one, then.'

She nodded. He filled her glass and his own, then enquired with a look whether he should also fill her husband's. She replied 'Yes' with her eyes, and even held his hand steady while he poured out a full glass. Then she pressed it into the drunk man's hand and shook him into consciousness.

'We're drinking your health,' she said in open mockery.

The other burbled unintelligibly and drained the glass. Immediately his mouth began to twitch: he got up, tried to take a step and crashed to the floor.

They got him on to his feet and the blonde succeeded, just in time, in leading him off to the lavatory, where Frank could hear him retching. She left him there and returned as though nothing had happened.

'He can't take it. It always ends up like this. Do forgive me and have another drink while I look after him.'

A tender, thoughtful wife indeed – to ridicule and humiliate her husband in this way in front of an old friend who had known him in very different days. Clearly, that was precisely what she had set out to do.

'Can I help?' said Frank. No, no, she shook her head, she was quite used to it, it wasn't the first time.

'Well, then, I think it's time I . . .'

Oh no, no, please don't go, I'm sorry the evening was such a mess, it's horrid for you, but I couldn't bear to be alone just now, let's have another drink – it's still quite early and anyway I'm told you keep late hours – no, don't say a word, you see I have heard a little bit about you – I'll just put him to bed and I'll be right back, it's good brandy and the bottle's still half-full . . .

She didn't say any of this in words, only by a gesture, but it seemed to Frank that this said everything.

So it was like that. Through the fumes of brandy Frank heard a voice in his brain saying Don't be a fool, get out while there's still time, this isn't for you and no good can come of it. But he didn't go, he sat down again – she attracted him, by God, and what did anything else matter?

He saw and heard her dragging her husband off, still hopelessly drunk, towards the bedroom. He offered again to help, but she refused. He wondered if she would undress him or at least loosen his tie and take off his shoes, or if she would just roll him on to the bed and leave him to get up in the morning as best he could.

She came back and, still standing, raised her glass to him and drank. Then she said: 'I must just go and clean up the mess outside – I won't be a moment, and then coffee will be ready.'

She returned once more, but without coffee. She said:

'Do come along, I can't stand this place, it smells of death. Come to my room, we'll be more comfortable there.'

It flashed across Frank's mind that this was his last chance to go, but he followed her like a spaniel. Her room was indeed more comfortable, she had furnished it with real taste, for herself alone. A shelf with a few chosen books on it and two modern paintings, not nudes as one might have imagined, but landscapes and worth a good deal of money.

She attracted him very much indeed ... Over the coffee and brandy she said abruptly:

'Tell me, what is it you have against me?'

Hallo, Frank thought, what's she up to now? But he was too much confused by the point-blank question to do more than reply: 'What have you got against me?'

She waved a finger and said laughingly: 'Oh, come now!' But Frank insisted:

'Why should I have anything against you? You attract me. You always have, since our first meeting.'

'You have a funny way of showing people that they attract you.'

Frank still could not guess what she was driving at. She went on:

'You tried to set him against me. Oh, it doesn't matter now. Perhaps it's a pity you didn't succeed.'

'Why should I have wanted to do that?'

'Of course you did. He'd been your friend for years and years and you knew right away that that was all over. In case you don't know, I had a bit to do with your being transferred away from here. It was silly of me.'

Frank grew alert again. Was this an invitation? Conversations that started this way usually ended in bed.

'Why?'

'It just was. It wasn't worth while.'

'Did things not turn out as you expected?'

'No, they didn't. But what I wanted then was to have him all to myself. You were in my way. He was always talking about you. As long as you were there, he wasn't all mine.'

'Did you love him?'

'Very much. He was the sort of man I wanted, the sort I'd been waiting for. Perhaps it was a mistake to insist on the

divorce and then marry him. He was marvellous as a lover.
We could have gone on that way.'

'What about Galovitch?'

She looked at him with surprise, tinged with amusement.
'What's it got to do with him?'

She could not possibly be dissembling to that extent. Frank
felt that he had been a fool to have harboured the idea.

'Well, do you think he'd have tolerated such a "slough of
immorality", as he would call it?'

'Oh, for goodness' sake! Have you never heard about bosses
and their secretaries?'

'Yes, often, and I've seen them too. But, if it suited somebody's book, it's been known to cost them pretty dearly.'

'Not as dearly as the divorce might have done. He was
scared to death of it. It was then that the trouble really started
between us. You see, I'd been in trouble because of my social
origin. And he, with all his billing and cooing, wasn't thinking
only of me. He was already thinking of his career and how he
could get to the top.'

Frank said nothing. No doubt his friend had been thinking
of his career, but wasn't it partly so as to impress this woman,
to cover her with reflected glory, to prove to her that he was
the greatest man in the world?

After a while he said:

'Weren't you thinking of it too?'

'How do you mean?'

'Well, did you mind his having a political career?'

'No, of course not. But I know people say I drove him into
it, and that isn't true. What came between us was precisely
the fact that his career came to mean more to him than I did.'

'Now you're trying to have me on.'

'Indeed I'm not. Look at me. Do I need it? What do I get
out of it?'

'Yes, but you may have imagined it all rather differently.'

'No, I didn't. I could be content with a piece of fish for
dinner and an old rag for a dress. What I wanted was a man.

But I made a mistake even there. There aren't any men nowadays. I thought he was one, but he wasn't.'

'I used to know him well. I should know whether he was a man or not.'

'Maybe he was once, but he isn't now. He's scared stiff for himself and his career, he's afraid of everybody and the result is that I live in this house like a prisoner. No one ever comes to see us, and he keeps on sniffing around to see if the walls are bugged. It's a life sentence, and there's absolutely no way out.'

'That car of yours is easily recognizable.'

Her grey eyes narrowed slightly.

'Oh, I don't try to conceal everything. It's a bore having to preserve the decencies. I ought to have sent you away long ago. But tonight I just don't feel like it. What the hell, I say . . .'

Frank stood up swiftly.

'I'm sorry,' he said, 'I really ought . . .'

'What are you so frightened of?' she grinned. 'Why are the whole lot of you so terrified? I thought you men were afraid of nothing – heaven, hell, the Germans. That's what they used to tell us, anyway.'

'It's . . . it's not on my own account.'

'Oh yes it is – what else? Your little job, your little place in the sun. Shall I tell you what you're afraid of? You're afraid of the report that Galovitch will have on his desk tomorrow, saying that you were here till early morning. With all the details: when the light in the big hall went off, when we moved into this room . . .'

Frank was stung by this. He said:

'Tell me, how many men have you frightened like this here?'

'*Touché*. Yes, all right, I'm frightened too. But I'm only a woman, I can start anything I like, but it's the men who decide whether I've really started it or not.'

Frank tried to switch the conversation into more promising channels, but she evaded him skilfully. He was attracted, very much so, but had she brought him here simply to tease? Or was it just that she wanted to talk freely for once, and he happened to be there? She attracted him and he wanted her. But how was it to be done? Things had to be brought to a head some time, it was nearly morning, he desired her and he realized that this was the only opportunity and that it was fast disappearing. But what to do?

Should he throw himself down beside her and clasp her in a passionate embrace? Should he kneel at her feet and declare his ardent love? Hardly his style, and not hers either. A night must develop gradually if it is to be worth anything, and she was doing all she knew to prevent this. She was making a fool of him, and there seemed no point in staying. Nevertheless, he couldn't bring himself to get up and go – he wanted her too much. He decided on a line of attack.

'That's a splendid portrait.'

'Do you think so?' She was obviously pleased.

'You're a beautiful woman.'

She had seen through his approach by now. 'Yes, I know,' she said. But Frank was not to be put off.

'You'd make a marvellous nude.'

She laughed – a clear ringing laugh. She stood up, took his head in her hands, kissed him and said; 'Oh, you are a dear.'

'I mean it.'

'I didn't know you did nudes. Tell me about them.'

'It's a complicated business,' said Frank, losing his nerve a little. 'You need about an hour between undressing the model and taking the picture. You see, the lens is remorseless, it picks up everything – the marks made by your girdle and the elastic of your pants, your shoulder-straps and brassière – all that has to disappear, the body has to be smooth and white all over . . .'

'I never thought of that.'

'Most people don't.'

'So you think I'd be a good model?'

'Perfect.'

She laughed again – long and merrily.

'I must say,' she gurgled, 'no one has ever tried that one on me before. The things you men think of!'

'I want you.'

'You're so gloriously clumsy, Frank – it's really marvellous.'

'I want you.'

'It's too late, Frank dear . . . That car of mine – I think you were trying to tell me that you've sometimes seen it in an unexpected place?'

'In several.'

'No, in one. Always the same one. At least, once or twice you may have seen it elsewhere, but never for long. I can safely tell you this, my reputation's ruined anyway. Once at a party I met a nice young man who looked into my eyes and said: "You're attractive and I want you." At another party, not long after that, I found under my handbag a key wrapped in a piece of paper with his address on it. Of course, I found out who he was first. I'm not the sort of woman who pretends to be interested in butterflies. But you – you're just a bungler.'

Frank understood. It was half past two, which is too late for a night to start – especially if it's to be the only one.

All the same, he desired her more than ever. It wasn't like Lisa, whom he had prowled around for so long. The way he felt about this one was different. He could do without her. It would be wonderful if it happened, but it didn't matter if it did not. It was a pity, though, to miss the unique opportunity. He could not help admiring her. There was more in her than he had imagined.

He looked at his watch, and stood up. She stopped him once more.

'No, no, stay a little longer.'

He was nonplussed, uncertain what she wanted.

'Why are you pursuing him?'

Frank made no effort to conceal his bewilderment.

'Yes, you are. You're on his heels everywhere. You avoid meeting him, but you keep spying on him. You never miss a single chance of being close to him. Don't try to look so innocent, I'm not such a fool – you think you see everything but I see one more thing, I see you as well.'

'Is this supposed to be a warning?'

'No, it's not. I'm just curious, that's all. I don't imagine, as

you once did about me, that it's some plot of Galovitch's. And
I don't think you want anything out of it for yourself either.
Listen, I've often watched you taking his photograph – what
does it mean to you exactly?'

'You know how to drive me into a tight corner all right.
But have you noticed something else? As for you – I never
photograph you at all.'

'I know he's on the way out. He's too far gone to know it,
but he's done for, it's only a question of time. It may be a release for me, although I live my own life anyhow. I'm not such
a child as you and everybody else may think, I can tell he's
written off and I can give a guess why. But, Frank, he's a dead
man anyway. He doesn't know it, but he's dead. And I would
hate it – not only for his sake, either – if you were to start kicking him when he's already dead.'

'That's the last thing I would think of doing.'

'You must have a wonderful butterfly collection, Frank.'

He smiled and said nothing.

'You know, I once held you in the palm of my hand. I could
have crushed you just like that, just by giving away one single
thing. You're proud of seeing everything, aren't you? What
about that time in the woods when you thought nobody could
see you? The people who were supposed to be watching didn't
see you, but I did. It's called a telescopic lens, isn't it?'

Frank gasped. 'You are fantastic,' was all he could say.

'And now here you are, sitting in my room late at night, in
questionable circumstances. Do you see what I mean?'

'You needn't ask.'

'I hate him. When he drinks, he gets ugly, and I'm terrified
every night. So I prefer – well, tonight you saw for yourself.
But that's something between me and him. He's alone and has
nobody. I'm not the happiness he was looking for. Sometimes
I feel sorry for him. That's what I wanted to tell you. You used
to be a friend of his.'

'What you're saying is horrible – horrible.'

'No, it's not. Look about you a little. It's perfectly normal.
It's the way we all live – we on our level, and you on yours.'

She stood up.

'And now you must excuse me, Frank. I don't look fresh as a daisy nowadays after a heavy night.'

Frank got up too, firmly this time. He kissed her hand. As they left the room she offered him her lips. A simple goodbye kiss.

'It's a pity . . .' he said. If she thought so too, she gave no sign of it.

Frank walked home in amazement. What a woman, what a marvellous woman! The following Thursday evening he made a point of driving along the ill-lit side-street. There, as usual, stood the showy Western sports car.

Eight

The café was warm and crowded. Students, editors, chauffeurs, police spies, lovers. Their conversations merged into a continuous buzzing roar. Nobody here cared about the man who lay dead a few hundred yards away. In a big city, lots of people are born and die every day. In any case, what did the dead man represent? Which of these young people had known him or had any contact with him? They knew of his existence from newspapers and photographs, but they knew and cared nothing about his past. The class war? Had there really been such a thing? The rising? Why did their elders keep dinning into their ears how they had fought and braved death and starvation for their sakes? It was an old story. Times were different now, and there was no reason why they should feel beholden for their lives to anyone . . .

In any case, less and less had been heard about the dead statesman for some time. His death was not a matter of yesterday or the day before. Frank could have given the exact date and hour of his death as a public figure. The press bureau bulletins bore on each separate sheet the date and minute of their issue. One day, a confidential notice on coloured paper had gone out to all magazine editors and radio and television directors, warning them that the statesman's name and photograph were not to appear in any articles or news items. That was the moment of his public death. He himself knew nothing about it : nobody mentioned the confidential bluish sheet of paper in his presence, none of the journalists gave anything away to him. There had been much amusement in Frank's office at his explosion of wrath on seeing a picture in the newspaper of Galovitch, and not himself, embracing the ambassador of a friendly country. He had summoned the director and threatened to make a clean sweep of his office. The editors thought it a splendid joke. Could he really be so isolated as not to understand what was going on? In the past, he himself had issued similar orders to the press bureau about people whose hour of death had officially struck . . .

Who could tell whether, in his last weeks of power, he had begun to notice that the people around him, his own people, were behaving differently – some with more reserve, and others with greater familiarity? The former because they feared that he would drag them with him in his fall, and the latter because they had helped to bring it about and were hoping for a reward in consequence.

Year after year, the public had watched the struggle for power between him and Galovitch. He had lost – in the last analysis, he had never really had a chance. But had anyone told him of his defeat? He went on summoning cabinet meetings, organizing conferences, discussions and banquets, signing papers, giving orders, administering – but he no longer really existed. What is not reported in the newspapers has no public existence.

Today, the papers had come out with black edges and with his official portrait staring at the reader from the middle of the front page. For two days more his name would appear in large letters on the front pages, and in a few days the weeklies would print his photograph, with appreciations and obituaries. The photograph would again appear, with shorter biographical notes, in the next edition of the official yearbook. After that, his career would be reduced to the briefest of summaries, with dates of birth and death. In ten or fifteen years' time his name would mean nothing to the great majority of people.

There were often streets named after people about whom nobody could remember anything. But this man would not even be commemorated by the name of a street. Three photographs of him would be preserved in the main registry of the press office, on the off-chance that they might some day be wanted.

Already nobody missed him. Even those whom he had injured in some way had thought, as they read the reports of his death: Well, he's dead, that's the end of that. Maybe the barber who had cut his hair might remember him because he gave good tips. Maybe one of his schoolmates, looking at the class photographs years after, might pause and say to himself: Who was that now? Oh, yes, of course, it was him ... And maybe someone was thinking at this moment: Well, that's the last I'll see of the fifty crowns I lent him twenty years ago.

All in all, not an impressive collection of memories. Of course there might be others, but they would be much the same as these.

Frank looked around the café and thought: Perhaps I'm the only person here who's thinking about him at all; and I'm not sorry he's dead, or am I? Frank, after all, had known him and knew what a mess he had made of his life, and for what.

Frank was about to get up and go when he felt a slap on the back, so vigorous that it hurt. He looked round angrily. The young people at the next table were also evidently struck by the vehemence of this friendly gesture: they fell silent and awaited the outcome with curiosity. Behind Frank stood an artist whom he recognized, an academician and recipient of the Artists' Order of Merit. This man, with an expression as though he had just won the big prize in the state lottery, said:

'Well, so your friend has died, eh?'

Frank snapped back in fury:

'Yes, he was my friend. But I didn't lick his ass like some I could name.'

The painter was disconcerted. He sensed Frank's irritation and realized that he had gone too far. He tried to avert a quarrel – 'Well, you needn't bite my head off.' But it was too late.

'You louse! You parasite! You think nobody knows who got you the Bastards' Order of Merit and what you did for it! And now he's dead you try to throw mud at him, eh?'

The painter looked round for a way of escape, but in vain. Frank pushed him on to a chair, hardly noticing the fact that the whole café had grown silent and everyone was staring at them.

'No, you won't go – you'll sit here if I have to nail you to the chair. Do you really think no one knows why the juries kept on awarding prizes for those daubs of yours year after year? How many state commissions did he get you for station halls and restaurants and those half-witted frescoes that you've plastered up and down the country? And do you think nobody knows what for? I do!'

'This is too much,' said the painter feebly. 'I'm not going to sit here talking to you.'

'Oh, yes, you are. I've got plenty to say to you and I'm going to say it now. Then you can go and complain to whoever you like, if you've got the face and the courage to do it. You started this conversation and now you can listen to what I've got to say. You're a dung-beetle, a feeder on carrion. If anyone dared to say the things to me that I'm saying to you, I'd grab him by the throat and not let go till I'd throttled him. But you – you're a coward, a parasite and a pimp! As long as that man was alive, you gave him the run of your studio and brought him all the whores he needed. That suited you down to the ground, but I won't sit and see you take it out on him now that he's dead. You're a louse and I'm going to make sure that everybody knows it. And now clear out, you filthy bastard!'

The painter did not wait to be told twice, but scuttled out of the café like a rat. Frank got up too; he already felt annoyed at having let himself be carried away. The incident had electrified every police spy in the place. Two of them followed him as he left the café. He paused and looked at them mockingly. Were they going to make a report? He knew them by sight, as they knew him. Would he be accused of insulting the memory of the dead man? Actually he had been defending it – and perhaps indeed that would be the charge against him . . . He could not resist saying to the men: 'What a life!' They looked sourly at him and disappeared. Frank watched them round the street corner with some relief. Things had changed. A few years ago they would have arrested him, and now you could laugh at them to their faces. Did that mean much or little? Frank didn't know, but it was certainly something when people no longer had to tremble at every step, no longer went in terror of their own thoughts even before they had put them into words...

Frank walked back towards the great hall, still annoyed at having given way to his feelings. What was the point? And what business had he to let fly at others for prostituting their art to official purposes? Did he not do the same with his photography? So why was he angry, what had he been shouting about? Why had he been so incensed at being called a friend of the dead man? Wasn't it true? Why, they had spent nearly half their lives side by side. Later on, things had gone wrong between them, but how could that erase the past from their memory, from their lives, from their consciousness?

Frank's chagrin increased. Why had he lost his temper in that way? Could it have been through fear of association with the dead man – fear that at some meeting, some day, he might be shouted down with the words 'You be quiet, you were one of his underlings'? Fear of being supplanted as a photographer of banquets? Some of his colleagues, he knew, would be glad to take his place – it was nothing to be envious of, but they did envy him. For a long time they had ascribed his success to his having friends in high places, or rather a friend... Actually, this was true only to a certain extent and for a certain time. Of course, Galovitch would rule the roost now, and he didn't like Frank. This funeral might be Frank's last grand occasion – from tomorrow onwards he might be doing edifying pictures of workers, milkmaids and damsels in national costume. Would it make any difference? Instead of microphones he would be photographing costumes, with some kind of faces attached to them. The technique would be exactly the same, but everything else would be different. There are gradations of rank among photographers too, and Frank had been at the top for a long time – that would now change. Frank had had a presentiment for some time past, he felt that this would be his last state funeral. And although he kept telling

himself that he was sick and tired of the job anyway, it was
quite a pleasant sensation to move amongst people of importance, to be able to talk to them and to penetrate to places
where others could not.

But was it worth while disowning his former comrade for
the sake of all this? Frank checked himself. Had he disowned
him? Surely he had been defending him against that scoundrel
of a painter? But it was no use deceiving himself – he had meant
to disown the dead man. He had been furious because the
painter had called him his friend, and he had flown at the
little wretch for fear lest he himself should be tarnished by
association with the dead statesman. Yet if Frank had had the
courage to ask himself whether he regretted having been a friend
of the dead man's, he would have found it hard to give a clear
answer. How could he regret the best years of his life, the years
which the two of them had spent side by side? What would
be left of them for Frank if the other were obliterated from
them? One cannot cancel one's own life, and Frank's own
life was to a large extent the man now lying dead here. The
man whom he had just denied in the hour of his utter loneliness, when he ought to have cried out: Yes, I do care about
him, I liked him, and in spite of everything I can and must
care even today – especially today!

Memories and episodes came crowding back into his mind
– like the time when they had fought each other – a fight to
the finish . . .

It had been when Frank was already a trained photographer.
He used to work in his studio till four in the afternoon and
then go to meet his friend on the river-bank. At that time
Frank was in love with a girl who used to join them every
evening after her work. When it was warm enough they bathed
naked in an inlet of the river, overhung with dense willow
foliage, and they prided themselves that they were helping to destroy outworn prejudices. There they were, two
young men and a girl belonging to one of them, and no absurd
bourgeois barriers amongst the three. They would watch her

entering the water like a slender mermaid, with the moon shining on her naked body; then they would dive in after her, and swim about for a good while, shouting and laughing – it wouldn't have been such fun with any two of them alone, this way it was marvellous. They both admired her, and why not? She was beautiful, supple, daring, a joy to behold, but she belonged to Frank, she was his girl and all three of them knew it. Each of them knew it and behaved accordingly.

One evening the two men were walking by the river as usual, waiting for the girl to arrive. Frank felt a little uneasy, she was late and this was not like her. He kept looking at his watch. Finally his friend said:

'Margaret's not coming today.'

His voice sounded strange. Frank looked at him sharply.

'What's the matter?' he said.

'Nothing. Why should anything be the matter?'

'Why wouldn't she be coming?'

'I just happen to know she's not.'

They stood and looked at each other.

'Has she said something to you?'

'No, nothing.'

Frank did not know what to think. The other was clearly making up his mind to say something that was not at all easy.

'Margaret and I are fond of each other.'

Frank still did not understand. What was he driving at? Of course they were both fond of Margaret. Why was he telling him this? What did he mean? Margaret was Frank's girl, everybody knew that.

'What do you mean?'

'Just that. We're fond of each other.'

Frank eyed him searchingly, but the other looked down. All at once, Frank understood everything. The bitch! Oh, well, they were all like that . . .

A moment later the pain began to tear at him inside. It was like a red-hot knife plunged into his breast, cutting, burning, hurting unendurably.

Then, without a cry or a warning, he leapt at the other's

III

throat, grabbed it and squeezed so hard that the hated face turned purple and the lips parted helplessly – then at the last moment the swine managed to prise open Frank's stranglehold. Frank kicked at him with such force that he thought he must have broken his ankle, but this only redoubled his fury: he threw himself on his enemy, hurled him to the ground, hammered away at his nose, mouth and eyebrows, dug his knee into the soft belly.

The other roared with pain, doubled up his legs, managed to throw Frank off and started to pummel him in turn. Frank felt himself weakening under the heavy blows, his strength and willpower were draining away, his ankle seemed to be in flames. He braced himself, threw off the other's weight with a supreme effort and, before his enemy could collect himself, caught him with a hook to the jaw. Then he hit him a second and a third time. He felt a sharp pain in his fingers and looked at his hand. The knuckles were maimed, the skin cut to pieces by the other's teeth. His rival tried once more to get up, but Frank knocked him down again with a final blow. Then he stood still, panting for breath and gradually recovering full consciousness of the situation.

The other lay at his feet in a bloody heap, incapable of movement. A rattling sound came from his throat, to prove that he was still alive. Frank seized him by the feet and dragged him to the shallow water, thrust his head in and then laid him on the bank. Once again his eyes went red and he planted a vicious kick in the other's side. Then he thought of something better – to kill the bitch, to kill her!

He could not have told how he managed to get to the street where she lived. He felt nothing and was conscious of nothing. He had to hurry, his foot was on fire with pain and swelling fast – he must drag himself along somehow, to get to where she was and kill her.

After a while he stood in front of the house, at the spot where he had said goodnight to her so many times. Suddenly he felt weak and wretched and did not know what to do next. The street was empty, but a ghostly figure came walking towards him along the middle of the roadway from the direction of the river. Frank dodged behind a chestnut tree, but too late – the other had seen him.

'Is it you?'

Frank said nothing, but the other was not deceived.

'I know it's you. Just you leave Margaret alone!'

Frank came out from behind the tree and walked painfully to where the other stood. Every step was torture, but he made his way with determination towards the shadowy figure in the middle of the dark street. The other waited, motionless. Frank took him by the throat: he offered no resistance. Frank loosened his grasp. It was no use: he couldn't do it. He took his hands off the other and moved slowly away. Hearing a thud behind him, he turned round and saw the dark form lying on the ground. He let it lie – his one thought was to get to the nearby hospital. At all costs he must make it as far as the porter's lodge ...

When the porter saw him, he held up his hands in horror. Frank groaned:

'In River Street – he's in River Street.' Then he moved another step, cried out with pain and collapsed on the hospital steps.

Before the evening was out they were sewing up and patching his wounds, his leg was in plaster and suspended from a hook. He refused obstinately to answer any questions, but a fight of that sort between such close friends could not be hushed up. The other was brought into hospital, and the town had its sensation. A policeman came to see Frank and tried to find out all the details; Frank kept telling him to go to hell, but he would not be put off. He cajoled and threatened, pointed out to Frank that he could get heavy damages for assault and battery, and reminded him that it was his own duty to start criminal proceedings against the dangerous ruffian who was responsible for Frank's condition. All Frank had to do was to sign the form which he had already filled in.

The authorities were only too anxious to lay the other by the heels and bring him to court as a danger to the lives and property of peaceful citizens. They wanted to turn the revolutionary agitator into a common criminal, to fill out his police record by making him an ordinary blackguard and a potential murderer. They did not care in the least what had really happened. It was Frank's friend they were interested in – even in those days they were afraid of him, knowing what he would grow into.

'But that's ridiculous, officer,' said Frank. 'The whole town knows what good friends we are.'

'We know what we know. And anyway someone must have knocked you about like this,' retorted the gendarme impatiently.

'Well, it's like this, officer. You wouldn't believe it, but I had a collision with a railway engine. The poor thing was derailed and it's still lying somewhere on the embankment,' Frank grinned. The officer lost his temper. All right, if Frank wouldn't talk it was his affair, but he needn't be surprised if they were both hauled up before the court.

'You know what you can do with your court.'

'You're insulting an officer of the law,' screamed the gendarme. 'You'll pay for this – there are witnesses here.'

He went on shouting till his voice was drowned by peals of laughter from the rest of the ward. The patients were having the time of their lives. Finally he made off, purple in the face with rage.

Next day Margaret came. She sat on the edge of the bed and took no notice when Frank turned his back on her.

'You're fools,' she kept on saying. 'Such a pair of fools . . .'

'Go away.'

She stopped talking, but she didn't go. She stroked his shoulders, which were quivering as he struggled with his tears. She did not go until he allowed her to stroke his hand, and smiled at her as he had used to do . . .

After a time, the three of them began to be seen again at the river. Everything was the same except for one small change. However warm the evening, they no longer bathed naked together.

Nine

Frank could not bring himself to go straight back to the hall. Instead, he stopped in at his office and handed his films to an assistant to be developed. She looked at him curiously. Usually he developed them himself.

He wandered for a while through the bleak streets and then went home to lunch, but found he had no appetite. Usually there was a scene when he left the food on his plate, but this time his wife made no fuss. She stroked his hair and said :

'You don't feel well, do you?'

He rejected her sympathy with a shrug of the shoulders and said :

'Oh, it's hell.'

'You should have given it up long ago. Other men publish big, expensive books, they get abroad, they have plenty of Tuzex coupons so they can buy imported goods . . .'

'Oh, give it a rest,' he snapped. He had heard this piece too often already. Not that she wasn't right, he knew that, but she had an unfortunate habit of always coming out with it at the wrong moment.

He got up, went into the dark-room and removed a screen from the wall. Behind it, his most secret treasures were arranged in meticulous order. Tuzex indeed – this was worth more than any Tuzex. The satisfaction of this passion had cost him thousands in paper and film alone. The result was a unique document, containing everybody and everything.

Once, for a short time, there had been on the market cellophane albums, three and a half by four and a half inches, in expensive imitation-leather bindings. Frank had bought twenty and regretted afterwards that he had not bought up the lot. The twenty, each containing fifty photographs, had been filled up long ago. Frank had marked them on the back with Arabic numerals and knew exactly what was in each. He had only to stretch out a hand.

He took out one of the small fat volumes, and opened it at the picture of a great man – another one, dead long since – standing on the balcony of an hotel at which he had arrived half an hour before. There he stood, full of pride and emotion, waving to the crowd assembled on the square below. He had been in the town for barely half an hour and already two thousand young people in light blue shirts were there to greet him, clapping their hands, cheering and demanding to see him. The great man, deeply moved, extended his arms to them. Such love, such admiration! How splendid our young generation was!

Another picture, from a different town. The same great man, wearing a miner's helmet and about to inspect one of the pits, accompanied by the director of the mine and a party of engineers. The mine had been named after him, and a placard bearing his name was attached to the main hoist.

The next picture showed a microphone. Behind it, the great man, no longer quite so great as before, stood with his right arm outstretched and proclaimed: 'I too, comrades, was found wanting in revolutionary vigilance and prudence, I too succumbed to the wiles of the enemy.'

Then the same mine again. A gang of convicts were seen about to enter the pit, and among them a familiar face, no longer surmounted by a peaked cap but by the usual convict's headgear. The mine, of course, had been renamed some time before.

Then the gates of a huge prison. The man was stepping out through them, bare-headed, with a small suitcase in his hand, looking round to see if anyone had come to meet him. No one had.

The open doors of an ancient synagogue, with a lorry standing in front, from which the man was unloading a large bale of compressed waste paper. Over the synagogue doors hung a notice : National Enterprises – Raw Materials Collection Point.

Finally a cemetery with a freshly-dug grave, and beside it a plain deal coffin. A Protestant parson, with an altar-boy bearing a cross. A woman in black, some other men and two grave-diggers. Protestant, because Catholics are not allowed to bury suicides.

A tragedy in brief – and on a grand scale as well. What name was it that had once been blazoned across the hoist of the great mine? Frank could remember it, but who else? One woman, and a few neighbours. How long was it since the date of the picture showing him on the hotel balcony? About fifteen years. Later on, Frank had been one of the few people who still greeted him if they met him in the street.

Today, however, even Frank's precious archives could not afford him pleasure or distraction. He got up and fixed the screen back on the wall. He could not settle his mind on anything.

'Will you be in for dinner?' asked his wife. There was a touch of anxiety in her voice.

'I don't know. Don't cook anything. If I'm in, I'll have something cold.'

She understood. So he'd be staying out again. She stood in the doorway as usual, watching him with the look he knew so well. All right, so you won't be in, but at least please don't get drunk. It always irritated Frank, but this time he turned round, took her head in his hands and held it to his chest. They stood like that for a moment without a word. He felt her trembling and wanted to say something affectionate, but it was probably better to say nothing. He kissed her goodbye, a thing he had not done for a long time. Why? Why did he not kiss her every day? Even after so many years, they still loved each other, and she did not have an easy time of it. With his salary, strive as they might, it was impossible to make ends meet. Frank was constantly going on trips and leaving her at home. He knew how apprehensively she always waited for his return, and this annoyed him too. After so many years she might have got used to it.

'I'll come straight home tonight,' he vowed to himself. Suddenly he felt immensely glad that he had her, that she was the kind of person she was and that she would be waiting for him. That he was not so lonely as he sometimes allowed himself to believe. He understood her and knew what she meant when she would say, out of the blue, 'Don't have anything to do with them any more. Do a book about dragon-flies – they last longer.'

Tonight, Frank said to himself once again, I'll come straight home, whatever happens.

Ten

Back at the great hall, Frank's attention was suddenly caught by a half-audible remark. He turned round sharply, and saw two unknown mourners leaving. As the dead man would have said, two unknown, faceless individuals: men in the street, anonymous representatives of the broad masses . . .

If the two men had been persons of any consequence, Frank would have known who they were. The experience of years had taught him to distinguish and recognize faces, and to remember them. He ran out, caught up with the two men, levelled his camera and snapped them. They stopped short: one of them paled and the other's face grew red. In a minute one would say bitterly to the other: Why couldn't you keep your mouth shut? We'll be in the soup for this. As a matter of fact they wouldn't, people no longer got into trouble for such remarks, but the two didn't know that – old terrors die hard. All Frank had wanted was to have a pictorial record of the voice of the People. That was what the insignificant character who had spoken represented – a man of the people whose tongue itched to say what was on his mind, who, the moment he had turned his back on the catafalque, had turned to his more or less trustworthy friend and confided:

'You know, he died of uraemia.'

Frank was startled, and not a little shocked. So the dead man had not been spared even this. For if a single insignificant private person knew it, it was quite certain that all the others would. He caught himself wondering if the widow knew, or the dead man's personal staff. The widow ought to have known – but did she?

Uraemia is an unpleasant disease.

The certificate of death had been signed by three eminent physicians, leading members of their profession. Its contents had been released as an official document by the government press agency, but not before a small alteration had been made: the cause of death was given as leukemia. The three eminent doctors had put their names to an official forgery.

Anyone at all might die of uraemia: Frank, the doctors themselves, or the man who had whispered the secret to his friend as they left the hall. But a statesman could not, was not permitted to die of it. No statesman had ever died of uraemia. A public man has no right to choose his own cause of death – at least not officially. As a private person he may die of anything he likes, but not in his public character.

Now the story would be whispered from ear to ear – not only about the dead man, but about the three who had forged his death certificate.

The whole business was absurd, and also terribly sad. Uraemia is a dangerous and repulsive disease. Certain organs of the body cease to function, and as a result urine gets into the blood, poisons and destroys it. To our squeamish and puritanical world, urine has offensive associations. Reading the newspapers, one would imagine that great men do nothing but make speeches, sign historic documents, receive eminent guests, pay official visits, confer decorations, warn, rebuke, or hold amicable conversations. That is their public, de-humanized, retouched personality. But who knows if they are sometimes full of doubts and complexes, or petty and malicious, if they have lovers – complicated and risky though it may be – if they put out their tongues and make faces at themselves in the bathroom looking-glass, if their elegant figures are due to the tailor's art, if they are fond of drinking or have in their libraries pornographic pictures which give them greater pleasure than works of philosophy? Or whether their home lives are happy and they beget children? It was the great man himself who, when they were schoolboys, had once startled Frank by asking him whether kings and queens went to the bathroom like everyone else.

Certainly it was not appropriate to the dead man's image that he should be known to have died from the presence of urine in his blood. Some people might think it unseemly. A statesman should die of a heart attack: that was the most dignified end, the heart succumbing under the weight of duties. Frank remembered the delightful passage in *Clochemerle* where the aged statesman has died in the arms of a prostitute and the speakers at his funeral proclaim that till his very last breath he was striving for the good of his country. Frank ran over in his mind the names of several eminent men in history who were known to have died of general paralysis of the insane, a fact tactfully passed over in their biographies. Marat had been murdered in his bath by Charlotte Corday – historians knew this and recorded it, but they did not explain why he had received her in such unusual circumstances, since this would, or so they felt, be placing the great tribune of the people in an unflattering light.

Frank could remember the exasperation of an old, retired Russian vice-admiral who, questioned about a meeting he had once had with Lenin, barked: 'Why can't you leave me alone? What's the good of asking questions? Lenin had red hair, but nobody ever writes about it, nobody describes that carroty beard of his. They all chatter about the historic paving-stones over which he walked, but in his day the streets of St Petersburg were paved with wooden blocks – they're asphalted now . . . Or they paint him in patent-leather shoes instead of the heavy boots he used to wear.'

The journalist with whom Frank had been visiting Leningrad had written all this down, but of course the censors had cut it out of his message. It was for them, and not some doddering old vice-admiral, to decide what sort of a person Lenin was. And woe betide any comrade who tried by such perfidious means to discredit the great men of the revolution.

Very well. Propaganda had always been there to retouch, embellish and dehumanize the great ones of history. But there was something called medical ethics, a doctor's honour, the Hippocratic oath. Medical institutions throughout the world paid strict attention to the enforcement of basic moral codes. A doctor who infringed them in any way was struck off the register, inexorably and for ever.

Three well-known, indeed famous doctors. And Frank knew a little more about them than did the members of the public who read their names underneath the certificate of death. For instance, the tall, good-looking one had been the dead man's personal physician – a man of excellent reputation from the professional point of view, though politically it might have left something to be desired. He had attended the dead man in his last illness and, realizing the gravity of his condition, had very properly called in two colleagues for consultation. Even had he wished to, he was not authorized to handle matters alone. The three specialists had conscientiously followed the progress of the disease and had doubtless done all in their power to save the patient's life. They had gathered regularly at his bedside, ascertained and discussed his condition, established a diagnosis and agreed upon the best method of treatment. They had all been with him at the last. Up to that moment they had kept an elaborate record of the course of the disease and the methods adopted, and copies of this had been sent to all the authorities concerned.

After they had conducted an autopsy and washed their hands, they had signed the final certificate of death. Frank did not know for certain, and probably never would, whether this document itself had given the cause of death as leukemia. What he did know, however, was that Galovitch had sent for the three physicians shortly after the announcement of the dead man's demise. He also knew Galovitch, and could vividly imagine what might have taken place at the interview . . .

Galovitch stood behind his desk and, in a grave voice which betrayed neither sorrow nor satisfaction, invited them to be seated. He himself then sat down on a hard chair – unlike other people, he kept a hard, ordinary chair behind his office desk and not a soft one. He remained silent for a moment and looked significantly at the document which lay before him, then at his three visitors. Then he said in his rough, unpleasant voice:

'We'll tear this one up, comrades, do you understand? The original and all the copies.'

The three doctors were taken aback. One of them ventured to ask why.

'We can't have uraemia as the cause of death, comrades.'

The doctors' confusion increased. One of them, incensed by Galovitch's tone and the air of authority with which he was meddling in their affairs, said angrily 'What do you mean?' Galovitch, who had been expecting this, replied with the imperturbable calm for which he was famous:

'Uraemia cannot be officially given as the cause of death, comrades.'

'But,' objected the bravest of the three, 'what you are suggesting would be a violation of our conscience.'

Galovitch looked at him ironically. Conscience, is it, you highbrow, you professor you? No wonder our universities turn out the kind of misfits they do, when their teachers fill their heads with a lot of rubbish about conscience. As for you, you rascal, do you think I don't know when you go to church and where, or when you were last at confession, you leading light of medicine? And now you have the impudence to come to me with your conscience and all the rest of the Christian folderol!

He spoke aloud:

'That's all nonsense, comrades.'

The doctors were appalled. The short, fat internal specialist with the big hands jumped up and made as if to leave the room, but it was only a gesture. He stopped half-way when he heard Galovitch saying behind his back:

'You must draw up a new certificate, comrades. Here and now. We have to get out the official report. It's urgent.'

The two who had remained seated looked at each other and shrugged their shoulders. A man who shrugs his shoulders has already made up his mind. Galovitch pressed home his advantage:

'I know nothing about medicine, comrades. That's your business. But we can't have uraemia as the cause of death.'

The dead man's personal physician understood. So did his colleague in the chair beside him. The personal physician had served other great men in the same capacity, including some on whose account he had later fallen into disgrace. His colleague also knew clearly enough where he stood. It would depend entirely on Galovitch whether this man became the chairman of the health committee of the cabinet, and perhaps later on a member of the cabinet itself.

The third man was a Catholic. He too knew what he had to expect.

So they drew up the new certificate, with the slight verbal alteration, and signed it. It had not taken them long to reach agreement. Galovitch watched them in silence, and then rose as a sign that the interview was at an end. So much for you, my fine intellectuals! I've got you in the hollow of my hand. You may twist and turn and get all steamed up inside and think about me what you dam' well please – I know what you think, all right – but when I want you to, you'll sign! When I told you to, you signed, and on the double too!'

That was roughly the way it must have gone. And Frank knew in his heart that only Galovitch could have brought the thing about. He imagined for a moment the situation of the three doctors. Would he have signed in their place, or not?

The chubby internal specialist – a Catholic, a man who believed in the Immaculate Conception. The fate of the institute which he had himself founded, built and enlarged had hung by a thread for years past on account of this ideological taint. Several times already his colleagues had saved it from disaster by warning the authorities – you can't do this, the man is world-famous in his own line, and the institute has achieved brilliant results in the cure of blood-diseases. Well, was this man now to destroy his own life's work with one Quixotic act – the institute which meant everything in the world to him? Was he to indulge in a fit of pride and obstinacy at the expense of his patients? The quack who had been foisted on him some time ago as a deputy would have asked for nothing better! Was he to hand the whole show to this man on a plate? He wasn't worried on his own account – he could survive and make a living somehow: he could perhaps make a new start in some secluded part of the country. But what was the sense in making a new start when he already had a well-organized institute with expensive foreign equipment and a first-class team of assistants? Had he any right to do so? Had he the right, by one act of defiance, to endanger the existence of an institute which had earned such a reputation and achieved such results? Was it right and honourable to accept the challenge of this barbarian and sacrifice his own position? Was it not rather his duty, however repugnant, to hold on to his place and defend it, to grit his teeth and get on with the job?

So he had signed; and Frank could not decide whether he had done right or wrong . . .

The second doctor was a man with an expert knowledge of the state of the health service. It was chaotic, weltering in a morass of unnecessary paper and red tape. The doctors treated people when they had time to, but their first duty was to fill up forms: they were overworked and underpaid, were treated with contempt and died young. The system was headed by an owlish bureaucrat whose main concern was not the nation's health but the production of neat, smooth, orderly reports. Once a year he would draw up a balance-sheet: so many hospital beds, so much devoted to investment, so many doctors and pieces of apparatus – the public were dazzled with figures, sums of money, statistics of persons treated. Not cured, treated. It was a cause of jubilation if the norm for the use of hospital beds was one hundred percent fulfilled!

The doctor in question knew what should be done about all this, how it should be tackled and what changes were necessary. He was not afraid of a fight or of the risks it might bring, and felt in himself the required energy and powers of organization. His appointment was expected within a matter of weeks, and it would be hastened by the shake-up that was bound to follow the great man's death.

So he had signed. Had he been right or wrong?

As for the third doctor, he had been attentively observing the yellowish whites of the eyes of the man of power who faced them across his desk. And he was saying to himself: 'Throw your weight about as long as you can, my friend. You'll need a doctor soon.'

So he too signed. He alone of those present understood the scene in its full significance.

Frank passed the three of them in the corridor as they were coming away from Galovitch's office. They walked heavily and in silence, with downcast eyes, sickened by their own thoughts. Frank understood why when he read the communiqué shortly afterwards. And he knew that at least two of them would, for a long time to come, feel sick with mortification whenever they recalled, even though it might only be in a dream, the shame and humiliation of that interview.

Would he have signed in their place or would he not? He still could not answer the question. He only knew that he was glad there was nothing he had to sign except accounts of travel expenses. It struck him that there was something to be said for being a mere press photographer, even a drawing-room one.

But how had the facts about the cause of death become known so quickly? Surely not through the doctors, who would be discredited by the secret leaking out. Galovitch? But he never betrayed secrets, his mission in life was to hear and preserve them. The widow? Did she herself know what her husband had died of? It was quite possible that she did not know, or even care.

How did such secrets get about? But after all, it was really not so mysterious. A laboratory assistant had been making blood tests. A nurse had been with the late statesman till the last. He had been in a separate, isolated part of the clinic, but the other patients knew he was there and were inquisitive, as people in hospitals always are. A comment here, an unguarded remark there. When the editor on duty in the press office was handed the communiqué, he grinned maliciously and said to Frank: 'It was uraemia.'

At that moment Frank understood the demeanour of the three specialists whom he had met an hour before. He understood, and he too felt sick at heart.

The public would grin, too, as the duty editor had. They would be grinning already. It wouldn't have been Galovitch's idea, he was too simple-minded to have thought up such a subtle intrigue, but, whether he had meant it or not, it was a shabby last trick to have played on the dead man.

So they hadn't spared him that either.

But then again, he had been a statesman – and no statesman that Frank had ever heard of had been allowed to die of uraemia.

Frank was so lost in thought that he became oblivious of his surroundings. He did not notice when they changed the guard, and when he next looked towards the catafalque, who should be there but Muklik!

Frank was furious with himself for missing this man's arrival on the scene, but he at once set about making up for lost time. He came out from behind the bronze doors and photographed Muklik from the front, back and sides and in close-up. The little man remained at attention, but his frightened, rat-like eyes darted nervously to and fro in search of a point on which they could come to rest and keep their owner in countenance.

Frank regretted violently that he had no sneezing-powder with him, but, as though the heavens had heard his silent prayer, the little man's nose suddenly wrinkled, his mouth opened, his hand twitched and, as if jerked by an invisible string, moved up to scratch one nostril. At once Frank had him in focus and had taken a snapshot. The other members of the guard of honour saw what Frank was up to and eyed him angrily, their looks saying: get out, don't spoil the show, give us a bit of peace. The eyes of Frank's victim were full of sorrowful entreaty: why are you tormenting me, what are you doing this for, stop it or I shan't be able to get through these next few minutes, Frank went on with the grotesque performance: he knelt down and took a full-length picture of the little man, and then raised the camera to a height so as to take him and the dead statesman together – he must at all costs have them together, little Muklik scratching his nose with the great man in the background. No one would ever see the picture or know what it was for, except Frank himself and the little man who well understood why he was being photographed so zealously.

The latter heaved a visible sigh of relief when the next guard of honour entered the hall. Frank followed their predecessors behind the curtain. Muklik, who was wiping the sweat from his brow, looked at the photographer reproachfully.

'Well, how was it?' asked Frank maliciously.

'Oh, leave me alone!' The little man turned away, tears starting from his eyes – tears at last in this house of grief. The little man, it was clear, would have thrown himself upon Frank if he had had the courage. Only the memory of cuffs and kicks in the past served to keep his rage within the bounds of decorum.

From his earliest years, Muklik had been a sneak and a tale-bearer. He blabbed about everything he knew, and what he did not know he invented. His schoolfellows beat him up, and he told tales on them for doing so. They beat him again, he told tales, they beat him yet again and so it went on. Even in those days everybody avoided him as something loathsome and unclean. You could see it in his eyes, his appearance, his walk. His big ears marked him out for life as an eavesdropper, a gossip and an informer. During the war he had edited a fascist rag in which he printed scurrilous attacks on Frank and the man now lying dead here, denouncing them and their friends as a gang of murderers and bolsheviks, sadistic sub-men and double-dyed traitors. In his very last article, the day before the Red Army marched in, he had written: We shall return and crush the evildoers.

His servile zeal and talent for mud-slinging were quite out of the ordinary. He reminded Frank of a pig rooting amongst garbage. For all that, his efforts went largely unrewarded, for the simple reason that he was a Lutheran. He was allowed to join the fascist party and even became an officer in the Hlinka guard, but heretics in those days got no share of the gravy. He was all right for dirty work, and that was all.

'We shall return!' he had screamed in his last article. But he himself had nowhere to return from – he didn't go away but merely went underground for a while, and as soon as things quietened down offered his talents and proved services to the bourgeoisie. From then on he foamed at the mouth, not on behalf of God and the nation, but in the sacred cause of democracy against the totalitarian hydra. The guiding star was different, but the vocabulary remained the same.

So it did later on, when he let fly against the bourgeois traitors, the hirelings of imperialism and the Trotskyist vermin. His articles were full of ranting about the dungheap of history and the excretions of sick brains. In this way he managed to keep alive during three régimes and to carve out a position for himself in the fourth.

When the dead man had come to power, he had driven Muklik out of his editorial office and out of town. 'The fellow poisons the air,' he would say. 'How the devil could you put up with him all this time?' In those days, the great man had been consistent. He had called for Muklik's dossier, and he and Frank had had a good laugh at the rogue's artless biography. To begin with, he had joined the Agrarian Party because he could not otherwise get into the hostel in which he lived during his studies in Prague. Then, for fear of losing his livelihood, he had gone into the Hlinka guard, but his party membership was nominal, as was proved by the fact that he had not paid any fees. In reality he had always been a convinced democrat and admirer of the Soviet Union: he had written anti-Soviet diatribes in order to conceal these sentiments and thus be useful in the fight against fascism.

During the rising, only a chain of unfortunate circumstances had prevented him from standing shoulder to shoulder with his heroic countrymen against the bloodthirsty occupation troops and the fascist murderers. His true attitude was shown by the fact that he had not betrayed to the fascists a certain editor whom he knew to be in touch with the underground movement. His writings? Any stylist could tell at a glance that their purpose was to discredit fascism: he had purposely written untruths and used coarse, scurrilous expressions so that men of good will would become disgusted with the wartime authorities.

He admitted with regret that even after the downfall of fascism he had not at once discerned the right path. For a time he had been deluded by the pseudo-democratic slogans of the mercenary bourgeoisie; but the victory of the working class had finally opened his eyes and shown him the way to salvation.

At the end, after the signature, came the following in manuscript:

'It is quite true that I wrote an Ode to Hitler. I was drunk at the time and I never meant it to be printed. How it got into the newspapers against my will is a mystery to me. I deeply regret it and am ashamed of what I did.'

The dead man had read all this and shaken his head again.

'How was it possible? Were all you comrades deaf and blind? How could he have been tolerated in that post for one instant?'

And, after a moment's thought:

'The quarry, that's the place for him. Let him work by all means, but at stone-breaking, nothing else!'

Muklik had made himself scarce. Frank, returning to the hall, glanced involuntarily at the dead man's face. He felt like shouting to him: Do you know who's just been mounting guard over you? Muklik! You remember him – he didn't break stones for long, you took him on as head of the press department of your private office. Were you deaf that time? Or how could you have done such a thing?

There was no need to ask: Frank knew how it had happened. When the dead man had become a minister he had given a huge banquet. Frank had been there on duty. It was their first meeting for many months. Frank was inwardly quite estranged from him, but he could not refuse the proffered hand.

'Come and see me at my office some day,' the great man had said. Frank had made excuses: overwork, lack of time, constantly on the move – yes, some day he would most certainly come . . .

'Nothing around me but bloody professors. They laugh at me, they may be afraid, but they hate me in their hearts. People like you and me who haven't been to school, they hate our guts. I can't trust a single one of them, I have to decide every least thing myself. But it's going to change, it bloody well is!' stormed the minister. Then he came out with it:

'In the country, in the old days, we were a good team, I had chaps I could trust. I'm going to kick out all these eggheads and put in people I know, from our own part of the world. But the trouble is, I don't know who to make head of the press office.' He paused, and looked at Frank speculatively. 'I thought perhaps you . . .' he went on.

Frank put on an innocent air. He was taken aback by the offer, and began rapidly to calculate what difference it would make in his life. Then he found words to reply, without actually accepting or refusing.

'You know,' he said cautiously, 'I'm not the desk type. I'm a press photographer. That's my job and I know how to do it. I wouldn't like to take on something I don't know how to do. I'd have to think it over.'

The offer was attractive, all the same.

'By all means, think it over, take your time. I'll pay you three times what you're getting now, and a bit more. We don't have to worry too much about the state tariff,' laughed the other.

Frank did not at once grasp what he was driving at. When he did, he flushed. So the great man wanted to buy him, to pay him hush-money? Perhaps he'd have liked to clap him in jail that time, but as he couldn't, he was trying to buy him instead?

Frank's pay as a reporter was miserable enough in all conscience. But there was something fishy about this offer. He bit back the words that came to his lips and resolved to reply in such a way that it would not cost him his present job also.

'I'll think about it,' he said cagily.

The other took this for a suitably veiled acceptance. 'Fine,' he said. 'Come along and we'll soon fix it.' But Frank did not go. It was the best way out. And it was a long while before the other found someone to take over his press office.

One day, he summoned a meeting of the chief editors of all newspapers and periodicals. Frank was sent to record the historic event, which was to be a milestone in relations between the government and press. When he entered the conference room, he started violently.

'It isn't – it can't be,' he whispered to the editor who stood nearest him. The other gave him a pitying smile. Much you know about it, my innocent friend . . . The statesman took no notice of Frank whatever. He got up and launched into a speech about prospects of development and the immense, inspiring and constructive tasks of the press – the Fourth Estate – the responsibility of journalists and the need to strengthen contacts between his own office and the correspondents of daily and weekly papers, so that they might get their news direct from the fountain-head.

'From now on, comrades, these meetings will take place once a month,' he proclaimed. 'The head of my press office, comrade Muklik, will be present to inform you all of our current problems of development and the tasks which lie before us in our glorious common effort for the transformation of human society . . .'

Muklik cast a glance of complacent triumph over the bewildered faces of the assembled newsmen. He was one to keep his end up all right – you could chuck him out through the window and he'd find his way back through the drains . . .

'Where the hell did he dig him up from?' breathed somebody close by. Everyone in the room knew who Muklik was. Frank shared in the general consternation, but he also felt foolish for another reason. He not only knew where the statesman had dug Muklik up, but why. To show Frank that he could get on without him quite nicely, thank you. Well, he had.

From that time on the statesman's vocabulary altered: it became more vulgar and more radical. Formerly he had been a brilliant popular orator, capable of expounding in clear, direct language the most complicated political and ideological problems. He could inspire, thrill and inflame to action. That had not been so very long ago, but since then his style had changed. His audiences began to be fobbed off with long, dry speeches composed in advance. He was an excellent speaker, but had no idea how to write. A single page was torture. That, perhaps, was why he detested journalists and literary men. The effect of reeling off written speeches and reports was completely to destroy his gifts as an orator – this voice became a monotonous drone, senseless and soporific. Actually, at this period no speaker dared to utter a single word without notes. People would turn up at discussion meetings with their three-minute contributions clutched in their hands. The notes were a guarantee of factual accuracy, precise and premeditated formulae. And boredom.

It wasn't from sheer perversity that he had taken on Muklik, not simply to show Frank that he could do without him. He didn't know how to write, and someone had to do it for him. Muklik was prepared to do anything. It wasn't long before he was raising a laugh at the press club at his chief's expense, and boasting about how he wrote his speeches. Once, while drunk, he had shouted at the top of his voice:

'The man wants to publish his works! Asked me to edit his speeches for him. Why, I wrote the whole dam' lot, and now he'll bring out a thumping great edition and pocket the royalties . . .'

Frank refused to believe it, but the speeches appeared. That is to say, they were printed, but they did not get as far as the bookshops. Galovitch had the whole lot called in and pulped, for political errors . . . Frank had a copy at home. Galovitch, with his sharp nose for errors and deviations, had done the book too much honour. It was nothing but a hodgepodge of the most devitalized phrases of the day.

However, when this took place the statesman's career had already entered upon its last phase. It was not long afterwards that the government press office issued its confidential directive that his name and photograph were no longer to be published.

Frank was dumbfounded when he heard that the dead man had laid upon Muklik the blame for all the political mistakes and deviations to be found in his works. But was there anything that couldn't happen nowadays?

Muklik understood well enough why Frank had been so anxious to photograph him beside the catafalque on which the dead statesman lay. But who could tell – maybe he would get off scot-free, maybe every member of the dead man's staff would be changed except this single one. With Muklik all surprises were possible, even the most fantastic.

Eleven

Apart from Muklik, Frank took only a few photographs that afternoon, enough to prove to his superiors that he had been at his post. Then he stopped in at the office and left two films to be developed. Groups of people were clustered around the showcases in front of the building. Frank had met this kind of interest before. Pictures of demonstrations, processions and funerals always attracted a certain kind of public. The people who stood and gazed on this occasion were not actuated by piety towards the dead man's memory. No, in photographs of this kind there were always a number of faces one could recognize. It might be mine, yours or somebody's that we know . . . On the following day the telephone in the photographic department would ring incessantly, and the office would be besieged by eager applicants for copies.

It was, no doubt, an ancient human longing to see one's face immortalized by means of a picture, photograph or film. To Frank, the agent of such immortality, this desire was inexplicable. There could scarcely be any family in the land without its album, and any member of the family about whom anything appeared in the papers would cut out and paste all the articles into the sacred volume. There was nothing people would not do for publicity, even down to committing crimes.

Frank had a good deal of experience of this, and most of the examples were comic enough. Once a stranger had pushed a hundred-crown note into his pocket as a reward for photographing him in proximity to some celebrity. On another occasion a young man and a girl had come to him and, after some beating about the bush, had asked him to go to their flat and photograph them making love. Frank had explained that that sort of thing was not allowed.

'But no one will ever know. We're married. We'll pay you well.'

Frank had still refused. He didn't feel like doing it. And, if they were married, what did they want the photographs for? They explained that they wanted to know what they looked like: from above, from the side, from below . . .

'Why don't you put mirrors round the bed?'

They had. But it didn't work, it distracted them. And anyway, they wanted to have the pictures to look at afterwards.

'Aren't you afraid they might get into the wrong hands? People pay a lot of money for that sort of thing.'

No, they weren't afraid. They had thought it all out. The man would go into the dark room with Frank while he developed the film. They would make one enlargement of each negative and then destroy the film together.

The girl, who was young and pretty, had reddened under Frank's enquiring gaze. 'You see,' she said in an embarrassed tone, 'we love each other, and I want to know what it looks like. As it is, I always have my eyes closed.'

Frank hesitated for a long time before finally refusing. He did not tell them the real reason for his refusal, which was – what would happen to the pictures when they divorced, as they certainly would do? People who think of such refinements in the first days of marriage are not going to stay together for long . . .

For some time afterwards he used to imagine the scene. The two of them on a sofa, floodlit from every side, and a third person looking on, walking from side to side, kneeling down, bending over them and taking one picture after another. They seemed to think that a photographer wasn't a man . . .

Frank, like most professional photographers, had a rich collection of female nudes. He knew from experience that there was scarcely any good-looking, well-equipped young woman who could not be persuaded to pose. And most of those whom he had photographed in the nude did not need any persuading;

some even asked of their own accord. But that was quite another matter. Try as he might, he could not imagine himself making love to a woman in the presence of an onlooker. Was such a thing really possible? Yes, of course it was, he had heard of parties where it went on, but in all such cases it was something different, a form of exhibitionism, which provided the excitement, not simply love-making as such. What these two young people wanted was something else – they wanted to capture for all time what was essentially transient. And yet, who could tell? – perhaps in half a century's time people would have photographs of that sort hanging over their beds in place of today's wedding groups, that is if marriage beds still existed any more.

Marriage beds ... Frank thought of one he knew, with an unusual picture hanging over it. A huge coloured photograph of the late statesman, on a speaker's platform, lifting a three-year-old child out of its beaming parent's arms. The father, who was a waiter in a large restaurant, had come to see Frank on the very next day after the picture was taken and led him in front of the show-case.

'Did you take that?' – Frank nodded.

'I want it. I don't care what it costs, I must have it.'

Frank suggested that he apply to the secretary for a copy in the usual way.

'No, I don't mean that. I want a big picture, the biggest enlargement you can make, and I want it coloured.'

'I don't do colouring,' Frank replied.

'That doesn't matter. I know a painter who'll colour it for me.'

'But what do you want with a photograph that size? Wouldn't a five inches by seven one do for your family album?'

'I want a big one to hang over the bed.'

'In your bedroom?'

'Of course – that's where the bed is.'

So Frank made him a huge enlargement, sixteen inches by twenty-four. And that was not the end of the story. A month later the man invited him to his flat, saying 'You must come and look at it.' Frank duly went and looked. The whole thing seemed to him a great joke. But was it any funnier than the thousands of oleographs which hung over thousands of other double beds? The guardian angel guiding a child across a narrow foot-bridge over a ravine? Christ weeping over the destruction of Jerusalem? A general on horseback surveying the field after a victory? It was absolutely unbelievable what pictures people would hang over their marriage beds.

Frank looked once again at the faces of the crowd passing before the catafalque. Neither grief nor satisfaction – and yet, at that very moment, it was possible that a certain waiter was staring at that picture on his wall and was grieving for the dead man's passing. What were his thoughts as he looked at the huge, expensive, brightly coloured photograph in its massive gilt frame? His attitude was certainly different from that of the crowd of official mourners. For him, the dead man was the greatest personality with whom he had ever come into contact. And this great and glorious personage was holding his, the waiter's own son in his arms – the son of an ordinary man of the people! Of course he had heard many tales about him, waiters hear everything, but that was all envy, gossip, scandal-mongering. The dead statesman had been a great and good man, for was he not clasping the waiter's son to his breast? He loved children, and no one who loves children can be really bad.

But what would happen to the picture now that the states-man had died? Little Billy had grown up, he was no longer of a size to be thrust into a statesman's arms. Meanwhile, the pictures of this great man had for some months past disappeared from all public places. No one had given orders about it – people can sometimes sense these things. In a few months more they would have disappeared altogether. His widow would clear the oil paintings off the villa walls and store them in some cellar or attic. And yet here would be one place where his picture would still remain for a long time. It would stay there until the young man who had fallen heir to the modest family estate got round to making a clearance and, in place of the grotesque photograph of himself at three years old in the arms of some unknown man, hung up a Modigliani nude or some specimen of the latest trend in painting.

Otherwise, the dead man was quite alone. Frank could understand the indifference with which people had received the news of his death. They had not sat with him for years on the same school bench or shared their last cigarette with him – and even to Frank these things now seemed distant and unreal. Had they ever happened? Was not Frank deluding himself, stylizing and idealizing his own past? Had the dead man been what Frank once believed him to be? If so, how was it that he had finished up as he had done? What had become of those qualities that Frank had so admired and almost envied? Directness, boldness in action, contempt for danger, love of risk, balance of mental and physical strength, sense of purpose . . .

Yes, the great man had always wanted to excel, to surpass others, to be in the lead. But when those others had recognized his outstanding qualities, enabled him to get to the top and made him their leader, he had suddenly ceased to be exceptional or to be a leader – he had stifled in himself the very qualities to which his rise was due.

When had this process begun? When, in the depths of his soul, had he started to replace the notion of We by that of I? Was this always part of his character, or had it been deformed and distorted by his new circumstances? And what good had it done him? Had his position ever brought him any happiness?

Shortly before his last illness, he had given an evening party for some foreign visitors. He stood at the door of the reception room and shook the hand of each new arrival. This always seemed absurd to Frank – why shake the hand of a colleague whom you saw only half an hour before? For his part, he tried to slip past unobtrusively. It was a depressing occasion: he would be running round photographing the great man in the company of his guests, but in the newspapers next day it would be Galovitch who was shown embracing the distinguished visitors.

The great man was unhealthily pale and tired. Perhaps he was already undermined by the disease of which he knew nothing. He was unsure of himself – he had felt of late that something was wrong, that even those nearest him were somehow behaving differently. He took Frank by the hand and looked at him searchingly.

'So you're betraying me too,' he said bitterly.

Frank bit back the angry retort, No one is betraying you except yourself. What was the use?

'We've created an atmosphere of poisonous distrust. Everyone suspects everyone else. Each one of us is alone.'

Frank thought, It's taken you long enough to find out. Still, perhaps better late than never.

'There's no friendship any more,' the other went on broodingly. Again Frank said nothing. It would have been easy enough to remind him of his own words about friendship in politics . . .

That was the last time Frank had seen him. Soon afterwards he learnt that his friend was ill and had been taken to the special section of the hospital reserved for important personages. He wondered whether to go to see him, but decided not to. Once, however, when he happened to be in the neighbourhood, he met the great man's personal bodyguard. He had known him for a long time, this was the same guard who had once so far forgotten his duty as to doze off in the statesman's car travelling at high speed. The guard misunderstood the reason for his presence. 'Are you going to see him?' he asked. Frank shook his head, and the other man stopped.

'It's tough on him. He lies there alone all day long and nobody goes to see him. His wife rings up every morning to ask how he is. Shouldn't wonder if she's glad when they tell her he's worse.'

'What's the matter with him?'

'Something serious, to do with his blood. But maybe it's better this way.'

Frank understood. He asked: 'What about you?'

'Oh, the next man'll need guards just the same. Although I have heard that they're doing away with us.'

'Did you like the job?'

'Well, it's the only one I know how to do, and it wasn't such a bad life. Always on the go, but I enjoyed it. Why don't you go and see him? He'd be pleased.'

Frank shook his head once again, firmly. Then, to his surprise, he heard the ex-bodyguard say:

'They all betrayed him, every one of them.'

This time, Frank uttered the words that he had not spoken to his friend's face:

'He betrayed himself.' And he was still more surprised when the other sighed heavily and said:

'Yes, I know.'

So even these men were not made of iron – they had their feelings, they could observe and understand, they knew what they knew. Muklik's thoughts, as he mounted guard that afternoon, must have run on different lines indeed.

Twelve

When he got home, his wife announced that she had bought tickets for a film. The theatres and cinemas had not closed, though the former had switched to serious plays for the next three days. The statesman's death had not been made an occasion for full national mourning.

Frank was sorry to refuse. It was a long time since they had been out together. But there was something he must do – the resolution had taken shape in his mind on the way home.

'Another time, Paula. I'm busy tonight.'

She said reproachfully: 'You never have time for me.' He clasped her to him. It always quietened her when he did that. She was right, he neglected her, and not always because of his job. However, he replied on this occasion as he always did:

'You married a reporter, didn't you?'

'Don't drink too much,' her eyes begged as he got up to go.

He found the place without difficulty – an old, tumbledown building. There was no bell, and he had to bang on the door with his fist. Margaret opened it.

'Hallo, Maggie,' he said, as though they had met the evening before.

She was glad he had come, and said so.

'I didn't know where you lived, or I'd have come sooner.'

What a stupid lie, he thought to himself. I only came because he's dead. While he was alive there wouldn't have been any point.

The place smelt of asphalt and mildew – a strange combination. Margaret noticed him wrinkling up his nose.

'You know what houses are like these days,' she sighed. And then, in case he should misunderstand:

'I wouldn't take a thing from him. Neither would Martin, after the way he treated him.'

She offered Frank a chair at the kitchen table – it evidently served as a living-room too. His thoughts went back to similar scenes in the small town in which they had both grown up, many years ago. But the kitchens there had been spick and span, with embroideries representing Dutch windmills and embellished with mottoes like 'God bless our home' and 'A stitch in time saves nine'.

Margaret hadn't changed, and never would: she was as reliable, simple and straightforward as ever. That was probably why her husband had thrown her over: she wasn't a sufficiently impressive ornament to his career.

Martin appeared from the next room, accompanied by a young woman.

'I got home earlier than I expected,' he said. Suddenly Margaret burst into tears.

'Do stop crying, mother,' said her son harshly. 'You've been going on like that for the past two days.'

What was he trying to make Frank believe? His wife withdrew tactfully. Frank took out a bottle of vodka which he had bought on the way, and stood it on the table. 'I hope you don't mind,' he said.

'Hardly,' laughed Martin.

So they sat and talked about all sorts of things except the one they were all thinking about. Before long Martin went off to bed: roadworkers start early in the morning. Frank remained with Margaret until midnight. They talked about old times, anything and everything except the dead man. Only when Frank was leaving did she say:

'There wasn't a soul with him at the last. He had driven everybody away. Even I couldn't think kindly of him. Not on my own account – that was long ago, and I never really blamed him at the time. If a man's determined to kick over the traces, nothing can stop him. But to throw his own son out of the house like a mangy dog...'

'It was the best thing that could have happened to Martin

though. He's made of different stuff, he could never have fitted into that life. The main thing is that he's found himself now, and found you. They took him away from you, but he's your son after all. It was good to see the two of you together this evening. I've been hearing nothing but sordid things all day long . . .'

'Tell me, Frank, what has happened to us all? Would you ever have thought it could come to this?'

'No. But that's what power does. We weren't prepared for it, we didn't know how to handle it and we still don't.'

'I couldn't live the way he wanted me to. It made me feel shy and ashamed. What use was a servant to me? How did that sort of life fit in with what we'd been fighting for? I didn't want to have anything that other people couldn't have. I felt all the time I was betraying something. What earthly difference was there between us and the pre-war bosses? We lived on the fat of the land while other people had ration cards. I couldn't look them in the face, it was like a reproach the whole time. When he wanted the divorce it hurt terribly, but now I'm glad. This is a musty, mouldering old house, but I'm happier here all the same.'

'Have you been to see him?'

'No, and I shan't. For me he died a long time ago. Perhaps I loved him too much in the old days to see him as he really was. The man who left me wasn't him, it was a stranger.'

Frank remembered how once in their young days, when he himself was let out of prison, his friend had smuggled out a message to him. It said:

'Take care of Margaret and see she doesn't lack anything. And tell her to look after the boy. He'll have a better life than we shall . . .'

When he wrote this about his son's future he had never seen him. He was in prison when Martin was born, and Margaret was not allowed to visit him with the child. When he came out and he and Frank were getting ready to take to the mountains, he said to her:

'It's our turn to fight now. You take care of the boy – that's your share. If it wasn't for our sons, what would we be fighting for?'

This was his answer when she had asked to be allowed to go with them. Women would be no use with the partisans, he said. Fighting was men's work.

She gave in. She always gave in to him, and so did everyone else in those days. But there were women who joined them in the mountains, and very valuable they were. They could stand all hardships, better even than the toughest men.

Today the dead man was a stranger to both of them, as he was to everyone else in the world. But Frank and Margaret had known him when he was different. From his earliest years, fighting had been his element. The gendarmes, who could think of no other way to handle him, had more than once flogged him senseless. The more prudent citizens of the little town were scared of him. They felt that if the threatened revolution was built on such material as this, it was no mere utopian dream, but an iron fist banging on the door of history.

As time went on he led strikes, he brought people out in mass meetings that filled the main square. The authorities tried in vain to bribe him, to discredit him, to reduce him to silence. They hated him, but they respected his strength of character. Wherever there was a need of men, there he was. When the European blood-bath was over, he was used in one emergency after another: as commissar for the restoration of the railway system, assessor in summary courts, special commissioner for food purchases and so on. In those days his home saw him rarely and for short periods – almost all his time was taken up in work.

What did he get from it all? Dark rings under his eyes for lack of sleep, and a host of enemies.

He began his new career as commander of the revolutionary militia. In that capacity he purged state offices, directorates and banks of their reactionary elements and threw light on one dark corner after another. His vocabulary at this time was a military one: attack, battle, encirclement, storming the enemy's entrenchments, pulverizing him . . .

Frank had once gone with him to the première of a film that was part of a trilogy about the life of Gorki. At the scene where Lenin installs an illiterate workman as manager of a Tsarist bank, the great man had shouted with glee. He never tired subsequently of quoting this scene by way of inveighing against the 'red professors' who interfered with the rise of the working class and objected to the filling of key posts with leading members of the proletariat.

He was one of those who performed the task of detecting enemies within the party. All kinds of scrimshankers, careerists, intellectuals, lightweights and foreign agents had wormed their way into its ranks – out with them, before they succeeded in wrecking the revolution!

So he conducted purge after purge. He became more and more trusted, and was finally give the mission of purging an entire area. His instructions were to be tough, decisive, firm, incorruptible and devoid of sentiment. 'Don't be afraid of severity,' they told him, 'and remember that when you cut down trees the chips have got to fall somewhere. Nobody's going to call you to account for them.'

So he set to work with his axe, and the chips flew. When his mission was completed, he was given a higher job still. He had cut his way through the forest, and in so doing had undermined the position of the 'cabinet of professors'. Did he already dream that he might one day be at the head of another cabinet, concerning which he could boast that not a single member had taken a university degree?

Cutting down trees is short work, but it takes time for a new forest to grow. His tragedy came when the work was accomplished, when there was no further use for the axe still poised in his hand. The giants had fallen, and there was no dead wood left between him and the sun. He towered over his environment, a giant himself. He had cut all the others down. That proved that they could be cut down – that he, a giant, could be cut down too.

It was somewhere around this point that he must have suffered a change in personality, a moral breakdown. The people he had helped to remove – how much had they known of his mission, of his plans and intentions? He and they would smile at one another, shake hands, swap stories and have a good time together, and then on the following day he would be denouncing their treachery. Smiles and handshakes were tactical weapons in the class war – yes, he still called it the class war at that time. But what was the difference now that he was at the top? The smiles and handshakes and jolly stories went on, but this time he himself was the giant and had to keep a sharp lookout for the glint and whirl of the revolutionary axe. Whom could he trust? Only those were trustworthy who had never wavered. He himself never had, he had remained faithful to the cause, but of whom else could he believe it? – and this meant in the end that he could only trust himself. The one last, single giant, still standing amid the debris of the forest.

In the doorway Margaret said to Frank:

'I don't regret anything. I was happy, and I suppose that's the most that anyone can say. But I'm glad he left me. I couldn't have borne to see him go to pieces in front of my eyes. It all began when he took up with that blonde. I did everything I possibly could to stop it. But he always had to have his own way.'

Thirteen

Frank stepped out into the frosty night. He had to walk carefully: the trees were encrusted with rime, the pavements covered with ice. He could not get the meeting with Margaret out of his head, and he did not feel like going home to sleep. As he walked past a certain tavern, it occurred to him that he had not visited it for a long time. He turned round and went in. Perhaps Lisa would still be behind the bar?

She was. But the place had come down in the world since he had last been there. Once it had been exclusive, and so had she. Things get old and worn out, and so do people. The upholstery round the walls was threadbare and greasy, and water seeping through the ceiling had made a dirty yellow pattern in the best tradition of abstract art. Frank wondered what sort of marks time had made on Lisa's smooth white body . . .

He did not go straight to the counter, but stood in the middle of the place and looked around him. It was half empty. One or two tarts sat waiting, not too hopefully, for a rich customer to turn up. In a corner, a youth in a leather jacket sat fondling a rather unattractive girl. The gipsy musicians were still there, but they looked much older than when he had last seen them three years ago.

The long side-wall was adorned by what had once been a huge and splendid oil-painting representing the blue sea and, behind it, the towers of Manhattan all in white. (The place had actually been called the Manhattan.) A luxury liner was seen approaching the Statue of Liberty, and on its deck a sunburnt gentleman with well-chiselled features was paying court to a beautiful lady. The paint alone for this enormous masterpiece must have cost a fortune.

None the less, time had had its way with it. The smoky atmosphere had turned the blue sea to grey and the sky-scrapers to a dingy yellow, not unlike the real buildings outside. Here and there the plaster had broken away. The lady's evening gown and the gentleman's white shirt-front had been disfigured by the contents of a glass of red wine which some reveller had hurled against the wall.

Once an exclusive night-club, the place had passed from private hands into those of the state, after which it had served for a time as a depot for electronic materials. Later it dawned on those in authority that the revolution did not necessarily mean the end of everything, that private life had to go on somehow or other, and that wine and spirits were a useful stock-in-trade. So the Manhattan Bar became the Dukla Tavern, after a beauty-spot in the Carpathians. This left the problem of what to do about the decoration. A fine painting, a marvellous work of art, but unmistakably representing Manhattan, the symbol of all that was evil and perfidious upon earth. Someone suggested adding a lynched negro to the Statue of Liberty, but it was thought that this might be going a bit far. So the only answer seemed to be to erase the painting, work of art or no. Of course the sea could remain and so could the ship – it would be a simple matter to paint out the flag, put the Don Juan into a boiler suit and his lady-love into national costume. Simpler anyway than a new painting – artists nowadays charged fantastic sums for village maidens tripping about over dewy meadows; what was more, they charged by the square yard, and the cost of this one would be prohibitive.

Then someone had the happy idea of not only saving the masterpiece but turning it to a propaganda purpose. When the place opened its doors again, the gently rippling sea was decorated by the inscription:

'Drone and spiv and profiteer
Dreamt their dreams of dollars here.'

In this way Manhattan was saved; and at the same time everyone who set foot in the place was reminded that the clientele had once been very different, and that it was only the victory of the working class which had thrown open its doors to all citizens without discrimination.

This evening, Frank was rather sorry to see that the inscription had disappeared. He wondered how long it would be before the Dukla turned back into the Manhattan. While they were about it, they might even freshen up the painting, which was badly in need of restoration. So was Lisa, for whose sake he had so often come here in the past; but she, alas, could not be rejuvenated.

There she stood, behind the bar as usual. Her once blooming cheeks were covered with an unhealthy grey, the mark of her profession. There were fatty wrinkles below her chin, and her buxom hips had become shapeless. When she went out behind the curtain to the kitchen, Frank noticed that she had varicose veins. She had, after all, stood there thousands of nights.

Her violet eyes, too, seemed dimmer. Only her coal-black hair was the same. She might have dyed it, but at any rate it wasn't blonde. And there was one other thing that hadn't changed.

'They're still as splendid as ever, Lisa dear.'

She smiled as she always had done when Frank sat at the counter and feasted his eyes on her protruding breasts. He used to threaten that one day he would lay them bare without ceremony.

She smiled again. 'You always were a flatterer – but they're not, you know. If it wasn't for this bra – oh, well, never mind. Your usual?'

'Yes, please, but put half a lemon in the vodka.'

'Lemon, eh? So you're getting older too.'

'Of course I am, but it matters more that you are.'

'Well, with this life, what can you expect?'

How beautiful she had once been. Beautiful and full of vitality – a bright star in the town's night-life. Sculptors, poets and officers came in dozens to drink rum at the counter and to gaze admiringly at Lisa's eyes, face and hair. So, for a long time, did Frank. He would have done anything for her. Once he told her so.

'You're a nice boy,' she smiled, 'but it wouldn't do. I'm happy as I am. I don't like makeshifts or half-measures.'

Frank refused to be put off. He paid court to her at every opportunity, and the rest of the time went about like a sleep-walker. At the most unlikely moment he caught himself mentally undressing her. He compared her with the women he had known and those whom he still met. None of them could hold a candle to her. Her resistance brought him to the verge of desperation. He told her so.

'You're a funny chap,' she said, stroking his hand. 'Even if your life depended on sleeping with me, I still wouldn't want to have you on my conscience.'

Frank was hurt by her mockery and went away, resolved never to see her again. It is easy to say that to oneself when one is cross. Sometimes, seized with longing for her during the night, he would get up and dress, make his way into town and walk to and fro before the entrance to the tavern, torn between his desire to go in and a voice that told him not to. In the end he had the strength to stay outside, and there he cursed himself for an idiot and Lisa for God knows what – she was a cheat, she was playing with him and all the others, maybe she was perverted or frigid or lesbian, in any case she was laughing at him and only wanted to humiliate him. No doubt she had some kind of fancy man whom she fed and clothed with the money she got from drunken students, artists and engineers who came to gawk at her face and figure . . .

So he didn't go in. He kept this up for a month or even longer, and he would never have gone back to the tavern at all if not for the telephone call he had received one day. He picked up the receiver casually, and at the other end of the line was Lisa saying: Frank, come over here for a whisky, if you'd like to and can spare the time.

He stammered something in reply, told his colleague he had an urgent job, and fairly ran out into the street. When he got to the large apartment house in which she lived, he walked round it four times so that she should not think he had come running at her whistle like a puppy-dog. They sat and drank together on the broad sofa, and she took his hand and said to him: 'Frank, darling, I've missed you, I know it's horrid, but what can one do, life's so complicated, things keep on winding and unwinding – you're very nice, Frank, I like you, I wouldn't mind going to bed with you, God knows it's easy, I've done it often enough, sometimes it doesn't mean a thing – a woman can have a hundred lovers and start again as if she were a virgin – but I can't live a second-best life, making love when it means nothing to me and nothing to the man either – if I do it at all, I want it to be full of passion and at the very dead of night – my skin can't bear the light of day, I don't know how to make love then, and what about my nights? My one night off in seven, every Tuesday – would that be any good to you? Would it really? Tuesdays from seven to midnight, when you'd have to go home – fifty-two Tuesdays a year? I couldn't stand it, and it isn't possible any other way. I feel sorry for those men at the counter who sit and sit and look at me and say nice things and wait and get cross when I have to attend to someone else – they pretend that they're there for the drinks, but really they're hoping that they'll make an impression on me, that I'll give in and go with them. And then at half-past three the head waiter comes along and says Closing time, please, gentlemen, and I have to sit for another hour or two over those stupid figures and write down all over again every measure of drink that I've poured out, and then by about five or half-past I manage to leave the place, dog-tired and with just one thought in my head – to sleep, sleep my fill, sleep until doomsday . . . You know, the other morning, one of the most persistent of them was actually waiting in his car at my house. I let him come up – what else could I do? The minute he lay down, he went straight off to sleep, and how glad I was! I'm no good to anybody, Frank. That's what I wanted to tell you.'

'But, Lisa, you can't live like this for ever – not you.'

'What else can I do?'

'Why, you could – ' He caught her ironic look and was silent.

'Yes, what? I could find a day job, couldn't I, and then you'd look after me. That's what they keep saying, anyhow. Some of them even offer to marry me, they swear they've no feeling left for their wives, they moan about how their marriage was a mistake from the beginning – poor devils, all misunderstood, all betrayed by life – it's enough to make you cry to listen to some of them. But I've had it all, Frank, I've been through one of these great, unique, magical love-affairs. How long did it last? A year? And the next one like it? Perhaps six months? Once, on this very sofa, a man swore to me : I'll take you away to the seaside, we'll stay there for weeks, it'll be marvellous. He never turned up again, I knew dam' well he wouldn't. It was some little engineer who'd spent a whole month's pay on that single evening. Oh, I know everything a man says to a woman, all men to all women. You're nice, Frank, I like you, I don't know why, you're exactly like all the others and yet I like being with you, I was sorry when you got cross. I missed you, and that's why I asked you to come.'

Frank suddenly felt an acute sense of depression and pity for mankind in general. She was right – it was all perfectly true. He could have said to her, Lisa, I can't live without you, I'll do anything you like, I'll leave my wife, I'll look after you – but she had said all this before he had had time to, and it was no use pretending that he'd been meaning to say it for a long time; she had heard it all before.

Her voice seemed to be coming from far away : 'Going to bed together is easy and ordinary enough, Frank – sometimes it can mean a great deal more not to.'

Frank moved to a chair opposite the sofa. He felt a new sense of warmth and gratitude towards her for what she had said and for not pretending or concealing anything, and of course all that she said was true. He had no doubt that she could have said quite other things if she had chosen – murmured words of passion, cries of delight, admiration, ecstasy. If she had fallen into his arms and whispered Frank, I love you, I can't live without you, he would have believed her, of course he would; but this way she was right none the less.

'But this sort of thing isn't for you, Lisa. You weren't born to be a nun. You have something, but it won't last for ever – and what then?'

'There is a man I'm fond of, Frank. Very fond. I don't know why, I just am. And it so happens that I can't have him. He's absolutely beyond my reach – our worlds don't touch at all.'

'Who is it, Lisa?'

'I won't tell you. You'd laugh at me.'

From then on Frank started going to the Dukla again and saw Lisa in her flat from time to time. A kind of tender intimacy grew up between them. Frank had someone he could talk to, and so had she.

On one of these visits it was different. She said:

'Come here, Frank. The years are slipping away. We're being silly . . .'

It was her free day, so that he stayed till the following evening when she had to go to work. It was unique, wonderful, breath-taking . . .

And it was the end. The end between them. He came back next week, and the two after that. Then he missed two, and later he ceased to come at all. Once upon a time there had been a beautiful woman called Lisa – once he would have done anything in the world to have her, to be allowed to love her . . .

Now, after all these years, they met as friends but not as intimates. Lisa was glad to see him, and he felt the same, though he missed the beauty and fire that had once been hers. Lisa, that Lisa, was somebody that had once lived. The woman who now stood behind the counter was a dear friend, nothing more.

Someone clapped him on the shoulder and he looked round. He knew the man – a Professor Fonda.

'May I join you?'

'Of course.'

'I didn't know you were such a night bird.'

'I could say the same.'

'It's a long time since we met.'

'It is,' said Frank. 'But it doesn't matter.'

'No. What are you drinking?'

'Vodka.'

The professor ordered a vodka and said: 'Let's drink to his memory together.'

'I've not been drinking to his memory,' said Frank savagely.

'Well, it's not too late. You know, I think he died at the right time.'

Frank looked at the professor in surprise. What did he mean? But it was really obvious enough.

'How do you mean?'

'Just that – he died at the right time. Death is sometimes merciful. It's saved him a good deal that would have been worse.'

'I can't imagine that you care much either way.'

'I suppose not. But, you know, life's a curious thing – I do care a bit.'

'You aren't going to tell me that you mourn his loss?'

'No, but I'm sorry for him. You knew him very well, didn't you?'

Frank wondered if the other could possibly mean what he said. Perhaps he did – he'd always been a queer customer.

'You're a queer customer all right...'

'Why do you say that? Because he went to the dogs in the end? That's another reason to be sorry for him. He did go to the dogs, of course, even I knew that. With all his opportunities, it would be strange if he hadn't.'

Why is he talking like this? thought Frank. To show how magnanimous he is? Is he trying to convince me that he liked and respected the man, after all that happened between them? Who is he trying to fool? How can he forgive a man who persecuted him all his life, who drove him out of the party and his professorship as well?

'What are you doing these days?'

'I've got a job in the city archives.'

155

'Had it long?'

'Two years.'

'Before that you had an industrial job, didn't you?'

'Before that I was in the mines.'

'Then what the blazes are you trying to pull the wool over my eyes for?'

'I'm not. Why should I? I saw you in here, I knew you used to be a pal of his and then you weren't any more, but now he's dead. As for the mines, I've never felt so well in my life as when I was working there. I don't hold that against him.'

'Why didn't you stay there, then?'

The other was silent for a moment. He was evidently hurt by Frank's surly tone, and was perhaps wondering whether to leave without further words. Then he thought better of it and said : 'I'll show you.' He pulled up his trouser-leg, and revealed an artificial limb.

'I'm sorry,' said Frank, appalled. 'I didn't know. I really didn't.'

'No reason why you should. I don't boast about it, but since you asked . . .'

'But, hell's bells, are you still trying to persuade me . . .'

'I've already told you, I'm not trying to persuade you of anything. Maybe I am a queer customer, as you say. Lots of people must think so. But I can't feel any hatred towards him. He was a man, the kind of man I would always feel inferior to. He couldn't have treated me any other way than he did. You may be thinking that he ruined my life and that my accident was his fault too, but it wasn't – I was careless, I had only myself to thank for that. And for everything else, I'm grateful to him in my own fashion. The way he treated me helped me to understand a lot of things. I found myself and, if one ever can say such a thing, the meaning of my life as well. I used to have all sorts of shallow ambitions, and it was he who forced me to live otherwise – not that I liked it at first. Nowadays I lead a quiet, humble life, nobody knows or cares about me, I work for a pittance at a job that nobody envies me or is going to try and do me out of. That's probably the nearest one can get to freedom in our time – to be in no one's way, to care for no one and not have to be afraid of anybody. There I am in the quiet world of books, and their magic means a great deal more to me than honours or money or a career. What's more, I have time to spare. I've taken up the study of Roman law – you may think it dreary and out of date, but it's an open door into world history. You can understand everything from it.'

'Even the present day?'

'Yes, above all the present day. It's incredible how people repeat the same mistakes in similar historical situations. It's been going on since the stone age. We're really all cavemen at heart, squabbling over bigger or smaller chunks of meat. All culture and all civilization are just a veneer we've invented to hide our real selves.'

'Aren't you exaggerating a little?'

'Yes, but only a little. You and I have known each other for a long time, you can remember how it was. He had a leadership complex – he always had to be first in everything. So did I in those days. It was inevitable that we should clash. Besides there was a woman.'

'That I could never believe at the time.'

'Strange that you couldn't. I always thought she'd have told you. You were all such friends together. Anyway, he soon realized that I was threatening his property, his girl that's to say. I believe she was yours once too. I wanted her, that was one reason I tried to get into your group. He saw what was coming, long before anything could have happened. But – there's no harm in my telling you after all these years – something might have happened, and that was why he could never stand the sight of me. I've often wondered if I would have behaved any differently towards anyone who'd tried to take away my girl. I don't think so. Of course I know you behaved differently, but then you were always his hanger-on. Even so, you half-killed him, or so I've heard.'

'Do you think Margaret was the reason for what he did to you?'

'Of course.'

'Aren't you idealizing him a bit?'

'Not in the least.'

'*Cherchez la femme*, eh? Well, I never believed it, I always thought it was just a pretext he'd invented.'

'I'd already met Margaret a few times. He caught us together once by the river. Not by chance of course, he'd been looking for us. He slapped her face in front of me and told her to clear off home. I just looked on and hadn't the courage to go for him. He'd have wiped the floor with me, of course, but I ought to have fought him just the same. That was when I lost everything, not only the girl – but it took me a long time to realize it. When I did, it rankled for longer still. There was only room for one of us – the stronger – and that was him.'

'You're wrong, all along the line. It was he who had an inferiority complex where you were concerned. That's why he had it in for you and never let you alone. You knew more than he did, philosophy, theory and all that stuff, and it made him feel a fool and out of his depth. He always hated anyone to know more than he did. He hated the intelligentsia.'

'It wouldn't exclude the other. The two things might spring from a single root. You remember what a weedy little chap I was in those days, more like a toothpick than a man? How could he have accounted for the fact that his girl, his very own girl, took up with a little runt like me? There was only one way to explain it – I must have turned her head with clever talk, the only kind of thing a stuck-up snob like myself was any good at – you know the attitude. All these self-made men suffer from inferiority complexes. And I was the obvious butt, with a rich lawyer for a father. He could take it all out on me and prove that he was bigger than I was and that he could squash me like a toad. If you think of the things he prevented me having, you realize what he wanted himself. And yet I believe that without him and others like him, we could never have won.'

'Who do you mean by "we"?'

'We communists, of course. I'm not a party member now – he had the power to stop that, and he did. But no one can prevent another man from feeling the way he wants to feel and acting accordingly. He was one of the strong men. Their job is to breach the enemy's ranks, but when they've done it, they don't know where to stop. You can't make limestone out of granite. That was his tragedy. Oh, well, it's time for bed. It was nice seeing you after all these years. There aren't so many of us around as there used to be . . .'

The professor – Frank still thought of him as a professor, from the time when he was dean of the legal faculty at the university – limped away towards the door.

'A queer chap, isn't he?' said Lisa.

'Yes, very.'

Frank was lost in thought. Where did some kinds of people get such strength from? Life treated them like a shuttlecock, hurled them down and trampled on them, and after all that they would quietly pick themselves up and go on in their own way, towards their own goal. He remembered how Fonda had come along wanting to join the workers' youth movement, and how they had looked askance at the lawyer's son with all his many advantages. Frank's friend, it was soon clear, felt especial mistrust for the young student – class instinct, it was called, but now it turned out that the reason was quite a different one. But was that the whole story? Would the dead man have behaved any differently towards the lawyer's son even if he had not seen what the other was after? And was it really for Margaret's sake that Fonda had sought their company and tried to become one of them? When his friend had brought about the rejection of Fonda's application for membership, he had done so on the ground that the other was a spy, a provocateur. Frank knew this was false and so did all the others, but who was going to stick his neck out and take responsibility for admitting the son of one of the richest officials in town? However, Fonda was undaunted by the rebuff: he looked round for other possibilities, and before long had founded a group of Marxist students. For this his father threw him out of the house, but Fonda stuck to his chosen path. Frank's friend denounced him all the more, as a splitter of party unity, and never ceased berating his comrades for having wished to take such a snake to their bosom.

When the fascist authorities had discovered the illegal group they had arrested Fonda with the others. But they had been subtle enough to sow seeds of suspicion by releasing him after a brief detention, while the other conspirators were beaten up with rubber truncheons. This, of course, was a fresh proof that Fonda was not to be trusted. Again appearances were wrong : he proceeded to organize a strong underground group which played an important role in preparation for the rising. Later, he worked as an editor of insurgent newspapers. Another bad mark! – or, as the partisan commander put it, 'a nice cushy job well behind the lines'.

After the war Fonda became a professor and eventually dean of the legal faculty. His students worshipped him and he was always surrounded by young people. When the statesman became head of the government, Fonda's university days were numbered. He was dismissed from the faculty on grounds of political unreliability. His students organized a monster petition in his favour – the *coup de grâce* : he was accused of incitement and expelled from the party, and could thank his lucky stars that his punishment was no worse.

After that, Frank had lost sight of him, and had soon forgotten him altogether. How strange to have met him tonight, and to have heard what his attitude had been.

'I liked him, you know.' Lisa's voice broke into Frank's meditations.

He was puzzled. Whom had she liked? Fonda?

'No, the man who's died. You were talking about him, weren't you? I liked him.'

'You never told me that.'

'Yes, I did. I once told you about a man I had liked very much. It was him.'

'So you had met him, had you? Did you know what sort of a man he was?'

'Yes. I heard a lot about him, most of it bad. But I liked him. He helped me once.'

Frank stared at her, feeling rather foolish. Lisa and the dead statesman!

'You're surprised, aren't you? But he really did help me once, when I most needed it. There are some things I've never told you – I couldn't. It's so long ago now, it doesn't matter. You know me by my maiden name, but I used to be called Stadler.'

Stadler, Stadler . . .? Could it be?

'Yes, that Stadler. He was my husband. A great organizer and a great communist. You remember, he organized a mass escape of captains of industry, as they were called in those days. They stole five brand-new cars from the sales centre and made off in them. The frontier guards were bribed and escaped with them.'

'As far as I remember, they took their wives too. What happened to you?'

'I didn't go.'

'Why not?'

'I didn't want to. Where could I have gone with that idiot of a husband of mine?'

'Idiot's a bit strong. He's made a name for himself on the other side. He's a director of one of the big international banks.'

'As far as I'm concerned, he's an idiot. I only prayed that the escape would come off so that I'd be rid of him. I never loved him. He bought me as you might buy a Persian cat. He had some sort of hold over my father, I don't know exactly what, and so I was married to him. He bored me to tears, and in the end I loathed him as well. We lived apart.'

'In the West, with your charm and your figure, you could have done absolutely anything.'

'Perhaps, but what kind of thing do you mean? Money and parties? I've tried that sort of life, and I didn't like it. It's one long bore. And besides, I didn't like the idea of running away. This place today, that place tomorrow – you can keep on escaping, but where is there security in the world, and who wants it anyway? If a woman like me wants to be provided for, she's got to get up at the same time every day, see the same people, hear the same things ... Listen, this year I'm going to the seaside. You've no idea what an adventure that is, how I'm looking forward to it, how splendid its going to be. What could possibly be so marvellous in the other life, what would I have looked forward to in the same way?'

'But, Lisa, surely you can't pretend that you're not bored here. You do get up at the same time every day, see the same customers, hear the same things ...'

'That's just where you're wrong, Frank. You don't know how much diversity there is in this little world, how many different kinds of people come and sit at this bar, the lives they lead and the things they talk about, and how fascinating it all is. Each evening is different from the last. Of course, there's always someone who makes eyes at me and tries to get me to go to bed with him, but even that's fun. Men are the comic half of the human race. I tell you, it's like a theatre here – a theatre just for me. You know, sometimes we close early – old Lajos the waiter stays, and the cook and the doorman, and we all sit in a corner together and Lajos gets his oboe and plays just for himself and for us, a kind of family party. No one else ever hears him play like that. And where in the world would I find anything to beat this kind of life? If I'd wanted to be rich, you know, I could have managed it without leaving here. There was an Englishman who came here for three years just because of me—he wanted to marry me and give me beautiful dresses and all the money in the world, but I wouldn't. I've tried living with one man. I've had enough of that to last me a lifetime. There are some things that don't suit me, but this place does. You realize that, don't you? ...

'... Of course, the bar's getting old and run-down, and so am I. You remember what a smart chap Lajos used to be – and look at him now, all old and bent. The men who hang around me have changed too – they still want me, but they're not the gay fellows they were. I'm not the girl I was either. Nowadays we get sailors from the Danube boats, beatniks, down-and-outs, all wanting the same thing as the people who used to come here years ago – a bit of life and experience, a chance to forget and dream. You know, there's not a single man who can sit here for an hour without telling me everything about himself. No priest has heard so many confessions as I have. And I'm fond of them – clumsy and irresponsible men who don't know what to do with their lives . . .'

'Perhaps you're right.'

'I liked him too, you know. He was the only man in my life that I really fell for, from the very first moment.'

'Yes. A lot of people liked him.'

'I heard lots about him. This is a place where you hear everything about everyone. The things they said weren't very nice, but I liked him. They say he didn't get on too well with his wife. Did you know her?'

'She was very like you, Lisa, but in reverse, like a negative. Didn't you ever see her?'

'They came here once in a big party after some reception. He came over and shook my hand and asked how I was getting on. He didn't care what his foreign guests thought.'

'Where did you first meet him?'

'Well, I told you who my husband was. When he ran away, I was put in jail.'

'Oh, I see . . .'

'It was stupid. They grilled me for a whole fortnight about things I hadn't the slightest notion of. The man who questioned me was an absolute prize imbecile.'

'And he – the other – was head of the security service in those days.'

'Yes, he was. Later on, he was sent into the provinces. Otherwise he'd never have got away from me . . .'

'And he had you released?'

'Yes. One day he had me brought into his office and came straight to the point. The police stooge stood in front of him like a schoolboy. He sat there and yelled at him: "Foreign espionage – the whole country's lousy with it and you can't discover a bloody thing, all you can do is to pester people who wouldn't know a foreign spy if they saw one. Tell me," he said to me, "why did you stay? Why didn't you run away when you had the chance?"

' "I didn't want to. Where would I have gone? There's no sense in it."

'He took a bit of paper out of a drawer, wrote something on it and gave it to me.

' "Here's the order of release. You can go. Nobody'll bother you any more. But get this straight – your old life's done with. The villa's gone anyway, you'll have to find somewhere else to live, and a job as well, otherwise you'll find yourself back here again. You can take your personal things out of the villa, but nothing else, mind – we'll be watching that. No jewellery – just a necklace, a ring and a watch. One picture, and no more. Enough furniture for one person. And don't do anything silly. Any letters you get from abroad, you're to hand over to us. And you'd better not write any abroad yourself."

'I can't explain, Frank, he was simply marvellous. He was a man, a person to be reckoned with. You couldn't help being impressed.'

'You might have found him less impressive later on.'

'I don't know. I only saw him once again, that night when they came here.'

'Did he never suggest anything or try anything on you?'

'No. I thought that I might have made some impression on him, too, thought he might ring up or make a pass of some kind. He liked the look of me, I could see that. And I wanted him to ring up or come to see me, but he didn't. Just a signature, and on to the next business. Actually, he did have to do with me one other time. When I took the job here, that lot – you know – wanted me to work for them. I refused, and they tried to frighten me by saying I wouldn't get the job if I didn't. I know he stepped in then, I heard about it later. If he hadn't, I'd never have been able to work here.'

Frank walked home with confused feelings. His head was full of the dead man's affairs – all day long his former friend had been thrusting himself on his attention, turning up at unlikely times in unlikely places, jogging and teasing his memory. He had no reason to disbelieve Fonda or to doubt Lisa's story. It was true then – the dead man was not so alone as Frank had imagined when he saw the listless crowd filing past the catafalque. There was someone who thought of him with pity, someone with respect, and someone who actually missed him. Fonda had said that he had died at the right time. Perhaps. Perhaps it really was high time for him to quit the stage. Frank imagined what his funeral would have been like if it had taken place a year or so after his fall from power. Then he would really have been alone, disgraced and outcast: no state funeral, no music, a humble grave in the corner of a cemetery, and a few people standing by. Lisa. Fonda. And himself, Frank. Not friends, but at least a few people who were not absolutely indifferent to him.

Would it not, after all, have been better that way? Had he really died at the right time?

Fourteen

Next morning Frank woke up with a headache, a feeling of nausea and a general sense of disgust with the world. He got up reluctantly and would not touch his breakfast, drinking only a cup of black coffee without sugar. That did not make him feel any better either. His wife looked at him reproachfully. Usually he offered excuses, but today he said nothing. She might as well think he'd been drinking – she always did anyway.

Out of doors, it was thawing. When he had left Margaret's flat after midnight it had been very cold, but on the way home from the tavern he had noticed that the wind was warmer. During the few hours he had been asleep, the weather had completely changed. Instead of glazed frost, the pavements were covered with black, slimy mud.

It cost Frank a great effort to make his way back to the great hall. Again and again he felt the impulse to return home and stay there, to go nowhere and talk to nobody – let them fire him, what in God's name did it matter? Paula was quite right: other photographers worked as free-lancers and published glossy albums in large editions, and they all had spruce summer cottages and decent cars, not the sort of rattletrap that Frank drove around. Then he laughed at himself. He, the revolutionary, the partisan – cottages, cars and thumping fees! How demoralized and bourgeois can you get? And the awful thing was that today millions of people were thinking in the same way: money, cars, cottages, jobs and reputation, those were the idols of the day. Fonda had been quite right. But in the stone age, had there been enough chunks of meat to go round? Nowadays there weren't all that many pickings:

cottages, cars and money, some people got them and some
didn't . . .

This isn't the way we meant things to be, thought Frank.
No, it wasn't, but that was how they had turned out. Of course,
there were still a few eccentrics left. Fonda didn't want money
or a car or anything else, he was self-sufficient and content
with what he had. Lisa – what did she want? An early-closing
night so that Lajos could give a concert on his oboe. Margaret?
To be able to live and keep her self-respect. The widow?
Not to be pursued by inquisitive eyes, to be free to live her
own life. As for Martin, he was content to be an unpolished
roadmender, neither more nor less. All these people had already tasted fame, money and power and had decided that
there were other things, perhaps more valuable.

The dead man might as well have gone on living . . .

Frank continued on his way. There was, after all, such a
thing as duty – his own job might be unnecessary and a trifle
absurd, but he had chosen it, and it was good for you to get on
with the job even when your whole being rebelled against it
and everything in and around you kept whispering; Don't go,
you fool!

The queue in front of the building was thinner than yesterday, and not so long. Were they afraid that the reserves
wouldn't last out?

When he got to his post, he was glad after all that he'd come.
What made him glad was that he was able to photograph a certain old lady, dabbing a white handkerchief to her eyes in front
of the catafalque. A tiny, unobtrusive old thing, well over
seventy, who had certainly been noticed by nobody else that
day and looked as if she had slipped through life equally unnoticed, from the cradle to old age. To those who would see
her picture in the newspapers tomorrow, she would be just an
ordinary old woman paying her last respects to the dead. Frank
alone realized who she was and was startled by her presence.
Had anyone told her anything? Had it ever come to her knowledge what alarm she had once caused by scattering a few
cake-crumbs on to the street from her third-floor window?

But who on earth would or could have told her? Above all, who could have told her that the dead man, entirely without her knowledge, had profoundly affected her declining years, had averted a thunderbolt from her defenceless head? No, she must have simply come of her own accord – a statesman had died, the former leader of the nation: it was proper to attend his funeral and pay tribute to his memory. And then the music brought tears to one's eyes, and everything around was so sad and solemn . . .

When Galovitch had become head of the security service he had introduced fresh methods. Greater zeal, ingenuity and persistence were necessary in order to seek out, render harmless and liquidate the class enemy. Galovitch, who kept for himself the political aspects of counter-espionage, had appointed as head of police operations a creature whom he had brought with him from the provinces and in whom he placed implicit trust, a morbidly suspicious individual named Jancuska. This man spent his days and nights in the pursuit of saboteurs, deviationists, spies and enemies of the régime. He pursued them in his office by day and in his dreams by night. He laid down drastic and original regulations for his staff.

'Everyone is an enemy,' he would say, 'everyone is a potential traitor. Human beings are evil and treacherous from birth. Your duty is to catch them in the act. Trust no one – not your friend, your brother or your own wife. Scrutinize your own every thought and deed. In our circumstances, to doubt or to waver is already to commit treason.'

His main directive could be summed up in the word: Exterminate! This was the slogan of his office and the sacred task and duty of those who served in it.

'Today's spies,' he told them, 'work in a different fashion from those of former times – they use scientific principles and the most modern techniques. Moreover, they preserve absolute anonymity: they merge into the throng. We too must go to work scientifically, and our technical means must be superior to theirs. Your task is to notice everything and everyone.

Investigate everyone, but especially those who are hardly noticeable. A blind beggar is unobtrusive, but of course it may be somebody else. Anyone, absolutely anyone you meet may be a deviationist. And your duty is to exterminate them!'

Such was Jancuska's gospel, until one fine day he began to shriek in the middle of a banquet:

'Don't touch the coffee, it's poisoned!'

Everyone present turned pale with horror. The coffee, of course, was instantly analysed, and proved to contain no poison other than caffeine. The banquet broke up in disorder and Jancuska was removed to a psychiatric ward, where they diagnosed an advanced stage of paranoia. Thus it was that Galovitch lost the services of one of his ablest operatives. He did not forget the episode: he never forgot anything. It was one of his duties not to forget . . .

The insignificant old lady tripped quietly out of the hall. She did not and never would suspect how bitterly the dead man had fought Galovitch and Jancuska for her sake.

It was Jancuska who had first brought her under observation. He himself had noticed her by pure chance (though as a Marxist he denied the existence of chance) one day when he was out for a walk, though naturally not off duty. It was also more or less by chance that Frank had heard about the affair. In the course of a train journey he had found himself sharing a compartment with an old acquaintance whom he knew to be an officer in the security police. By cautious degrees, the other had brought the conversation round to the subject of Frank's friend, the statesman.

'What do you want me to tell you? You know him as well as I do.'

'Yes, but you see him, don't you?'

'No, I haven't for a long time.'

'Well, at least you can tell me whether he's the sort of chap one can talk to.'

The officer looked round nervously to see if anyone might be within earshot. Then he burst out:

'The whole thing's a bloody nonsense! We spend our time chasing shadows when the people we ought to be catching are somewhere quite different.'

Frank did not reply. It was risky enough to listen to a single word from anybody in that outfit. True, this one had been a pal of theirs in the old days, but there was no knowing what he was like now. And what did he want of Frank? – for it was clear that he wanted something.

By this time the other had regained his composure. He continued in a low voice:

'Take this case I'm on now. It'd be a joke if it wasn't so cruel and senseless. I've had enough – I simply can't go on with it.'

He obviously couldn't wait a moment longer to get the matter off his chest. Frank felt that he would have done so even to a total stranger.

'You know what my job is, of course. Well, at this moment I'm the head of a special group whose one and only duty is to keep watch on an old, retired schoolteacher. We've been following her movements for the past week. Just now I'm on the way to interrogate a woman who's sent her a postcard – maybe her sister or sister-in-law or something of the kind. You know Jancuska, don't you?'

Frank nodded.

'He's off his head, ripe for the looney-bin. Last week he came into my office like a whirlwind. Hatal, she's called, he said, Veronica Hatal. Nothing on her file, but last evening around dusk she stuck a white cloth out of her window and shook it up and down three times. And I don't need to add that her house faces the frontier...'

'No!' exclaimed Frank involuntarily.

'Yes, I tell you. So he put me at the head of this group to find out who the old girl's in contact with and how. By now we know all about her – we've stuck microphones all over her flat, even one in the lavatory for good measure, and been through the place three times with a tooth-comb.'

'Why didn't you refuse?'

'Refuse?' said his friend incredulously. 'In our job? That'd be the quickest way to get arrested and tried yourself. And what good would it do? Someone else would get the job who wanted to suck up to Jancuska, and where would the old girl be then? As it is, we know every blessed thing she does, what she buys, what her income is, what she has for breakfast, when and where she goes for walks – ten of us, ten well-paid men spying on her every footstep! This postcard is the first mail she's had in all that time. Jancuska reckons that's suspicious in itself – he thinks it's fishy if people get mail and fishy if they don't. He told me to come and see who the sender was covering up for. When I told him she saw nobody but other old widows like herself, he got all the more suspicious. I tell you, it's an out-and-out farce. We've been to the window where she waved her dishcloth and we've photographed the entire view from it with a telescopic lens, we've looked for a secret observation post with special field-glasses, we've rigged up a film camera under the eaves to operate automatically whenever the window opens. I sometimes wonder if every single one of us is nuts.'

'Can't you throw up the job altogether?'

'Don't be ridiculous! That would be desertion, high treason. The only way you can get out of our job is by a heart-attack, or with a bullet in your neck as sometimes happens, or if you get the sack or get put in prison. But I've had just about as much as I can take. Listen, a year ago we arrested a bunch of archaeologists who were digging up there by the old castle. Jancuska got it into his head that they were making an underground passage across the frontier. For Pete's sake tell me, is it any use going to your friend and warning him of the kind of things that are going on in our shop? Has *he* still got any gumption left?'

Frank shrugged his shoulders:

'You can always try. He may not do anything, but you'd have nothing to be afraid of – he wouldn't take it out on you, because he hates Galovitch.'

'It's risky, I know, but I'm going to try it. He can only throw me out, and that's better than ending up in a madhouse.

Listen, why don't you come and have a look at the old girl next Friday? She always meets her friends then for coffee and cakes at the Grand Hotel.'

Frank went to the hotel, and sat down at a table beside his lieutenant friend.

'There she is – the one in the little black hat.'

Frank saw five little old ladies sitting at a round table, no doubt talking over old times and lamenting the degeneracy of modern youth.

Leaving his office a week or two later, Frank found the lieutenant waiting for him outside. He was clearly in good spirits.

'Well, I went. He's a good man all right. It must take some courage to tangle with Galovitch. I wonder what sort of a raspberry Jancuska got. He told us today that our group was dissolved – mission accomplished. But I'm getting out anyway – I'm being moved to the transport section.'

Frank was surprised. He hadn't credited his friend with sufficient courage to do anything in the matter. But one can never quite tell what others are capable of ...

The insignificant old lady had been gone for a long time now. Had she ever noticed, he wondered, that for a time mysterious dark shadows were moving about her, watching her comings and goings? Why should she have? How could she suppose that anyone would take an interest in her?

Clearly, she had come today without any personal motive. An old, retired schoolteacher, trained to respect authority ...

Fifteen

The next person he noticed in the queue was Judith.

Sun-tanned, with prominent cheekbones, her nose a little narrow, herself somewhat thin and with greying hair. She wore a fur coat which had obviously cost a good deal of money. Frank was startled to see her, and watched her closely. Her eyes were expressionless and so was her face, which was angular as though cut from stone.

As he watched, Frank began to feel annoyed with her for coming. She need not and should not have come. The man was dead now, past making amends, atoning or repaying. If she had come to gloat over his death, it was mean and unworthy of her.

Judith remained for a moment in front of the catafalque, motionless, without the flicker of an eyelid. Then, quickly and nervously, she walked past the queue back to the entrance door. Frank stopped her.

'What are you doing here?' he asked reproachfully.

'I just came . . .' she said irresolutely.

A guard motioned them away from the entrance. 'Come and have some coffee,' Frank said. They walked down the stone steps.

'It's been a long time,' she said in a low voice. Frank counted mentally. Yes, it had. Ten years? No, not so much – they had met for the last time on a certain evening . . .

'Why did you come?'

'I don't know why, I just came.'

'Where do you live, Judy?'

'Still in that little country hole of mine.'

Frank looked puzzled.

'In the cottage. They didn't take it away from us, you know – I suppose they must have forgotten.'

'What do you do nowadays? What do you live on? Evidently . . .' He felt her coat appreciatively.

'Oh, yes, I manage quite well. You'll laugh – everyone does when they first hear about it. I breed dogs.'

Frank stopped short. Breed dogs? What the devil did she mean?

'You breed what?'

'Dogs. I run a dog-kennel. Thoroughbreds, you know?'

Frank still did not understand.

'How do you mean, you breed them? Of course I know people breed dogs, cats, canaries and parrots, but surely that's not a livelihood?'

'Indeed it is, and a very good one too. My kennels are right up in the mountains. It's a lovely place.'

'Well, I never heard of such a thing before.'

'Then you have now. Have you any idea how much people will pay for thoroughbred dogs?'

'What kind are they? Wolfhounds?'

'No. I started with those some years ago, when the army and frontier police wanted them, but now they breed their own. I go in for boxers and pinschers. Come up and pay me a visit and you'll see. It's glorious up there in spring, and you can choose a puppy for yourself. You could do an interesting story about it, and the publicity would be good for me. You may not know it, but pinschers are quite fashionable nowadays. The whole thing pays so well that I'm afraid the state will take it over one of these days.'

Frank was still shaking his head in bewilderment.

'Didn't you realize that that sort of thing was possible any more? But it is – there are lots of little private enterprises. Take the places where they breed insects to feed aquarium fishes on – that's even more profitable than dogs. Have you any idea how many private aquariums there are in this country, or what the fish live on? Well, with me it's dogs. For a long time I was officially recognized as an industry of importance to national defence. There isn't a single salary-earner in the country who makes as much as I do out of my kennels. Of course I pay high taxes, but even so I can live on the fat of the land. For every puppy I export, I get part of the price in Tuzex coupons. Dog-lovers and dog-breeders come to see me from all over Europe. And I go abroad to international exhibitions – I've won a gold and two silver medals for my chuvashes ...'

'Oh, for goodness' sake, Judy ...'

'Why? Don't you like the idea? What else was I to do? They took away my licence to practise medicine. They wouldn't even let me work in the local sawmill. Yes, the authorities had it in for me all right, they wouldn't let me get a start anywhere. But I enjoy being among my animal friends. Dogs are as different as people, but at least they don't betray you.'

Frank felt the bitter reproach in her voice. But that could wait, he wanted to hear more about the dogs first. He still wasn't sure that Judith was not making fun of him.

'What made you think of dogs, anyway?'

'It wasn't my own idea. I thought it was absurd too at first. But I was up against it, they wouldn't let me work anywhere. I could have moved to another part of the country, but I thought I'm damned if I will – I'll starve, but I won't give in. Whenever I applied for a job they'd be glad to see me at first and make all kinds of promises, but as soon as they saw my papers they'd shake their heads – very sorry, the job has been filled meanwhile, the establishment has been cut, the wage fund wouldn't cover it. Somebody or other was blocking me at every turn, they wanted to drive me to desperation. Then, quite by chance, I ran into Horvat – you remember, he was with us in the mountains. By this time he'd become an officer in the frontier guards. He was pleased to see me, we went and had some coffee together, and I told him the whole tale. He helped me. He said: "Judy, we need dogs down here, wolfhounds, our kennels aren't big enough. I could get you a thoroughbred bitch and a dog to mate her with." I looked at him in the same way as you looked at me just now. I thought he was laughing at me, but he was serious. "You could run a splendid kennel from that cottage of yours. Don't worry about finding buyers, leave that to me." I began to like the idea, it was crazy but it suited me. Horvat spent a long time talking me into it, he told me all kinds of things about dogs and kennels. He even offered me a loan to get started. You'll see, it's an almost uninhabited valley, filled from morning till evening with the noise of barking dogs. I'm a member of the International Dog-Lovers' Club, I attend congresses and all sorts of people come to me – counts, bankers and their women – they think nothing of chasing off from Paris to a godforsaken Slovak village to get advice or to buy a puppy or to bring a bitch to be mated. Besides, dogs are becoming fashionable in this country too. The ladies of our new society go in for pinschers in a big way.'

'And you mean to say that you declare an income from this and pay taxes? And keep a record of every specimen with details of purchase and sale, receipts and expenditure, numbers of stillborn puppies and all the rest of it?'

'Exactly – in strict accordance with the laws governing private enterprise. But the main point is that I enjoy it. Dogs are splendid creatures. Of course they're as individual as people – they can be moody, jealous, brave or cowardly, some of them are afraid of the dark and others of thunderstorms, some have strong characters and others are slavish. Bringing them up can be a lot of fun – and a lot of worry too. Sometimes, when I have to sell one I'm particularly fond of, I feel like crying. I have two boxers that I won't ever sell. They're lovely creatures with all the right points, I won prizes with them at an international show. People have offered me pots of money for them, more than they're worth even, but I always refuse – I pretend it's because I want them for breeding . . .'

'How is your husband, Judy?'

'I haven't one. They let him out of prison first, and he divorced me while I was still inside. Horvat was a good friend to me then. He gave me help and advice and he didn't drop me, he wasn't one of those who cut me in the street. A good many did, Frank.'

She spoke this time without bitterness, but Frank felt that the 'many' was meant to include himself. He said:

'I only heard about it all much later.'

'It doesn't matter.' She shrugged. 'It's over and done with.'

But it wasn't. Memories of the past are not like flies that you can brush away. The memory of that day, that evening, that night . . .

It was when the great man had been visiting a small town in a remote valley for the purpose of laying the foundation stone of a new factory. It was not long since he had become head of the government, and great things were expected of him. The population had come from miles around to hear him speak. After the ceremony there were open-air festivities which were interrupted by a downpour. The guests of honour made a dash for their limousines. Frank was looking about him for a lift when he heard a voice behind him saying: Come on, get in. He obeyed.

The next part of the function took the form of a banquet in the chief town of the area, in the uncomfortable dining-room of an uncomfortable hotel. The doorman stopped Frank politely, but his friend said: It's all right, this comrade is with me.

As they advanced towards the laden tables, the statesman said:

'Mind, we don't want you photographing this little lot.'

Frank was struck by a difference in his tone. At this time their relations were already a trifle strained and they met only on occasions like the present one. But the statesman's manner today was a new one: patronizing, condescending, even a shade contemptuous. He felt like turning round and walking out.

The feast began with grilled trout. Frank was surprised at this: it was the close season, protected by strict laws. But laws were evidently not binding everywhere and on everybody, least of all on their authors.

Frank sat at the extreme end of the table. He could not stand these official dinners, where you might get trout but you also had to listen to a lot of stupid toasts, where the jollity was forced and your head got heavy from drinking too much wine too quickly, and everyone jostled for a position near the guest of honour so that they might be seen in his company, exchange a few words with him and perhaps seize the opportunity to wangle a building permit. He did not envy his friend these all too frequent occasions when the great man had to listen to a babble of commonplace and feign interest in all, grin and slap people on the back, scatter promises around which he would forget as soon as possible, and generally be bored to death.

Only one thing induced Frank to stay to the end of these junketings. It amused him to watch the boredom of the others, each one talking and none of them listening, all giving themselves airs, bluffing and showing off, and the whole thing trailing off into a round of silly and badly told jokes about people called Moses, Cohen, Isaac and Sarah.

Tonight Frank decided he had had enough. He got up and made for the exit – perhaps he might still catch a train home. Half-way to the door, he was stopped by the great man's voice from the high table:

'Hey, where are you off to?'

Frank shrugged his shoulders.

'Don't be a fool, wait, I'm leaving too in a minute. Sorry, comrades, duty calls.'

Frank waited for him. He would get home quicker by car than by the express, even supposing he hadn't missed it. When they were driving, he could not resist saying:

'It's the closed season for trout, isn't it?'

'Oh, never mind, it was a great day for these people. Bloody good trout, too.'

On the outskirts of the town he made a sign to the chauffeur to turn right at the next crossroads.

'We're going to pay a visit here. You'll get a surprise.'

Frank was not too pleased, but there was nothing for it. They stopped in front of a large villa surrounded by a handsome garden. There was a light burning over the door.

They got out of the car, and the statesman told the driver to come back in two hours. He said nothing to the bodyguard, who knew his duty. They went through the wrought-iron gate and up to the front door. The statesman rang, and Judith appeared.

'Frank! How marvellous to see you,' she exclaimed, and threw her arms about his neck. Her greeting to his friend seemed to Frank a little constrained. But by this time the others had come forward: a white-haired lady, an elderly gentleman with large spectacles, and a youngish man who proved to be Judith's husband. The old couple welcomed Frank's friend like the prodigal son. Judith's mother beamed: 'What an honour! What an honour!' When the old doctor congratulated him on his new position, he replied:

'Oh, forget it. In this house I'm still the same as I always was. You know,' he said, turning to Frank, 'this is the house I used to hide in in the old days. If it hadn't been for Bela here, I wouldn't be alive today.'

Frank had not known this. He knew his friend had hidden in a doctor's house somewhere in the town, but he did not know it was with Judith's parents.

Their hosts led them into a large hall, from which an elegantly carved wooden stairway led up to the first floor. In the middle was a table laden with food – they had evidently been expected.

'We've already had dinner,' the statesman protested.

'Oh, but you mustn't disappoint us,' cried Judith's mother. So they sat and ate, Judith waiting upon them. When they had finished supper she withdrew to a corner. Frank was glad to see her again. They had not met since the war days, and he only knew that she had taken her doctor's degree at Prague. It was a pleasant atmosphere: Frank did not know when he had felt more cheerful, though he was conscious of a slight tension, due perhaps to the silence of Judith's husband, who was also a physician. Old Doctor Polonec was in his element. Eventually he disappeared for a few minutes and returned, humming a song, with an armful of dusty bottles.

'Here,' he said with mock drama, 'is a wine the like of which you will not find in the length and breadth of our country. Do you remember,' he said to the statesman, 'tasting it when it was young? It is now precisely the right age.'

'Have you got much of it?'

'No, not very much, but it's not every day that we have such guests. It's two years since you came to see us.'

The great man certainly felt at home here, perhaps even more than at home. The old doctor was in excellent spirits. It was a pleasure to see the youthful zest with which he opened the bottle, smacked his lips, lifted up his glass to the light, tasted the wine and rolled it on his tongue, made more appreciative noises and pronounced: Well, here goes . . .

'I've got an air-conditioned cellar to keep it at the right temperature.'

They talked for a long while of old times, and the doctor expatiated to his guest on the need for an annex to the local hospital, of which he was the director. Before they knew where they were, he had opened a fourth bottle of the heavy wine. The conversation began to ramble; their speech thickened a little. The statesman had drunk more than the others: he fell into a kind of trance, neither speaking nor listening, aware of nothing around him, his mind far away. His eyes shone strangely, his jaw became rigid. He went on drinking, however – draining glass after glass, partisan style.

Suddenly he got up and, like a sleepwalker, made for the stairs leading to the first floor. The doctor tried to direct him elsewhere, but he obviously did not hear. He reached the landing, opened a door which led off the wooden gallery, and went in.

'That's Judy's bedroom,' called the doctor after him. They looked at one another in astonishment.

'He's had more than is good for him,' Frank said.

Judith rose from her corner and quickly ran upstairs. The doctor said in an undertone:

'It used to be his room . . .'

Suddenly the silence was broken by a cry from Judith. Frank

jumped up, rushed upstairs and threw open the door to her room. On the threshold he stopped, dumbfounded. The statesman was naked and had pinned Judith to the bed, where she was struggling desperately. Her torn dress lay on the floor. Frank leapt across the room, grabbed his friend and pulled him away from the bed, shouting: 'You bloody halfwit, what the hell do you think you're doing?' Judith ran out and the statesman, tearing himself from Frank's grasp, hurtled down the stairs after her, still naked. Judith was screaming. The others looked on aghast at the crazy scene. Judith managed to reach a lavatory, where she locked herself in. Her pursuer battered on the door, attempting to stave it in.

The first to regain his presence of mind was the old doctor. 'Brandy – give him some brandy!'

Somehow they got him to take a huge swig. He coughed violently, and a moment later calmed down and became as meek as a lamb. He let Frank take him back upstairs and did exactly as he was told. Frank had to help him to put his clothes on – he was incapable of doing it by himself.

'It's a trauma,' was the doctor's verdict. 'A fit of exhibitionism. Too much of the heavy wine. It can't be helped – these things happen sometimes.'

Frank led his friend downstairs. Judith, her husband and the old lady had disappeared.

'I'm really very sorry,' said Frank. 'I'd better take him away.'

Suddenly the other began to retch, and vomited on the carpet. Frank and the doctor led him off to the bathroom, washed his face and wiped the mess off his suit and shoes. None of them said a word.

The car was waiting outside. Frank and the bodyguard laid the drink-sodden statesman on the back seat, where he instantly fell asleep. Frank walked back to the front door where the light shone.

'This is a terrible business,' he said to the doctor.

'Yes. It's a trauma. He probably hasn't the slightest idea what happened. He was in a complete state of trance.'

Frank held out his hand to say goodbye.

'You must come again. Come whenever you like.' It didn't sound very sincere, and that was not surprising.

Frank sat down beside his snoring friend and thought over what had happened. No doubt the doctor was right: a traumatic state, a fit of exhibitionism... For two whole months the man had lived without stirring from that room. Judith had brought him food and drink, and one day he had laid her on the bed. She had let him, and he was probably the first man she had given herself to. He was always successful with women, and for her he was a mysterious, romantic hero, a fugitive from the Hlinka guard, the police and the gestapo. Her parents probably knew, and turned a blind eye. Then, years afterwards, when he was three-quarters drunk, the fumes of alcohol had conjured up those scenes in his brain once more. Very likely he hadn't known what he was doing at the time and would never realize it afterwards. Certainly Frank wouldn't tell him, and neither would the others. But it was a stupid, unpleasant, painful business. Of course, he had never known how to hold his liquor. Luckily the old doctor, who had seen a thing or two in his life, had treated it as a bagatelle, the kind of thing that sometimes happened, and not half as bad as many others that he could recall if he chose.

The statesman was still insensible when the chauffeur stopped at Frank's house. The bodyguard came up to him and said:

'What happened at that place?'

'Nothing. He drank too much, that's all.'

Catch me telling you what happened, he thought to himself.

At the next opportunity he looked searchingly at the statesman to see if his face registered any awareness of what had passed. It didn't. Evidently he remembered nothing, or at all events not everything.

Two years later, Frank happened to be passing through the same town. Looking up, he was pleased to see the new hospital annex gleaming on the hill-top. So the statesman had kept his word. Suddenly Frank felt he would like to talk to

Judith. He left the main road and turned right at the cross-roads as they had done that night. The house should be easy enough to find – it was set among tall, leafy trees. He stopped at what appeared to be the place, and got out of the car. Somehow it didn't look quite right. Was it the house or wasn't it?

It wasn't. A group of toddlers came out, led by a kindergarten mistress. Evidently his sense of direction had failed him.

He drove to the end of the street and back again, but could see no other building that reminded him of the villa. Was this the right street at all, or could it be the next one? He stopped at a tobacconist's, bought some cigarettes and asked the old woman where Doctor Polonec lived, but she was apparently deaf and made no reply. Still, how could she sell cigarettes if she was deaf? He repeated his question more loudly.

'I don't know. Leave me alone,' growled the old battleaxe. What was bothering her? Or perhaps she was simply a newcomer to the place.

He went back to the garden where the three-year-olds were playing, stood by the trellis-work fence and addressed the mistress.

'Doctor Polonec? You're a friend of theirs, are you?'

Frank nodded.

'This is the place all right, but they moved two years ago.'

'But that's impossible!'

'I assure you, nowadays anything's possible.'

'But the villa belonged to them.'

'Well, as you can see, it belongs to the state now.'

It began to dawn on Frank that there was something amiss, something he did not want to think about and refused to believe. 'But why? Can you tell me why?'

'I know nothing whatever about it. You'd better ask someone who does.' She turned away.

When, after much beating about the bush, he asked the waiter in the local restaurant if he knew what had become of Doctor Polonec, the man suddenly became very busy. 'He must think I'm a spy,' thought Frank. The whole town seemed to be in a psychopathic condition of fear.

Frank remembered that an old acquaintance of his was practising here as a lawyer. He went to his office.

'What is your interest in the matter?' said the other cautiously.

'Judith, the daughter, was with us in the mountains. I simply can't believe she'd be capable of anything wrong, or her father.'

The lawyer was clearly hesitating whether to speak. Then he burst out:

'It was a damned shame. Everybody around here was angry when they were put in prison. People were fond of Polonec.'

'When was it?'

'I can't remember exactly, but I could find out for you. The lawyer who defended them is a good friend of mine. If you want the details . . .'

'No, not specially. But can you tell me what they were arrested for?'

'Yes – it was some rubbish about conspiring with foreign intelligence agents.'

Frank had suspected as much.

'But surely that was utterly impossible.'

'Of course it was. Foreign intelligence had nothing whatsoever to do with it. To be sure, the old man was imprudent. He used to write letters to a friend who had emigrated to Israel, telling him everything that was going on here. As you knew him, you'll remember that he had a pretty sharp tongue. Also he was simple enough to suppose that the authorities respected the privacy of correspondence. Naturally his letters were intercepted and copied. I imagine it happened with all letters to or from that country. A few sentences out of context made things pretty black for him in court. He couldn't deny that he'd written them, and it was no good explaining that in context they meant something quite different. They simply shouted him down. "Did you write this or didn't you? You confess it? That's enough." '

'All right then, the doctor wrote the letters. But why did

they lock up Judith and her husband as well? They hadn't written anything, and they could have been ignorant of the old man's correspondence.'

'They weren't even put on trial – just kept in custody, pending examination. The young doctor was let out before long, but Judith's still inside. There must have been something more behind it all that we don't know about.'

'And the old lady?'

'She died of a stroke brought on by the shock.'

'But that's ghastly.'

'It is. It was a dirty business.'

'Can you by any chance remember when they were arrested?'

'No, I've forgotten. I know it was around the end of summer.'

'Let me help you. At the end of summer there was a ceremony here, the foundation-stone of a new weaving-mill.'

The lawyer reflected. 'It could be ... Wait a minute ... Yes, I think I remember. The ceremony was on a Sunday, and they were arrested at the end of the same week. What are you driving at? Have you got some specific point in mind?'

'Do you think it would help if someone disclosed the real reason for their being put away?'

'Not much. Come to that, I have my own ideas. But there is one thing I don't understand. They had a highly-placed friend, a powerful man, and what's more he owed his life to them. How he could have left them in the lurch ... But you must know more about that than I do.'

'I suppose there's no chance of the case being reopened?'

'None whatever. He wrote the letters, they proved it and he confessed. Legally, that made him guilty. Whatever you may think about the law, it's there and it's valid and that's all there is to it. The town was up in arms about it, but you know what people are like. Soon afterwards they began to build the new hospital and the villa was turned into a kindergarten. Anyway, we've seen too many injustices nowadays to bother for long about just one more.'

Frank pondered whether to tell the lawyer what he knew.

'Let me put it like this – supposing new facts came to light showing, for instance, that there was a sordid political background to the whole thing. Suppose they were put out of the way because they knew something which might have caused a public scandal and made things very unpleasant for a certain highly-placed personage. If this was proved, could anything be done then?'

The lawyer looked at him sharply:

'Do you know something?'

'Perhaps I do. But you haven't answered my question. Could anything be done?'

'There's no simple answer. You spoke of a highly-placed personage. It would depend a good deal on how his political stock stands at the moment.'

'Haven't you heard anything yourself? Didn't any stories go round the town about things that happened at the villa?'

'I don't know what things you mean. All they said in the town was that Doctor Polonec had plenty of good wine and used to give cheerful parties from time to time.'

Frank made up his mind.

'You're a lawyer. You are bound by obligations of discretion and secrecy in regard to your clients' affairs.'

'I wouldn't put too much trust in that if I were you. Times have changed. Under our present statutes I'm also bound to cooperate in the detection and liquidation of the class enemy.'

Frank found this candour reassuring. He went on:

'I'll risk it. It might be just as well if the story went a bit further anyway.'

So he told the lawyer about the evening at the Polonec villa.

'Yes . . .' sighed the lawyer after a long pause. 'I see how it was. We all knew there must be more in it than met the eye, but we put the opposite interpretation on it. We thought it was all a plot against Polonec's powerful friend. There was a long struggle over the appointment of the director of the new hospital. Polonec had a strong rival, not a doctor. Do I need to tell you his name, or can you guess?'

'You needn't.'

'We all thought it was a question of prestige. Of course what you've just told me explains everything. You say you actually saw the whole thing?'

'I was there. It was I who poured the brandy down his throat to finish him off. What do you think? If the matter was presented properly . . .'

The lawyer shook his head.

'You wouldn't get anywhere. Whom would you tell? The judges? They're scared to death of losing their posts. Galovitch? Of course it would be grist to his mill and you might help to bring about a cabinet change, but it wouldn't help Polonec, not one little bit. In fact, the only result might well be to bring down trouble on your own head. No, the only thing that could help Polonec would be to go for a pardon, amnesty, conditional release. And I doubt if even that's possible. Judith is bound to be let out soon – she wasn't convicted and they can't have anything against her. My advice to you is keep the whole story to yourself. I won't say anything. I'm just a drab old family lawyer, I still have some principles left. But what's one to do nowadays?'

He emphasized his words with a helpless gesture.

'No. The best thing is for you to forget it all. I know my colleagues, not a single one of them would touch it.'

Then he looked at Frank quizzically and added:

'May I speak openly too?'

'Of course.'

'How is it he didn't have you put in prison?'

Frank was taken aback. This had not occurred to him.

'Assuming that what you suspect is true, I can't see him stopping half-way. Can you?'

'Hardly.'

'So mightn't there be some quite different explanation after all? The dates might be a coincidence. Or supposing someone else got wind of the story and wanted to get the details out of Polonec?'

Frank remembered the bodyguard's question on the way

home. What had he been doing all that evening outside the villa? Could he have seen or heard anything?

'I doubt it. If they knew anything at all, they must have known that I was there too, and in that case they wouldn't have let me alone.'

'A puzzling business.'

'Yes. Everything is nowadays.'

So ended Frank's investigation.

'And do you live all alone with these dogs of yours?' he asked Judith when they reached the café.

'Father's in Canada.'

'They gave him a passport, did they?'

'Yes, soon after he was released. They would have given me one too, but I didn't want it. What would I have done in Canada? I already had the dogs by then.'

'What about your husband?'

'Oh, that was only – you know.'

Frank understood.

'Tell me, Judy, why did you disappear so completely after the liberation?'

'I didn't want to be a burden to him. He was married and had a son. In the mountains it was different, but he loved his wife – I knew, you can feel these things.'

'And so now you breed pinschers.'

'You are silly. Why shouldn't I? I've known less innocent hobbies. What's so odd about a person who feels lonely surrounding herself with living, sensitive creatures?'

'Yes, but why did you come today?'

'Why . . . he's dead . . . I wanted to see him once again. You deserted him, all of you, and I feel sorry for him. You say that he changed, but as far as I'm concerned he hasn't, he's still exactly as I knew him, strong and upright. It is a shame about him. He wasn't to blame for everything, and he couldn't have helped us, they'd have used it against him. Father wrote to him from prison, but I suppose he never got the letter. He'd have helped us if he could.'

God in heaven, was she as naïve as all that? Was that her idea of how things had happened?

'Judy, did it never occur to you that there might be a different explanation of it all?'

Obviously it had. She bit her finger nervously: 'I don't know what you mean.'

'Oh, yes, you do.'

'It isn't true,' she said angrily. 'He could never have done a thing like that. How can you, of all people, say that about him?'

She still loved him, she had loved him all along. He had been her first, perhaps her only love, and it was unthinkable that he could have been so base. She had known him as a strong and upright person, and in her mind he had remained so despite all that had happened. But she was wrong. It wasn't other people who had deserted him, it was he who had trampled on everyone who had cared for him, loved or respected him. It was curious how, on this day of his supreme loneliness, almost all those who remembered him kindly were people whom he had injured – Judith, Fonda, Martin, Margaret . . . What about himself, Frank? No, he could not say that the dead man had injured him. He remembered the lawyer's question – why had nothing happened to him over the Polonec affair? Could Judith be right after all? Neither Frank nor anyone else would ever know. Perhaps it had been only a coincidence, perhaps there had been a plot against the great man. He had been on friendly terms with a traitor, had visited his home and drunk himself into insensibility . . .

Frank couldn't tell. It was possible, everything was possible. But even so, it was none the less shameful to desert a friend who had sheltered him and taken such risks for his sake, to abandon the woman who loved him and to whom he had made love in the mountains – to let both these people be ruined and not lift a finger to help them . . . No, Judith could think what she pleased, but even if she was right it did not alter Frank's opinion of the dead man. Kicks had been the reward of everyone who had known him. This above all had been the cause of his downfall, of the inglorious end from which he had been saved only by death.

'Tell me, Judy – do you remember Fero Cigel?'

'The bricklayer? The one we had to carry when he got wounded in the mountains?'

'Yes, that's the one. Do you know what he's doing now?'

'No, what?'

'He's a bricklayer.'

'Well, why shouldn't he be? What made you think of him? He's all right, isn't he?'

'He would be perfectly all right but for one thing. There was a time when he wasn't a bricklayer. Instead, he was the manager of a big hotel in a certain country town.'

'I still don't understand. Several of the men we knew in the mountains became managers. Some of them still are.'

'Well, Fero isn't. And I shouldn't wonder if some of the boys we knew are jeering at him and saying: "He was a fine pal, that great commander of yours, and no mistake. When you were in the cart he didn't lift a finger to help you." And I expect he answers back the same way as you did to me and says: "He couldn't have done a thing, it wasn't possible, he had powerful enemies of his own, they'd have used it against him" . . . I myself once had a stand-up fight with him about it.'

'I still don't understand what this is all about.'

'I'll tell you, Judy. In the place where he ran his hotel there used to be some sort of shindig every month, a conference or a celebration or what have you. And so they kept coming along to him and saying Look here, Fero, we want a dinner for two hundred tonight, or hot food continuously for two days or whatever it was. Fero began to get a bit nervous, I was there once when he asked about it. "It's all very well," he said, "but who's going to pay for it?" You know what our friend told him? "You're a member of the party, aren't you? What have you got to worry about?" All right, Fero was a good communist, he asked no more questions. One fine day, along came the state inspectors. Fero was sitting pretty, or so he thought –

he let them inspect as much as they liked. Well, they went on inspecting until they'd discovered a deficit of a million crowns. A party member, was he? That made it far worse – he had shamefully misappropriated government property and abused the confidence of the state. Seventeen years he got, Judy – seventeen, and he served two thirds of it. And to this day he swears that our friend couldn't have done anything, that they'd have used it against him . . .'

'Well, they would have, wouldn't they? What could he have done?'

'He could have done one thing, Judy – the only right and decent thing. He could have come before the court as a witness. The judges were all at his beck and call anyway. He could have explained how the deficit came about. I'd like to have seen the public prosecutor who would have dared to ask him any embarrassing questions! But did he say anything? Not a word! Of course he could have done something! Why, damn it, he could have resigned when he saw what was going on in the country and where it was all leading to. In any case he could have prevented Fero's trial, and once he had let it happen he could have admitted his own responsibility.'

'What about you? If you knew all about it, why didn't you do something?'

'I wasn't living in that part of the country then, and anyhow I couldn't have helped. Only he could have told where the missing million had gone. I did go to the trial when I heard about it. Fero never got a chance to speak, every time he tried to explain anything the judge shouted him down and said it wasn't relevant. When he threatened to have him removed for contempt of court and to hold the rest of the trial in his absence, I couldn't stand any more and shouted at the top of my voice that it was a bloody outrage. I was thrown out, of course, and there was the devil to pay afterwards. That's the way it was, Judy, all along the line. He never stood up for anyone.'

Frank felt that he had touched her on a raw nerve. She seemed to shrink into herself, struggling desperately with thoughts that she could not throw off, try as she would.

She did not speak again until they rose to leave. Then she said :

'You know, I like being with my dogs. I feel better up there . . .'

Frank promised that he would go up and look at them some day, but he doubted if the idea gave her much pleasure . . . He drove her to the airport, as she had to be back with her dogs as soon as possible. He did not go back to the great hall. What would have been the use?

Sixteen

Frank spent the evening putting some prints through the glazer. Few instruments can be so lethal as a camera in the right hands. He was especially pleased with one picture of Muklik, towering like a giant above the small, insignificant figure in the coffin. Frank knew his camera, and could juggle with perspectives to his heart's content.

As he filed the picture away in his secret collection, he smiled at himself wrily. Why was he doing it? To anyone but himself, the snapshot would have neither point nor value. No one would know who the giant Muklik was, and before long no one would know who the tiny dead man was. But Frank would know who they were and why he had taken the picture, and why it was worth taking.

He took out an album and started leafing through it. His first pictures, showing the dead man in his teens, Margaret and the other companions of those days. Bathing in the mill-stream, picnicking in the mountains. The plays they used to put on once a year, with Frank's friend always in the part of the young lover. Street fights, demonstrations, election meetings. The dead man as a soldier, returning from manoeuvres. The last peace-time meeting, and then the mountains again, with them and their friends as partisans. There were many gaps, of course – things which had survived only in Frank's memory. He took a longer look at some of the pictures, and cast his mind back into the post-war days.

Here was the dead man as Commissar for Reconstruction, standing on the footplate of the first locomotive to be driven through a reopened tunnel. Here again on the first train to cross over a rebuilt bridge. Again, stripped to the waist, welding a pickaxe at the head of a group of roadmenders. A dramatic scene in which he was shown in the act of removing a reactionary politician from his seat of office. A martial scene in which he led the militia, clad in blue overalls with a red band on his sleeve. Then provincial scenes, for instance the one of him thrashing the behind of a village harridan . . .

In those days he was still the right man in the right place. He had not yet dug himself in behind an administrator's desk, and there was practical work in abundance. A hundred problems clamoured for solution: materials weren't coming into the factories, trains were delayed, the farmers held out on deliveries and wouldn't join cooperatives. Endless discussions, lightning trips to crisis areas, urgent decisions, manpower shortages, investment programmes that ran into millions. Then the Catholics got obstreperous, there were village riots, the Pope launched his excommunication and the state in reply demanded declarations of loyalty from the parish priests. Some of them balked: they announced their decisions from the pulpit, there were dramatic scenes of farewell, revolts by whole villages in which the faithful mounted guard over their pastors day and night, armed with hatchets, pickaxes and sometimes even firearms they had kept since the rising.

The great man's area happened to be one of the worst. Reports poured in of attacks on official cars and the beating or even murder of their occupants. It was his job to stop it: this was his own part of the country, it was for him to show if he was capable of restoring order.

One day it was reported that the inhabitants of a certain village had barricaded the main highway. Frank was in his friend's office at the time. The latter's face grew red with fury: he leapt to his feet and summoned the captain of the militia.

'I want a hundred men, this minute.'

Then he took a pistol out of a drawer and said: 'Come on.' They went down into the courtyard, which was already seething with armed men from the factories, his own private reserve. A hundred of them jumped into the waiting lorries and off they went.

The barricade outside the village could be seen from a long way off. Frank took his pictures. An old man with a double-barrelled rifle stood on the improvised rampart and gesticulated furiously at the driver of the first lorry. Behind him, a crowd of women brandished pitchforks and large rocks.

Frank's friend stopped the driver immediately in front of the barricade, which consisted of uprooted paving-stones. He sprang out first, paying no attention to the excited old man, who took aim at him with his gun. The militiamen jumped out and formed up in front of the barricade. Their commander bellowed at the villagers:

'Disperse, all of you! This very minute! And send your menfolk here. This road has got to be fit for use in an hour, or I'll know the reason why!'

The villages stood their ground. One of the women hopped on to the barricade and displayed her naked hindquarters to the militiamen. Another began to scream hysterically: 'Beat us, kill us, shoot, you devils!'

'Yes, you'd like us to shoot, wouldn't you?' growled the commander. Then he ordered tersely:

'The cudgels!'

These had been stacked in the lorries, ready for use. He sprang on to the barricade and wrenched the gun out of the old fellow's hand. Then he shouted:

'Tan their asses for them!'

He himself sought out the woman who had shown her buttocks to the soldiery, whipped her with a hazel switch and sent her scuttling away into the village. The women screamed and scattered in all directions, throwing away their weapons as they went, howling with pain and fear. When the militiamen got to the barricade at the other end of the village, there was not a soul to be seen.

'Now the men. Pull them out of the houses!'

Within half an hour they had collected about a hundred angry, but silent and cowed villagers.

'Get them on to the road. Leave one truckful of men here to keep order. That road's got to be cleared in an hour!'

Then they brought out the priest, who wriggled and made excuses. He had signed the declaration, he said . . .

'You ought to have had more sense than to let this happen. We've got nothing against you, but you're coming off to town with us. No more masses here.'

After that, he called a meeting of the village committee and said to them:

'You're discharged. There'll be new elections, and I'm putting in a commissar meanwhile. The first thing he'll look into is deliveries . . .'

Frank could not help laughing as he remembered the scene. The old virago had tripped over in her flight, the commander had lifted up her skirts and was laying on with the hazel-switch . . .

There was no other way of keeping order in those days. Scars heal, but shed blood is indelible.

No other way . . . He looked at the next picture. It showed a group of embarrassed villagers standing in the great man's office, nervously twisting their hats and sheepskin caps in their hands. He had kept them waiting an hour before he rang for Mrs Hornak and told her to let them in.

'Well, what's the trouble, comrades?' he enquired in an artless, almost tender tone, in which only Frank could detect a note of malicious glee. 'If you've come to ask me to let your parish priest off, you're wasting time.' He knew quite well that they had not, and he knew why they had come.

One of them plucked up courage to speak. No, it wasn't about the priest. They knew now that he had been an evil counsellor to them. The villages round about had priests too, but nothing had happened to them. It was theirs who had put them up to the whole business. But what they had come about now was – well, you might say it was about the electricity.

He looked puzzled. What about the electricity? They had it in their village, didn't they? He seemed to remember it being installed years ago.

The men coughed and shuffled, groping for words. Yes, they

had it, indeed they did, but it was that silly great oaf – if he wasn't in hospital now, by golly they'd ...

The commander still pretended not to know what it was all about. Let them stew in their own juice a bit.

'I still don't see what the trouble is. Can't one of you explain? What great oaf, and what has he got to do with the electricity?'

Well, it was all the priest's fault really – the priest and the sexton. The sexton had egged them on. The women, silly creatures, had been keeping watch at the priest's house, and one evening a lot of cars came that way, so the sexton climbed up into the tower and started ringing the alarm bell. And then that silly thirteen-year-old lad – what can you expect at that age? – had shinned up the telegraph pole and cut the wire leading into the village with a pair of shears. Nearly did himself in, too, because he trod on the broken wire as it lay on the ground. And it turned out the people in the cars were foresters, not militiamen at all ...

Frank noticed his friend's mouth twitching at the corners. It was all the latter could do not to burst out laughing, but he put on a severe look.

'This is a serious matter, comrades. More serious than you may realize. Those wires are made of copper.'

Yes, they mumbled, they knew the wires were made of copper. But couldn't they sort of – you see, it was dark in the village, and lots of them had electric motors, and now they'd have to cut the chaff by hand ...

'But don't you also know there's a five-year plan?'

Of course they did, everybody knew that.

'Well then, that means, comrades, that copper is more precious than gold. We pay hard-earned foreign currency for it to the capitalist countries, and even then they won't sell us all we want. So we have to save every little bit we can lay our hands on. Where do you think we can get any copper that hasn't been budgeted for?'

'But it's only a tiny piece ...'

'That's what you think – only a tiny piece. That piece might be needed to bring electricity to a village that hasn't got it yet. And what about electricians? They're all urgently wanted in important sectors of the economy. No, comrades, I can't help you, I really can't. Your village isn't covered by the plan. I'm sorry. You must just make do as best you can. Maybe you've got a few oil lamps left somewhere . . .'

One of the men spoke again. They were a peaceful, law-abiding village, he said. It was the women who'd got these silly notions into their heads. And as they weren't trying to get anything for nothing. Surely a little bit of wire like that could be raised from somewhere. And they'd pay the workmen what was proper, they weren't skinflints . . .

'What?' thundered the chief. 'So you're trying to bribe me, are you? That was the way things went on in the old days, but it won't work with me. And now I've got an important meet-comrades. I'm sorry, I can do nothing for you.'

The men moved towards the door, disconsolate. When they had reached the outer office he followed them.

'You said something about the chaff, comrades. Having to cut it by hand.'

They stopped. Could there be a glimmer of hope after all?

'Cutting chaff by hand is inefficient, certainly. That's why the state provides current for machines. And what do you do on your side? How about meat and milk? Chaff is milk and meat. Have you fulfilled your quotas?'

Oh dear, so that was it. Those wretched deliveries, no, they hadn't completed them. But it wasn't their fault, it had been a bad year.

'Oh, a bad year, was it? Well, in the next village to yours, two miles away as the crow flies, they didn't have a bad year, they've punctually fulfilled their contract with the state. And, let me tell you, they don't go damaging public property either, they don't have a pack of women who get silly notions into their heads. And now you people come along to me and talk about a little piece of copper. Sure, a little piece, but even that little piece has got to be made in a factory, by workers, and the workers want to eat. And what are they going to eat if every village defaults on its deliveries like yours? You can't eat ration cards if there's no food to honour them with. So now, comrades, let's see you bringing along a certificate that you've completed your meat and milk deliveries, and we'll see what we can do. Perhaps in that case we might manage to lay our hands on a little bit of copper, and perhaps a workman as well.'

With which, he let them go. Frank said to him, half in jest: 'You shouldn't have been so cruel.' He replied:

'Don't worry, they'll come back all right. The state they're in now, they'd sign a pact with the devil! As it is, all they'll have to do is to sign a special agreement with me. If they fulfil the plan they'll get their electricity, if not they'll be cut off. Once people have had electric light they don't want to sit around with oil lamps, especially when there's no oil for them. So they'll have a nice little five-year plan all for themselves . . .

That was the way he used to run things, and in those days it was the only way . . . Another time, he got a letter from a mountain village which had long been known for its recalcitrance – an abusive letter, signed by all the inhabitants including the village committee. The gist was that they needed nothing and nobody up there, the state could go and bugger itself, they weren't afraid of the gendarmes, they had their own machine-guns, thank you, and they hadn't the slightest intention of fulfilling any cockeyed plan . . .

Frank came upon his friend, holding this missive and shaking with laughter. 'What d'you think of this one?' he gurgled. 'It's like the history books – the Zaporog Cossacks hurling defiance to the Sultan!'

The letter didn't seem to Frank so funny as all that. It was a challenge all right, and if the village wasn't brought to book it would mean an end to all government authority throughout the area.

The great man was still laughing heartily when he took up the receiver and asked for the local director of communications.

'Listen, comrade, this place Pohora, it's got a post office, hasn't it? And the telephone? When was it put in? Six months ago? Right. It's to be disconnected until further notice. No mail's to be collected or delivered either. The postal official there is to go on unpaid leave for an indefinite period. Send him a letter saying so. What? On whose responsibility? Mine, of course. Yes, sure, you can have it in writing, with the greatest pleasure. Never you mind, it's my affair, I haven't gone mad, I know what I'm doing.'

He pressed a button on his desk.

'Get me the bus controller.' They put him through. 'How often do buses go to Pohora? Twice a day? Then cancel the service till further notice. On my responsibility, mine and no one else's. Yes, I know the place'll be cut off, that's just the idea. Don't worry, I've got my reasons.'

He pressed the button again.

'Get me Comrade Hric at the power station . . . Look here, Hric, I want you to cut off the supply of power to the village of Pohora. Immediately and until further notice. Hell's bells, what's the matter with you all, of course I'll take responsibility. Yes, I'll give it to you in writing. When? At once, today, in an hour if possible.'

He buzzed again. The captain of the militia.

'I want a hundred of your best men. You come along too. Be ready to start in half an hour. I'll explain on the way. Yes, armed, of course. And bring a couple of axes.' He put down the receiver and murmured, wiping his eyes, 'Oh, you bloody Zaporogs! . . .'

They stopped the trucks at the village hall and got out. The place appeared deserted, but Frank could see sharp eyes at every window, watching to see what would happen. Actually nothing happened at all. Frank's photograph showed the commander chopping down the wooden post which marked the bus-stop. When they had tossed it into the truck he said:

'Right. Get on board again. We're driving back.'

'Is that all?' said the astonished captain.

'That's all.'

When they got back to town, they stopped at the bus station. He and Frank got out and went to the office.

'When does the bus leave for Pohora?' enquired the chief. The official, who did not know him by sight, answered:

'It doesn't. The service to Pohora's stopped as of today.'

'What for?'

'They've all gone crazy up at the town hall, that's what for. We've just had an order . . .'

The chief made no reply. They went out and looked at the timetable. Meanwhile the loudspeaker was screeching that the Pohora bus was cancelled, no service would run until further notice.

A small crowd of people were waiting at the station. Several of them looked startled at the news, and two men went inside to make sure they had heard correctly. When it was clear that they had, the crowd dispersed, grumbling loudly, and set out on foot.

'You'll see, they'll be on their knees to me in a week.'

The crestfallen villagers turned up in three days. He kept them waiting in the corridor for three hours, then let them in but did not offer them chairs. The letter was lying on the desk in front of him. He picked it up and waved it at them.

'Which of you signed this?'

None of them replied. Evidently they had all signed it.

'Is there anyone in your village who didn't sign it?'

They looked at one another, perplexed. Was there? They couldn't remember.

'You don't know, eh? Well, if there's anyone who didn't sign, let him come here a week from now – no sooner. One week! And now get out – I've nothing more to say to you.'

A week later, a group arrived consisting of the parish priest, the schoolmaster, the chairman of the village committee and four farmers. He received them at once and addressed the chairman.

Did you sign?'

The man hesitated.

'Out you go! I'm not talking to you! Your Reverence, have you read the letter?'

The old priest assented. Yes, he had read the letter, and he and the schoolmaster had tried to persuade them not to send it. They had pointed out that it was rebellion, mutiny and that no good could possibly come of it. And now it was clear that they were right.

'It would have served you right, comrades, if we had sent this letter to the security police. Every single person who signed it has broken the law! Now listen to me. Tomorrow, you're to call a meeting of every man, woman and child in the village, and you're to make a neat pile of all the arms you've got hidden there. We'll search your houses, and if we find so much as a single rifle, God help you! Then we'll see how well you can manage without the state!'

Next day the village inn, in which the meeting was held, looked like a small arsenal. The militiamen carried the weapons out and piled them on to trucks. The meeting had been a short one. The commander was the only speaker. He fished out the letter, read it through, and then roared at them:

'If you people want to have leaders like this it's entirely your own affair. We couldn't care less! You've made your bed and you can lie on it. We won't ask you for anything. You needn't deliver anything if you don't want to. You can live without the state. But remember this: the buses and telephones belong to the state, and it's the state that provides you with electricity. So you can take your choice. Try, if you like, and see how well you can get on without the state. The state can manage without you, you can be sure of that. I might have had the whole lot of you tried and sentenced, but what would be the point? So just you try and sort out among yourselves what bright spark it was that gave you this advice – it's of more concern to you than it is to me. I'm giving you a week to think it over. In a week's time you can send your spokesmen to me, but I warn you that I won't discuss anything with anyone who signed that letter. Maybe then I'll sign a private agreement with you, a sort of little footnote to the five-year plan. That's all!'

He marched out, brushing aside the schoolmaster who tried

to stop him. He and Frank jumped in the car and off they went.

When the villagers next came, he was most cordial. He offered them plum-brandy and did not say a word about what happened. He nodded approvingly when they said they wanted fresh elections. He smiled when they showed him a certificate of completed deliveries.

He pressed the buzzer on his desk. The power station. 'Comrade Hric: the supply of power to Pohora is to be resumed immediately.'

He pressed it again. The telephone lines to be reconnected. A third time. The bus station. 'Resume service to Pohora this evening. And you can sack the controller for telling people that we'd gone crazy up at the town hall.'

Episodes like these made him respected in the villages and popular in the factories. Naturally they were told all over the countryside. Only Galovitch was not amused. Why all the showing off? he growled. But it was the only way of doing things . . .

Frank came to a photograph which showed seventeen cows tethered to a fence outside the local district court. They belonged to a village called Hanovce.

'Come on,' the chief had cried to Frank, 'we're going to the Hanovce village meeting.'

The villagers, assembled at the inn, appeared taken aback by the unexpected visit. The notables welcomed their guests, stood in a huddle behind the table on the dais, and were silent.

'Carry on, comrades, don't mind me – go right ahead as though I wasn't here,' said the chief. No response.

'All right, then, I'll say what I've come about. As we all know your deliveries are pretty good, especially of meat – in fact, you exceed your meat quota and the newspapers keep praising you for it. Milk, eggs and grain, not quite so good – one might almost think your cows don't give any milk. That's what I came to talk about. I find it hard to understand. I wonder if you can help me . . .'

The chairman of the committee set out to explain. The burden of his somewhat nervous statement was that it was a sort of custom, not a law of course but it was often done, that you could, for instance replace meat with eggs or eggs with meat, or milk . . . they had fulfilled their meat quota by three hundred and sixty per cent since the beginning of the year, and if you converted that into other products it still came out that they had more than fulfilled their quotas, overall – and meat was the most important thing, as the newspapers were always saying . . .

'Three hundred and sixty per cent, eh? How much of that was in heifers, comrades?'

The chairman began to explain at length that it was all a question of weight . . . the fulfilment of quotas was measured by weight. How many heifers? Since the beginning of the year, he thought there had been seventeen . . .

'Seventeen. And all of them called Malina, isn't that right, comrades?'

Frank saw consternation on every face. The cat was out of the bag with a vengeance!

'And now, comrades, I'd like you to explain to me how it's possible to fulfil your norm by three hundred and sixty per cent and be praised by gullible editors for doing so, and still not deliver a single kilo of meat. You don't want to tell me, comrades? Lost your tongues? Then I'll have to explain it to you myself. There happens to be a law – a good law, passed in the peasants' own interest – that the sale of a cow is equivalent to the fulfilment of one's meat quota. If a man sells a cow, he has no surplus and can't afford to deliver meat. But laws, and this law in particular, are not passed to make things easier for speculators. What applies to the individual cannot apply to a whole village. Our contract is with the village, not with this or that farmer. And you, comrades, have fulfilled it in percentages but not in meat! What you've done is, you've sold and resold to one another a single heifer, Malina by name, seventeen times, so that each farmer has sold a heifer and is exempt from delivery! Isn't that right, comrades?'

He stood up.

'You people owe me seventeen cows! The village of Hanovce owes the country seventeen cows! I expect to see them in front of my office tomorrow. That's all, comrades. You can go on with your meeting, you don't need me any more.'

They went out.

'Do you think they'll bring them?' asked Frank on the way home.

'Of course they will. They know what happened at Pohora.'

On the following afternoon Frank was able to photograph the seventeen cows – fine, glossy, well-fed beasts.

Frank remembered other incidents of that time. Once, in a frontier village, they had come across a gang of smugglers, sixty strong, making their way with heavy sacks towards the frontier in the immediate vicinity of a customs post. An hour later the chief had personally arrested the commander of the post and dismissed all his men. On another occasion they blew up an illicit distillery, cunningly hidden in the countryside, and punished the village concerned by cutting off its power supply for a month. It is easier, and surely better, to govern a country by cutting off electricity than by means of bayonets . . .

And all this time he was holding meetings, conferences and assemblies, writing reports and records, travelling day and night, going without sleep. Everywhere there was something amiss, something which called for intervention, for a helping hand or a sensible decision.

In those days he was truly a great man – capable of anything, equal to the demands of the time. It was a period when you had to act, to take decisions and risks, to master situations at a glance and above all not be afraid. All this he did, and reaped a reward of popularity and affection. He became a legendary figure throughout the region . . .

When and how was it, then, that the flaw in his character had developed? Had it come about suddenly, sharply, or gradually and imperceptibility? To Margaret this was a simple question:

it was the blonde woman who had led him to his doom. Frank had sometimes thought the same – it was the first thing that had come into his head when he made her acquaintance in the chief's office. But was not the truth really quite different? Was she not an effect rather than a cause? Had the chief not been surrounded by too many flatterers who daily sang his praises and his unparalleled qualities and persuaded him that his life, his time, his person were unique and irreplaceable – that this entitled him to demand more, to demand everything – that an exceptional being has the right to live in an exceptional manner?

Frank remembered a certain member of the government whom he had met shortly after his elevation to that position. When Frank offered congratulations he had replied: 'They shouldn't have done it to me. I'm not fit for the job, I'll make a mess of it, I'll be thrown out...' As time went on, Frank had watched with amazement the change which had taken place in this individual. After a few months in the ministerial chair he became a pasha, manipulating millions by the stroke of a pen and looking distrustfully at his colleagues and associates as if to say: How is it that I was discovered so late? That my talent was not recognized? Which of you was it that held up my advance to this post, when I had such a clear claim to it? Of course he did not make the grade, and of course he was thrown out. Nowadays he went about with an injured and embittered air, explaining to anyone who would listen that his fall was due to a conspiracy against him, to dark doings that he could unfold if he chose...

The next photograph was taken in their home town. The chief was addressing a large crowd on the very square where he had once delivered inflammatory speeches. The audience had changed – it now consisted mostly of the sort of people he used to denounce. Frank turned back a few pages. The old fellowship, the old companions. They had remained at his side, they had followed him wherever he went. At all times he was their respected and acknowledged leader. No one had ever challenged the position he occupied among them – it had evolved naturally, of its own accord.

This afternoon, Frank recalled, a delegation of some fifty people had come from their home town to take leave of the great man as he lay in state. Frank had looked in vain for the face of any member of their former group. Not one of them had come.

Nor had they come, on that earlier occasion, to listen to his great speech in the main square. Frank examined the picture he had taken of the official stand. Anything up to two hundred people, and not a single old, well-loved face among them. He looked at the audience : there were none there either. They had not come – the brave boys, the veterans of desperate fights into which he had led them. And yet they were expecting him – he must, he would come to see them. Frank knew where they would be waiting – in the tavern where they had all met together in former times. Sure enough, he found them there, all those who had survived. As he entered, the whole place fell still. They had been expecting to see their former chief – Frank too of course, but him especially. When they saw Frank, they knew that their expectation was in vain.

An old comrade shouted to Frank from a corner of the room :
'You're a crow with gilded claws too!' The whole place burst out laughing. Frank turned round without a word and went out into the cold air. Tears of anger and humiliation stung his eyes. 'A crow with gilded claws' – he knew what they were talking about. Once, when they were boys, they had caught a crow. A local tramp, who was supposed to raid crows' nests and eat crow-soup, met them as they were walking proudly along the river-bank with their prize. He had said :
'Is it alive?'
They showed it to him. It was.
'Then paint its legs and tail with bronze paint and let it loose among the other crows. Only you must make it drunk first.'
So they made it drunk and painted its legs and tail with the paint they used for nuts at Christmas-time – the legs gold and the tail silver. Then, with a great hullabaloo, they took it back

to the river where the crows nested. They frightened a great crowd of the black creatures into the air and set the painted one free among them. The others pecked it to death. Frank had long since forgotten about the painted crow – it was an unpleasant memory, and such memories are forgotten soonest. But some of the others had not forgotten . . .

His friends ran after him. Don't be a fool, they said, we didn't mean you, it was just a silly joke – but Frank had not returned with them to the tavern. He could not, because he knew that they were right. He was no longer one of them. They had come home from the battlefield and gone off to relight the factory fires. They had followed with pride the rise of a member of their group, the best of them. He's our man, he won't forget us or betray us, he'll use his brains to go on fighting with us and for us. We trust him and we'll stand by him . . . Later on, they had been puzzled by certain things – what's he trying to do, what kind of a set-up is it? They had been waiting for him to come today so that they could tell him what was on their minds. But he had not joined them, because there was a big dinner at the hotel and his presence was required at the head of the table. His neighbours to right and left held him fast, they drank him under the table, they gilded his legs and silvered his tail. He did not show up in the tavern, and he had better beware of doing so in future. If he did, he would be pecked to death . . .

Well, this was understandable, but why should Frank himself be cast out in the same manner? And yet after all it was fair enough – he had moved too long amongst the gilded tribe, and even though he had always sat at the bottom of the table, some of the gilding was bound to stick. His condemnation was cruel but just. They had disowned not only their one-time commander, but himself as well.

'He's done for,' thought Frank. 'It's only a question of time. He's betrayed his own people, and they have rejected him.'

Frank was wholly immersed in this strange biography, whose chapters he had painstakingly assembled over the years, page by page and scene by scene. He paused over a snapshot which he had once taken in a spirit of open mockery. It showed the statesman in the company of two foreigners, a man and a woman, and a uniformed gamekeeper with a massive red beard who had stepped straight out of the picture-books. The foreigners had come on an important political visit and the great man was looking after them. A full programme had been planned. He had given a big reception, accompanied them to the opera and to a model cooperative, shown them the sights of the town and taken them on a whirlwind tour of the country-side, pointing out mountains, dams and other features as they swept past. They made a two-hour stop at a newly-built factory, where they addressed the assembled workers about friendship and the need for peace, and assured one another how gratified and honoured they were by this meeting and how they should strive to come together oftener, to develop mutual understanding and to remove the differences that still remained.

But what about the Saturday? This, as they knew, was not a working day in their guests' country. So the organizer of the visit (Muklik, none other) had hit on the happy idea of a trout-fishing expedition.

'Do you like fishing?' enquired the host over supper in their private room at the hotel. The eyes of the guest of honour lit up. Was fishing in the programme too?

It was soon arranged. The guests were delighted, and the host was as proud as a peacock. What a programme! They wouldn't forget us in a hurry, and they would carry home the best possible memories.

Early next morning, the party left town in six stately black limousines. After twenty miles or so they turned off towards the nearby mountains. Frank was there of course: you could not have a diplomatic fishing-party without a photographer. The Swedish guests were in high fettle. Trout was a noble fish, almost as good sport as their own salmon. What a charming little country this was, to be sure!

No doubt they had their own mental picture of what trout

fishing was like. A wild, thundering mountain stream, the scent
of burdock – a fleeting shadow in the clear water, imperceptible but for the fiery spots on its back – an unsuccessful jump,
another jump, and the splendid creature has surmounted one
more obstacle on its tireless journey upstream ... They must
indeed have been impressed. Really an admirable country!
Only a few miles from the capital, and trout-fishing!

The six cars came to a halt beside a meadow surrounded by
a fence. The iron gates were open, and there stood the majestic
gamekeeper with his bushy, fiery beard. After welcoming the
guests he led them to a part of the meadow where there were
three small lakes – his work and his pride. The chauffeurs got
ready the fishing-rods. An angler's paradise indeed! The
lakes were swarming with trout – now and then a fine specimen would leap high out of its rather slimy pool. The great
man and his entourage, fired with enthusiasm, scarcely noticed
their foreign guests. The gamekeeper surveyed his domain
with pardonable pride. They're hungry, these fellows, I took
care not to feed them so that they'd bite properly. They'd go
for an unbaited hook if you let them!

The Swedish guests were standing to one side. They seemed
embarrassed and a little awkward. Perhaps they were not such
keen fishermen as they had made out the night before.

'They're rainbow trout, aren't they?' said the Swedish
woman with pretended naïveté. The gamekeeper launched
into a long account of his charges. Yes, *bitte schön*, rainbow
trout, they breed well here, they come all the way from Canada
but the climate here suits them to a T, they grow faster than
our river trout, *bitte schön*, and they spawn better too ...

The slim, elegant Swedish visitor listened to his explana-
tions with a curious smile. When he had finished, she asked
the interpreter whether 'bitchen' was the native word for
trout. Her husband made no attempt to feign even polite interest. He stood aloof with a disgusted look on his face, and
watched with unconcealed contempt the enthusiasts who had
got tired of waiting and were already hauling fish out of the
muddy water – a trout at each cast.

The host began to grasp that something was wrong. Could anyone have offended the guests? He beckoned to the interpreter.

'What's the trouble?' he asked in bewilderment. The interpreter shrugged helplessly.

The guest of honour could bear it no longer. He walked rapidly across and said in an angry tone:

'Will you please tell our host that I'm a sportsman and not a murderer!'

The statesman was nonplussed, but he looked daggers. Who had had the impudence? Had anyone made a blunder of some kind? Surely they couldn't have called his guests murderers?

The tall Swedish woman tried to save the situation. She said:

'My husband doesn't feel well. If you don't mind, we'd rather go back to town.'

Without waiting to see whether they minded or not, she walked off briskly to where the cars were waiting. It was still a little while before the host understood what everyone else had grasped by now. Frank saw his face suddenly go crimson with anger.

'The bastards!' he fumed as they drove homewards. 'Bloody high-and-mighty bourgeois swine! Everybody knows where their famous standard of living comes from. Millions of men killed on the battlefields, and they were selling steel and iron ore to Hitler!'

Next day Frank went to the airport. The honoured guests were seen off by the Chief of Protocol – and of course Muklik.

Holding the picture in his hand, Frank caught himself murmuring: A crow with gilded claws ... he can't go back to his own people, but to the peacocks he's still a crow ...

With a sigh he closed the album and put it back in its place. A life-story, soon to be completed – the life itself extinguished already. Tomorrow he would insert the final picture. Something would then be at an end – something concluded ...

Seventeen

That night Frank could not get to sleep, which was unusual for him. His wife lay beside him, breathing deeply and regularly. Frank lay on his back, gazing into the darkness. Or perhaps not into the darkness, but into a long-distant past. He told himself in vain that the dead man was a cypher unworthy of attention, that he had long ago seen through him and found him wanting, that he had no feeling whatsoever for him, that the other had met the end which he deserved. In his mind he knew this to be true, but man is not a creature of mind alone: he belongs, among other things, to his own past, and for Frank the past was unimaginable without the dead man – they had been through too much together. A man may repress such things for a long time, but a moment will come sooner or later when they crowd in upon him and he is forced, willy-nilly, to come to terms with them. Old loves and sufferings, old, forgotten events and sensations revive with unexpected poignancy; shameful acts that we have no wish to remember come back to mind when they are least welcome; we may deceive the world but never ourselves. Each of us experiences in his life at least one such hour of trial: and the fewer they are, the more painful – those hours of unvarnished, importunate truth, when we have to recognize ourselves as we are, stripped of disguise.

I wonder if you too had to face yourself, Frank addressed the dead man. What did it feel like? Where did it come upon you? When did you realize that you had betrayed yourself? Were you able to admit the truth at all – you who were once an upright man? Do you realize how much people loved you, and what a precious boon that is? How did you respond to it? How did you treat those few people who, tonight, are still thinking about you – how did you repay their devotion and their love? By taking, always taking. All your life, from childhood onwards, you did nothing but seize and grab. Instead of requiting their love you fobbed them off with patronage, you allowed them to catch a few rays of the sunshine that fell on you. In return for affection you tolerated them – it was more flattering to you that way . . .

There was always someone to envy you and dance attendance on you: always – from your schooldays onwards. I myself was your shadow and satellite for many years, I stood by you and sought you out and watched over you and you were glad of it, because after all I was not a nobody, I had my own value and strength and pride, but I succumbed to your charm and your authority: we began as equals but you became first in everything, it was a matter of course. A born leader – there are such people. You were a leader, beyond dispute, everyone respected you, your enemies were afraid of you – they soon realized what a danger you were to them and they tried to destroy you. They did not succeed, but you did. A leader who can no longer govern himself has lost the right to rule others . . .

When did you surrender to the delusion that you were more than human, that you were everything and that everything was permitted to you? We used to bathe naked together in the days when Margaret was my girl, although she was my girl – that was the kind of confidence there was between us, silly and romantic perhaps, but it was there. And yet, when you talked Margaret into loving you it wasn't down there by the river in the evening, it must have been somewhere else behind my back, so that I wouldn't suspect anything, and it must have been deliberate on your side at least – Margaret was far too young and pure and straightforward to have led you on. All right, so you took her away from me, and it was with her consent. I expect she loved you more than me, you must have impressed her more. And I had it out with you in my own way, the way men ought to settle these things.

But what did you do with Fonda when he tried to take her

from you, when she had already become your property for all time? Why didn't you follow him at night to some lonely street and push him up against the wall and say: Fonda, you get out of my way or I'll make mincemeat of you? That's how you and I settled things when we first shook hands after that fight of ours. But you – you pursued Fonda for years afterwards, you hated and persecuted him, and in the end you ruined him for having dared to cast an eye on Margaret – the action that you had regarded as your own manifest right. What's more, you continued to hound him down long after you'd cast off the woman who'd been the cause of it. You cast her off because she'd become a burden to you – all those years of life together, and then you suddenly found her standing in your way, you were ashamed of her. She was a back number, wasn't she? She couldn't or wouldn't fit into the new conditions which were appropriate for you. Neither her appearance nor her manners were ornamental enough. She was a simple girl, and simple she's remained up to this day. And you took her son away from her. You had no right to him, not even a legal right, but you took him because you wanted to own him as you always wanted to own everything and everybody. Of course he was your son, your offspring, your own flesh and blood, the heir to your undying name. You wanted to do all you could to make sure he grew up worthy of the honour. And what did you do with him in the end? If he wasn't really and truly your son, he could hardly have survived the way you treated him. You kicked him out at the time he needed you most. And it was just as well you did, or there'd be one less honest, rough-mannered roadmender in the world.

Do you remember the time when you were on the run, with a price on your head, and some decent people had the courage to hide you although they knew what it might mean for them? How did you treat them afterwards? What did you do to Judith, Doctor Polonec and his whole family? And what about that blonde wife of yours, who once loved you with an ardent, eternal love and who greeted your death as a deliverance?

But above all what did you do to yourself, you black, fearless eagle? What dragged you down from your serene heights to our drab, petty world, the dust and the twittering sparrows? Was it giddiness that seized you? Did you get bored with the heights and want to see them from Below? Did you want to eavesdrop on the jealous babbling of those who could not fly as high as you? Or was it some curious derangement of the brain which made you seem to rise when you fell and fall when you were rising?

Or perhaps you were afraid? Of what? Of that black raven Galovitch? Couldn't you see that in order to stand up to Galovitch it is necessary not to be afraid of him, to prove that you are not afraid of him? That it is the law of nature that once somebody is not afraid of Galovitch, Galovitch is afraid of him?

Yes, you were afraid. More and more afraid. First of Galovitch, and then of everything. Were you most afraid of shadows – the memory of the people you had hounded down, kicked out and ruined? Were you already afraid when you said to me that there was no such thing as friendship in politics? Of whom were you thinking then? Of those who stood in the way of your career, or already of yourself? Or were you thinking that one day you too would stand alone, glancing fearfully to right and left to see where the axe would fall? Did you say to yourself: the more power, the greater security? Was that why you kept concentrating more and more power in your own hands, why you kept buttressing the positions you had gained, and not always honestly?

In the old days you were strong, healthy, resilient – and happy. Did power increase that happiness? Or did it give you something else, something more intense? If so, what? Happiness in love? Did you love and did women love you? Did you love the blonde, for instance? Probably – certainly. But how long did it last? By the end, she was making you drunk to get rid of you, and locking her bedroom door. She despised you and laughed at you. Or were you happy with the floozies that came your way by permission of the security guards, when you couldn't tell who or what they were protecting, or against what, or even why?

Or was it work that made you happy – the consciousness of something achieved, of work well done? That exists all right, it suffices for many people, it is indeed a great deal. But what is your achievement, my noble friend? You ran this country at a time when it took a great step forward in its development. Nobody denies that – it's visible, tangible, indisputable. But how much of that progress is yours? A braver and wiser man than you could have achieved more, given the tremendous effort the people were ready to make. You were afraid to take decisions, you were afraid to lead. You were always worrying about your position – what if you took a false step which might be used against you? So you lapsed into doing nothing and making empty phrases which no one took seriously, least of all the yes-men around you. You were afraid to take risks – but without risks no one ever got anywhere. And you got nowhere in spite of all your honours and position, in spite of those three rows of medals on your chest.

What other happiness? That of an exhibitionist, who cannot resist performing? The pleasure, or at any rate the intoxication, of applause? But didn't it sometimes occur to you that they clapped for your predecessor just as loudly and will do the same for your successor? An actor or a pop singer at least knows what he's being applauded for. Did you ever know? And what did you do between one round of applause and the next? What were your feelings then?

Very well then, it wasn't love, and it wasn't achievement.

There might be another kind of happiness though – singular enough, but it's possible: the happiness of power. To demonstrate to all eyes that one is greater, that one can make sovereign and unquestionable decisions affecting the destiny of others. Perhaps there is happiness to be found in raising a man up in order to strike him down, or vice versa, or in raising up some and striking down others. Is that pleasant? Does it satisfy a man's desires and his passions, to avenge himself on others for his own shortcomings, to take out his frustrations on those who dare to smile when he frowns or frown when he smiles?

No, that cannot be happiness either. How about fame?

That, now, is a powerful intoxicant. Rulers have led whole nations to victory or destruction for it. Today people would still do anything for fame, popularity or publicity. Fame is a pledge of immortality, a notion that haunts anyone who considers himself exceptional. But what does your fame amount to, my friend? If you had walked about the streets these last few days, I should not need to tell you. And your immortality? Buried deep in my secret archives! In ten years, or eleven at most, the historical almanacs will cease to mention you. Was it worth enslaving, destroying, betraying yourself for this? Once upon a time men followed you into the cannon's mouth, and two days ago there was no one to close your eyes.

Power, my friend, is neither good nor bad in itself – it depends on the man and how he uses it. Was power in your hands a good or a bad thing, or was it a mere end in itself, a hobby-horse, a toy? If it had been good, many people today would be hymning your praises and lamenting your death; if evil, they would be cursing you and rejoicing at your inglorious end. But no one is mourning you, except perhaps one or two who knew you best, and they with what bitter overtones of doubt, what painful memories! And is anyone cursing you? Even those whom you personally injured are saying now that it was probably not your fault. You spend twenty years and more persecuting and doing your best to ruin a cultivated, decent man and last night he proposed a toast to your memory, and meant it seriously. No, my friend: neither grief nor hatred, but indifference. Utter and complete indifference – that is the shroud in which you will take your last journey tomorrow.

There have been funerals of a different kind, my great and good friend. Even state funerals, and recent ones too, at which not a dry eye was to be seen. And there are dead men, including some you helped to their death, whose names are still on people's lips. These men, thanks to you, were once accursed, disinherited, and forgotten, but today monuments are erected to them, tablets unveiled – yes, even streets named after them, my famous friend!

But there is a man lying in bed here who knew you. Lying

in bed, and sleepless. He at least is with you in thought, is enduring with you this long and heavy hour. He knew you and he knew what sort of a man you were, and he is trying desperately and in vain to answer the question – what became of you? At this moment he is lighting his fourth cigarette, and he will light many more before he recognizes that he will never know the answer to his question. He asks himself whether you are to be pitied and he replies, No, no one is to be pitied who has shaped his own destiny. You were free to shape yours as you did, but you might have chosen otherwise. The road you took is a hard one, perhaps the hardest – that of immense endeavour ending in nothingness. Your sleepless friend here can think of only one answer to his question, and that an inadequate one. Power corrupts.

Tell me, you who lie dead – what was the taste of all that power that you held in your hands?

Frank's thoughts were broken by a gentle moan from Paula at his side. She stirred in her sleep as though she were having a bad dream. He drew her head towards him, without waking her, and placed his other hand on her breast. He did not behave towards her as he should, he knew, but she belonged to him, she was his wife, she was what he possessed upon this earth. Love? Was there still love between them? They were accustomed to each other. They might get on each other's nerves when they were together, but when he was away from her he often felt a painful longing for her presence. They knew each other's ways, they had no need to pretend. Was this love, or something at once greater and less? But what else could love be?

What did Frank have in life? A meagre salary, a job that bored him, a hobby he could divulge to no one – and this woman. To have someone, and that someone a woman . . .

Paula awoke. She made no sound, but Frank knew that she was no longer sleeping: he could not see her eyes in the dark, but felt that they were open. She was breathing more quietly, her breast rose and fell at a different rhythm.

'They're still beautiful.' It was what he always said when he caressed her.

'Oh, Frank,' she said softly. It was like the invitation to a miracle.

'I've no one but you, Paula, my sweet.'

She stroked his hair. She knew what he was trying to tell her and why. Something more than love – silence, full of understanding . . .

Eighteen

The funeral procession was due to leave the great hall at precisely ten o'clock. The fifty eminent persons who had been bidden to the ceremony were already assembled there. Outside, a crowd of several thousand people was lining the route. As Frank crossed the street he caught sight of Margaret amongst them. He purposely took no notice: she had evidently wished to be alone, lost in the crowd. So she had come after all. Frank was glad, not so much for the dead man's sake as for hers. She had not changed. Perhaps, if he had not met the blonde, everything might have been different. Perhaps – but he had met her . . .

The crowd stood and waited. A funeral like this was an impressive show, they would not miss it on any account. On the square, to one side of the hall, stood two hundred young men and girls in light blue shirts, under which they wore thick pullovers. Their duty was to carry the wreaths that covered the catafalque and filled the laurel bower. In a side street twenty shiny black limousines were waiting. Army and militia guards of honour were drawn up a little further off. The coffin, reposing on a gun-carriage, was to be drawn by an army vehicle manned by helmeted soldiers. The dead man's last journey would take place to the strains of a military march.

Frank knew the programme by heart. At ten o'clock the orchestra in the hall would strike up an extract from Dvorak's Requiem. There would be only one speech, delivered by Galovitch. The six generals would carry the coffin, draped in the national flag, to the gun-carriage. The army and militia guards of honour would head the procession. Next would come a general bearing the cushion on which rested the dead man's orders and decorations. Then the wreaths, followed by the gun-carriage. The widow would walk behind the coffin, supported by her father-in-law. After her would come the most eminent figures of political and public life; then a group of six high-ranking officers, and then the remaining official guests. It was expected that the procession would be joined by the public lining the streets. In this way it would cover the distance of a mile and a half from the hall to the Residency which had been the dead man's official abode. There, a member of the government would take leave of his former chief in a short speech. Frank had not been able to find out who this would be. The fact that the name was being kept secret might mean that the person in question was the dead man's chosen successor – chosen by election of course, though this formality was not to take place till two in the afternoon. After this speech, the coffin would be transferred from the gun-carriage to a hearse, which the twenty black limousines would escort to the city boundary. Another short speech, and the dead man would be conveyed from the place in which he had lived and worked to a crematorium in a distant town. On this part of the journey he would be accompanied only by his father and widow. This had been her wish, agreed to after long debate. Another wish of hers to which they had agreed was that there would be no ceremonies at the crematorium and nobody else present except the necessary attendants.

Such was the planned order of events. Frank's own task would be over as soon as the coffin left the great hall. Other photographers had been assigned by the head of his office to cover the rest of the programme.

The strains of music from the orchestra, out of sight in the gallery, fell silent. For a few moments there was no sound except that of subdued coughing. Then Galovitch advanced and stood beside the catafalque with its coffin draped in the national flag. In his hand was a red folder containing the text of his speech. He opened it, and gazed about him. He began his address to the dead man's widow and relations and to the assembled company. Galovitch spoke.

Except for a few tufts of grey hair at the temples, Galovitch was bald. His skull was knobbly, his face and form cumbrous and uncouth. So were his thoughts and his delivery. This was what distinguished Galovitch from all the other notabilities who were present. Always, and in all circumstances, he was clumsy and graceless.

It was a graceless speech. Galovitch was a poor reader. He misplaced accents, marred literary phrases by his provincial brogue, raised and lowered his voice at the wrong places and mangled any foreign expressions that came his way. Frank thought of him humorously as Comrade Vietman, having heard him refer at least a dozen times to the 'Democratic Vietmanese Republic'.

Galovitch's speeches were all alike: dry, drab and full of clichés. They had obviously been written for years by the same man. Whoever it was, he was no genius.

The film camera buzzed and the lights were switched on to full power. Frank took one picture after another. The eye of the television camera was fixed on Galovitch as he ploughed ponderously on. The widow was seated on a small chair, her head bowed, her expression inscrutable beneath the heavy veil. When Galovitch referred directly to her, she raised her head slightly with what seemed to Frank a look of defiance, as if to say: What right have you to be addressing me? But perhaps her thoughts were running on the same lines as Frank's.

Frank's former chief had once had a great opportunity. At the time in question, Galovitch's position had been badly shaken. Public opinion, inarticulate though it might be, was strongly against him. Those who had feared him began to lift their heads. Scurrilous gossip and ugly stories went the rounds about him. People said that he couldn't sleep at night if he hadn't had someone arrested during the day. This was an exaggeration – but public opinion is prone to this kind of embellishment. But the stories were an index of what people thought about him.

At that time people expected that somebody would come

forward with the courage to denounce Galovitch's misdeeds and expel him from public life. And they had a clear idea who this person ought to be, namely the statesman. He was the only one who could stand up to Galovitch and give him his deserts. Everyone knew that they had long hated each other. They were like two cocks on a dunghill, bound to fight it out sooner or later – and now seemed to be the time. Galovitch's position was so weakened that people avoided him at receptions, where he sat alone. His fall seemed to be only a question of time.

The statesman's intervention was awaited eagerly. Surely this was the last day of Galovitch's power! But his rival kept silent – he was afraid. On that day he lost everything. No one expected anything of him any more. If he had acted, everything would have been forgiven and forgotten, and all his old acquaintances, including Frank, would have been jubilant – so he is still the man he was, after all. Of course he too would have got up to all kinds of tricks – who wouldn't in that position? But by deposing Galovitch he would have proved that he stood for something new, something as yet only dimly surmised, but which must come sooner or later.

He was afraid, he held his peace and did nothing. At a stroke, he forfeited all liking and all respect. Was it Galovitch he feared? Hardly – there was no need to at that time. No, he was afraid that if Galovitch's wrongdoing were brought to light there would be a chain reaction, the balance of power in the leadership would be upset and the whole house of cards would start to tumble – and that would be dangerous, for once it began, where and at whom would it stop?

So he did nothing – nothing to dislodge from his key position the man of the 'hard line', the universally hated man. And by this inaction he pronounced his own doom. The opportunity passed. Galovitch maintained and strengthened his position, and learnt from what had taken place. He realized that the way to safety was to concentrate all available power in his own hands. Unlike the dead man, he knew what power was and how to handle it. For a while longer, his rival enjoyed some show of power. Galovitch had never been one for shows, he preferred to remain in the background. But it was he, Galovitch, who ruled from then on.

Galovitch was still speaking.

'With profound relevance' – he paused, realized it was the wrong word, wondered for a moment whether to correct himself, decided not to – this was all quite in his usual style – 'with profound relevance and sorrow we bow before the mortal remains of our unforgettable comrade, faithful friend, beloved son, husband, father – a great statesman and a great man . . .'

Frank looked round to see about whom and in whose name he was saying all this. The dead man's father was genuinely moved. The widow was not. As for the son, he was not present – a fact which the writer of the speech could hardly have foreseen. Friends – where were the dead man's friends? Who could remain friends with a politician who proclaimed that there was no such thing as friendship in politics?

From other lips, these words might have sounded appropriate enough; but the man who spoke them was Galovitch. Everyone knew how things had stood between him and the dead man. He was the last person who ought to speak over that coffin, but he had elected to do so, and those most in touch with affairs could guess why. Galovitch was playing for the main stake: by taking his place on the stage immediately after the dead man he was demonstrating that he was there, a man to be reckoned with, that it was he who would decide the fate of others and not they his. Galovitch was not going to be stopped by anything, even a corpse.

A great statesman? Yet Galovitch himself had forbidden the appearance of the dead man's name and photographs in the press and newsreels, on radio and television. Still, what else could he say in a funeral speech? He could hardly depict the dead man as he really was. Anyway, the dead man was irrelevant: what was at issue here was the authority of his post, the seat of office, the ministerial chair. The chair is dead, long live the chair. Of the chair, *nil nisi bonum*.

The speech went on.

'A true son of the revolutionary working class has left us . . .
He sprang from that class, fought for it, represented it . . .'

A pity you weren't in the tavern, thought Frank, that time
when the boys who were expecting him called me a crow with
gilded claws. But even if you had happened to put your nose in
and hear what they thought of him, I suppose you couldn't
say anything else . . .

'A brilliant organizer, a hero of the struggle for liberation
from fascist tyranny, the organizing genius of our glorious
peacetime victories . . . One who, to his last breath, loyally
served the people's cause . . .'

His last breath . . . Galovitch could have told them more
about that if he had been so minded . . .

In the last years of his life the dead man had fallen victim, like
many another high officer of state, to the passion for hunting.
There was, to be sure, no harm in that. Hunting is a healthy
recreation, a chance to relax and get away from daily cares and
the hustle of a smoke-filled office, out into the open air and
the quiet forests. But hunting should not become a statesman's
sole or main activity, and our man before long did scarcely
anything else. Hunting was to him a refuge from the monotony
of his not too successful career, an excitement, a compensation
for this or that failure, and, not least, an assurance that he was
still as much of a gay fellow and a crack shot as he had been in
the old fighting days. It was his ruling passion and perhaps
his last. When the fit came on him, as it did more and more
often, he threw his duties and timetable to the winds and disappeared without even telling his immediate staff where he
had gone. His absence did not in fact make much difference.
Letters and documents for signature piled up on his desk, but
they could always wait.

At one of the regular meetings of political leaders under
Galovitch's chairmanship, the great man's chair was empty. It
was not the first time – his colleagues were used to it and knew
what to think. Galovitch, having opened the meeting, read his

letter of apology for absence – also nothing new. What was new was that Galovitch at once proceeded to declare the meeting strictly confidential. The others sat up and took notice. Something was afoot...

'It is my disagreeable duty to inform you of certain facts which are in flagrant contradiction with the statements in this letter. Discipline is binding on all. The more highly placed a comrade is, the more strictly he must observe it. Unfortunately I am obliged to tell you the nature of the urgent public affairs to which this letter refers. Such affairs are indeed a valid excuse if they are in fact urgent and public. But what is the position about the ones mentioned here? Comrades: exactly two hours ago, the writer of this letter shot a doe . . .'

Galovitch sat down and looked searchingly at each of those present in turn. Neither they nor he were surprised at the news he had just announced. What he was concerned with was to judge whether the moment had come for a decisive step. He had chosen it well. The look of disgust on every face was not wholly feigned. To shoot a doe, a female animal, whose numbers were strictly protected by law – and in the closed season too! Why, it was the act of a common poacher, a criminal act! Galovitch's colleagues were also keen huntsmen.

Galovitch went on, thundering with indignation.

'I have evidence that this is not the first case of gross violation of civic and official discipline on the part of the comrade in question.'

The others had by now recovered from their initial shock and begun to see which way the wind was blowing. Apparently this was not just a simple case of denunciation for a crime, but something more. Was this the moment they had been waiting for so long, not without apprehension? Was Galovitch about to strike a decisive blow, or would he for the time being be content to establish the facts?

In fact Galovitch intended to keep his heavy artillery in reserve. He felt he had judged the situation correctly. He would take a vote on the question of an admonition to the offending comrade. An admonition sounds harmless enough. If he proposed anything stronger there would certainly be a long argument, and he was far from certain that the vote would go in his favour. So they voted for an admonition, with relief and with surprise that he had not asked for more. But in fact he was out for total victory, and this was an adroit tactical move in the game. The others did not perceive that they had given him exactly the vote he wanted, the necessary weapon with which to deliver a decisive blow.

On the following day the press office issued a directive to the effect that the statesman's name and photographs were not to be published until further notice – which meant until the incident had been fully investigated and appropriate action taken. By Galovitch, of course. Whatever he might decide as a result of the investigation was bound to be approved by the others – they had, after all, voted for the admonition, and could not now go back on it.

That episode was the statesman's end, his official death. Only his fatal illness had saved him from worse disgrace. In the circumstances, even Galovitch did not dare to proceed to extremes, and in any case there was no need. Galovitch, the guardian of public morals, was not fond of scandals which cast a cloud over the authority of public men. It would be simpler and neater to announce that the statesman was prevented by illness from carrying out his important duties. As it turned out, even this was unnecessary. The case was closed by the death of its central figure.

Frank had grinned maliciously when he had heard the official reason for the enigmatic press directive. It had been high time, in all conscience, for the statesman to divest himself of functions which he was incompetent to perform. Thanks to him, costly and harmful mistakes had been the order of the day. His intellect and vision were insufficient to prevent them; what was more, he lacked the necessary will-power, he shrank from responsibility and would not take decisions even on trifling matters. In short, there were plenty of grave reasons why he ought to have been deprived of a position for which he was unfitted. And now – he was being dismissed because he had shot a doe!

Yet after all, Frank had thought, it was not so incongruous. The ground for dismissal matched the statesman's true weight, his dignity, his authority . . .

Galovitch's speech was droning towards its end. He saluted the dead statesman with the words:

'You are alive and will always be alive among us . . .'

Taste, tact and a sense of moderation had never been Galovitch's strongest points. The meaning of delicacy was unknown to him. Very likely it did not occur to him what a gruesome role he was playing as panegyrist for the dead man. But to allow anyone else to perform this function would have been unthinkable: it would have cast a reflection on the whole solemn act of state.

As Galovitch concluded his speech, Frank suddenly felt pity for the dead man. Of course, there was much for which he was to blame. He had destroyed public confidence, not only in himself but in the social system he represented and the movement in which he had grown to manhood. He had frustrated the hopes placed in him. He had committed many base actions, abused power that did not belong to him alone, brought sorrow and misfortune to many; but all these were in a sense natural human failings. His motives might have been impure, his impulses and actions unworthy, but they were those of a fallible human being, and at times of a wretched and unhappy one. Frank was not seeking to justify him but only to explain, to understand. He had known him when he was another sort of being . . .

But Galovitch was of different clay. Galovitch was infallible. Throughout his period of office he had never made any mistake. He was a monster of absolute morality, without weakness or passion, perhaps without desires of any kind. Galovitch never lost any sleep – he lay down nightly, closed his eyes and slept the sleep of the just. His conscience – a word he would have abhorred – was always clear. And, strange as it might sound, he never took any step for reasons of personal interest. He had no personal interests. Duty was his law, the only form of honour he understood, and, if the term may be allowed, his passion. Joy and sorrow, to him, were meaningless notions.

The dead man had spent years trying to concentrate absolute power in his own hands. There was always someone in his way, someone of whom he had cause to feel jealous or afraid. Galovitch had no such impulse. When, finally, all the power in the country was concentrated in his office, it was not because he had in any way personally desired it. For him, power was not an end but a means. He did not lust after it, or abuse it for the sake of his own advantage or prestige. It came to him of its own accord, gradually without effort on his part. And he was admirably fitted by nature to hold on to it during the crazy era of universal mistrust. His measures might be harsh and cruel, but he never committed a base action from the personal point of view. He acted according to law – the law in force, as it stood embodied in decrees, regulations, proclamations. He always did his duty and nothing else – the rest of life was of no interest to him.

The dead man had hated him, impotently, with an instinctive, passionate and elemental hatred. When they were still in the provinces Frank had more than once experienced his outbursts of rage and frustration against Galovitch. He was afraid of him. When he became head of the government he had openly exulted – this was his great day, his day of victory over Galovitch. He believed that at last he was out of the other's reach, outside the scope of his authority. But soon afterwards Galovitch had risen to his present post, and the great man was again afraid.

Galovitch was afraid of nothing. He probably felt no personal hatred for the dead man. All his hatreds were class hatreds, the only kind he recognized. But his task was to protect the morals of the nation, and this he did all the time and everywhere. No one escaped his vigilance. Patiently he had collected reports of the other's deeds and misdeeds – they might come in handy some day. He did the same in regard to men and women against whom he would never have to take any steps. He needed to know everything, it was his duty to, and he did.

The dead man had run a large house, with much glitter and circumstance. He loved social pomp and enjoyed parties. His wife, whom he came to loathe in time, accompanied him to them: she was decorative and, at least outwardly, a tangible proof of his success.

Galovitch had refused to accept a villa and lived in a three-room flat in a large building. He disliked appearing in public. He felt awkward in society, he did not know how to behave or how to use a knife and fork properly, his tie was always askew. He never took his wife to parties: if he could not get out of going to them, he would go alone. At one time he had even had a rule made that no officials should take their wives with them to public functions. The result was to make receptions look like homosexual gatherings.

His wife was a stout, dumpy, rather stupid woman, whom hardly anyone had met. Frank had seen her perhaps four or five times in the course of his career. No one took any interest in her: it seemed irrelevant whether Galovitch was married or not – his private life was unknown, unimportant, uninteresting.

Although he was robust, healthy and without doubt sexually potent, it had never been so much as whispered that he might have a mistress: such a thing would have been unimaginable to others, and to him as well. An interest in women would have been contrary to his principles; a frailty, a vice, and, worse still, a security risk. If by any chance he ever desired a woman or found her attractive, he was careful not to let it be noticed – he crushed the disgraceful weakness within his own bosom. It was by overcoming and suppressing impulses that the revolutionary steel was forged. Weakness in a revolutionary was always the first symptom of his downfall, the beginning of a road which led irrevocably to treason.

Was it conceivable that any woman should be interested in

him? Women are manifold and their desires unpredictable – why should not one of them take it into her head to subdue, to enslave, to weaken the strong man? Many a beauty must have visited him to plead for mercy for her husband, arrested or condemned. With some of these it would have sufficed to stretch out a hand towards an imaginary couch. Galovitch must have heard many a hint in this sense, many an outright offer. But he was as hard as granite. He was a warrior fighting for human happiness, for the brave new world, the granite world of morality.

With all this he was not stupid. He understood human weaknesses and how to make them serve his purposes. To abstain from alcohol was to him a self-evident revolutionary duty. When official toasts had to be drunk, his glass would be filled with water coloured to resemble the appropriate wine.

He went to and from his office on foot. If he ever went away for a holiday, he travelled by rail, third class, at his own expense. He was careful to observe which officials used government cars for private purposes. This information too might be useful some day.

He was always on the job, always on duty. He scarcely ever chatted to anyone. At parties he stood aloof and on the watch. He had never had any friends. He regarded friendship as unworthy, degrading, sentimental, a fetter and a clog.

This solitude was the source of his strength that the world feared. He was known to be vigilant, hard and incorruptible. Beyond that, no one knew anything about him.

Galovitch never doubted the rightness of his acts; he believed that doubt, even unexpressed, was the twin brother of treason. He never hesitated to pursue to its uttermost conclusion whatever course he regarded as in the interest of society.

A fanatic? No. Fanatics are passionate, impulsive, sometimes incalculable. Galovitch was a machine for the purpose of grinding people – an infallible being of rock-like probity. He never claimed to be exceptional or superior to others, yet by the totality of his virtue he was an exceptional man.

A man? A human being?

Was it not precisely this quintessence of all virtue which made him a dreaded monster, a bogey feared by all? His own absolute morality was the mirror in which he discerned the principles and criteria of public morals. Whoever in the slightest degree offended Galovitch's code was unfit for his position. If he got drunk today, he would commit treason tomorrow.

Pity and clemency were merely names for treason. The revolution could not afford such luxuries. Indulgence towards mistakes and failures had meant the downfall of states, systems and régimes. Galovitch could only have respected someone even more virtuous than himself, and woe betide those who were worse. Nor did he recognize any overtones or shades of alteration. Good was good, evil was evil, and there was nothing in between. Only hypocritical intellectuals – weaklings, as he described them, with undeveloped muscles – prated about the complexities of human evolution. He, Galovitch, was not to be caught with such chaff. Nothing could be humane which was not progressive, or progressive which was not revolutionary. No one had ever dared to ask Galovitch how he defined 'revolutionary', and if they had, he might have been puzzled to reply. But not for long: he would have answered with a brass-bound cliché.

Thus Galovitch destroyed, rough-hewed and pulverized humanity in the name of revolutionary purity. The faintest breath of suspicion, ludicrous though it might be, was to him a proof. After that, matters could be turned over to the investigating services, whose business it was to convict. Detect, convict, liquidate – Galovitch's vocabulary was a small one.

What had enabled this man to remain for so long at the top of the pyramid of power? Did others not realize what manner of person he was? Indeed they did, and that was why he kept his position. The dead man here had once been reputed fearless, but even then he was afraid of Galovitch. To the rest of the country it looked as if there were two strong men, two fighting-cocks at each other's throats. But only one of them was really strong – only one was a fighting-cock. Perhaps Galovitch felt that he needed the other, that they complemented each other and thus guaranteed each other's existence. None the less, he had not hesitated to destroy his rival when he had the power to do it. Not from fear, not from envy, but on principle. By so doing he had attained the topmost rung of personal power, but had he not at the same time destroyed himself? Gradually, unobtrusively, positions of importance were being occupied by young men, unencumbered by the old mistrust and prejudices. There were more and more such men and they slipped through Galovitch's fingers, they would not play his game or be caught in his toils. Their elders had been obedient, almost every one of them had a past and knew that Galovitch was aware of it; but about the young ones he knew nothing. He had never had or needed a friend, but now he was alone, the last strong man, the last of the old guard. It had after all been a mistake to get rid of the statesman lying here, it had troubled the waters – even his very own machinery of obedience creaked here and there; there were people who refused to dance to his tune; something unknown and incomprehensible had come to birth over the years, something against which Galovitch's tried methods were powerless. There were people who disdained the rules of the game as he had played it, unruly trouble-makers without respect for the laws of the revolution as enacted by Galovitch, bent instead on acting according to their own judgement. Their own judgement? That, to Galovitch, spelt treason. And there were even others who openly mocked him, a new, terrible thing, previously unheard-of. Galovitch trembled for the revolution when he thought of these disruptive influences.

He was still powerful – he had never been so powerful. Today he held in his grasp the fullness of actual power, and he had under his command an apparatus whose task it was to defend that power against intruders and to see that it functioned effectively. And yet he himself felt that he had reached the end. With the dead man an entire era had passed away, an era of which Galovitch was the sole survivor. In future he could only be a hindrance, a stumbling-block. This he had long been, but not many had realized it – the dead man, not he, had been the scapegoat of public opinion. From now on it would be himself and no one else. He had been like an owl hunting by night; now he would be thrust into the light of day, to be swooped upon and pecked to death by all the birds of the air. Sparrows, tits, thrushes, swallows – all of them would descend upon him with furious cries. He was the lord of darkness: in the world of living men he would be impotent and ridiculous. And one day someone would shout fearlessly to his face: We know what you are against, but tell us if you can, are you for anything? And that challenge could not be answered with slogans about revolutionary vigilance . . .

Frank had taken a picture of Galovitch making his speech over the coffin of his victim. The strange knobbly head, the steely, half-closed eyes. He was pleased with the picture, which would be the last – the last page in his photographic chronicle of a life and of a death.

Galovitch had finished speaking. He went to where the widow was sitting and extended his hand to her. The others present did likewise in their turn – even Frank, though it is not correct for a photographer on duty to offer condolences. As he took the widow's hand she whispered: 'If only it were over.'

It was over. The unseen orchestra struck up a funeral march. The six generals shouldered the coffin and moved slowly from the hall.

Frank did not follow them. His task was done, his colleagues outside were waiting to take over. Two attendants closed the heavy bronze doors. As if at a signal, men in overalls appeared from the back of the building and extinguished the artificial memorial torches. The light of the great chandelier went out. Their foreman called to the two men who were removing the black curtain: Mind out, now, be careful of that velvet . . .

No one took any notice of Frank. As the men removed the wooden blocks on which the catafalque had rested, the last remnant of the funeral furnishings, he looked at his watch. They had taken not quite half an hour. The film men still had to roll up their cable, and then the hall would again wear its normal aspect. But not for long, because it had to be set in order and festively decorated for the inauguration, that afternoon, of the new head of government.

In the street Frank met Margaret, who was carrying a black shopping-bag. He did not mention that he had seen her before. She burst out:

'The scoundrel! He really ought to be ashamed.'

She must have meant Galovitch and his speech.

After all, thought Frank, things have not changed so very much. Someone has died, but Margaret is still the same as she always was. The very same . . .